THE GAMBLE

S.E. Welsh

www.BOROUGHSPUBLISHINGGROUP.com

THE GAMBLE
Copyright © 2020 S.E. Welsh

ISBN: 978-1-951055-59-2

For my husband
Two gifts you gave to me, this one I give to you
Love you

ACKNOWLEDGMENTS

Thank you a million times over Mel. You keep me on track, answer my stupid questions and kick my arse when I need it. Also, Romance Writers of Australia needs a special shout out for all the support I've received from members and the organization over the last two years. Without the conferences, OWLs and pitching practices, I never would have had the wherewithal to publish.

THE GAMBLE

6

white feather
noun
a white-coloured feather used as a symbol or mark of perceived cowardice. During the First World War young men seen not wearing uniform were sometimes presented with such a feather, as part of a campaign to induce men to enlist for military service. —Oxford Dictionary

Chapter 1

Ghosts don't always sleep where bodies lie.

Connor picked up his rucksack and stepped down from the buggy, the tightened skin of his back stretching over barely healed wounds. As he shrugged off the pain, he took a deep breath of fresh mountain air, rich with the scent of dusty eucalyptus. The last time he had seen this place, his mother had been on the porch, farewelling him with forced smiles and tears. In the distance, a figure on a horse had waved at them. *Caleb.*

Caleb, whose hero-worship of his big brother had often pushed him to stupidity. Like forging his age on his enlistment forms and running away to Sydney.

Like letting a white feather kill him.

The old homestead reeked of neglect. The wide veranda was dust-covered, gardens his mother had tended daily now weed-filled and overgrown, tinged with hints of brown.

There were no smiles or hugs of welcome, no baked goods for this returned soldier. All that was left was an empty house and memories. Ghosts.

"You sure you want to stay here tonight, son?" Mr Graham asked from the seat of the buggy.

The old stationmaster never forgot a face and had made him wait until the last train for the day lumbered through, so he could give him a ride here.

"I'll be fine, thank you, sir. There's work to be done." And there was. Broken fences glared at him, daring him to fix, mend. Now he had to build a new life without his family.

How am I supposed to do that?

"Boy, you aren't the healthiest-looking piece of horseflesh this side of the mountains. Even if you are in that uniform the ladies love." A wry smile flit across Connor's face at the words. "Give yourself time to rest. Grieve."

Connor's smile disappeared. "There's no rest for the wicked, Mr Graham." His tone was mocking, but there was a truth in it he didn't bother to hide. Connor was wicked. Or at least, people would say that if they knew his plans.

"Suit yourself," said the old man. "But don't say I didn't warn you. You youngsters are all the same, happy to make martyrs of yourselves a dozen times a day. Why, when I—"

"Thanks for the ride," Connor said, eager to hurry the old man on. "But I'd best see what food I can scrounge up before the light goes."

The sun was disappearing quickly behind mountains. Mr Graham muttered to himself, no doubt about the stupidity of the young, as he clucked at his old mare, urging her into a slow trot down the dusty road. At best guess, Connor would have a little less than an hour to take stock of the stores and see how the animals fared in the house yard.

No doubt the chickens would be fine. The henhouse and yard his father had built spanned almost the length of the house itself. And the church matrons wouldn't let those animals starve. Connor knew better than most how the community looked after its own.

This wasn't the first time they'd helped him pick up the pieces.

He dropped his kit bag on the veranda, moving out the back toward the henhouse. The chickens squawked angrily as he raided their nests. By the time he was finished, Connor was stocked for the week and felt a smattering of satisfaction that despite the neglect, the old homestead was still looking after the family. The thought of fried eggs for dinner made his mouth water, a luxury he'd missed while bogged in the trenches.

But he'd have to face the memories in the house to cook them.

It was with relief that his eye caught movement in the small paddock near the house yard. His brother's chestnut mare grazed peacefully, waiting for the master who'd never return. On impulse, Connor raided the barn for a curry comb and brush, ignoring the cobwebs for the moment, but adding it to the list of repairs that was steadily growing.

The chestnut ambled across to Connor, her well-rounded stomach suggesting the animal hadn't suffered in the absence of the family. It lipped at his clothing, searching eagerly for the treat it thought to find there. Spoilt. The matrons had a lot to answer for.

Running through the old motions was soothing, and Connor realised he no longer felt that stiffness around the eyes that accompanied one of his headaches. There was something about working with animals that made you loosen up, made you forget the things that chased you through the dark, if only for a moment.

It didn't last long enough. He gave the old mare an affectionate tap on the behind, startling her into a quick sidestep, then returned the grooming gear to where he'd found it.

The house hovered before him, full of the echoes of the past. Only three steps stood between him and the veranda, another four to the door. The distance seemed impossibly long, the fly-screen door a thing of nightmares. Lord knows it had featured enough in his to inspire terror. The stained glass in the front was nearly as bad. His mother's pride and joy, a frivolity his father hadn't been able to refuse. Another more expensive item his father had struggled to afford to keep her happy.

Constant creaking came from the left, drawing him away from the darkness. Connor remembered when his father had made the enormous swing. Connor had been eight years old, Caleb five. His mother had laughed, though delight shone in her eyes. "What will we do with a swing that large, Jacob?" she'd asked, shaking her head.

"Those boys of ours are getting bigger," he'd replied with a grin. "If we want to fit all four of us on it, we'll need the extra space."

They had loved afternoons on the porch swing, watching the sun slip behind the mountains. First, their mother would join them, taking a moment to snuggle each of her boys into her ample curves, the smell of flour and sugar a scent they'd never tire of. Then their father would arrive. His return from whichever part of the farm held his attention was the most eagerly awaited part of the day. It always coincided with the falling of the sun, the tall, beanpole of a man on his equally stringy horse, silhouetted against the sunset.

The boys had inherited their father's height, their mother's stocky frame and her sparkling blue eyes. The only difference was Caleb had the shocking red hair of their Scottish background, Connor the darker hair and skin of the Irish. As youngsters, they'd held the potential to become powerful men. It seemed such a waste that only one would get the chance.

The swing continued to creak back and forth with the wind. A bone-deep weariness settled in Connor's bones as he lowered himself onto it. Maybe he'd rest out here for a second. Postpone the inevitable confrontation with his ghosts.

Lulled by the rhythmic rocking and the scent of home, Connor's eyes drifted shut. He stayed that way 'til morning.

He had his first dreamless sleep in an eternity of nightmares.

***

The bell above the bakery door jingled its cheery hello when Margery burst inside.

"Did you hear, Sarah?" The irrepressible young woman hadn't even managed to close the door before her mouth opened. Sarah sighed. Much as she loved her best friend, she didn't share her enthusiasm for gossip.

Marge knew everything that happened in a five-mile radius of their tiny hometown. When old man Graham caught Jessie-Claire Tilbot and William Duncan in a compromising position behind the train station the year before last, Marge had known about it even before the irate stationmaster had dragged the culprits by the ears to their parents.

She'd spread it halfway around town before Jessie's pa had gone after William with a shotgun, telling the young man he'd better be ready to marry his daughter, or else.

Luckily the pair had been heading in that direction anyway and were now about to be proud parents, but it was no thanks to Marge's wagging tongue.

"Margery Anne Cleary, you know how I feel about gossip," Sarah said tartly, opening the enormous oven and removing the first tray of pies. A rush of warm air followed, the rich aroma of beef and thick gravy carried with it stirring her hunger. She swiped an errant lock of red hair from her sweaty brow. Sarah had been at the bakery since well before sunrise, a regular occurrence lately. The sickness devoured more of her Pa with each passing day, so Sarah took up his burdens herself.

Lord knew, her sister Isabel would never set foot anywhere she'd have to work.

Sarah was in desperate need of a slice of toast and a cup of tea, but her friend looked crestfallen, so with a sigh, she relented. "Go on then, tell me what has your knickers in a twist." The bright smile that graced Marge's face made up for any irritation she may have felt.

"Connor Williams is back in town." Six words. Six words and Sarah's heart went crashing through her chest.

The tray went crashing to the floor.

"Oh Lord," Sarah moaned as she dropped to the ground, scrambling to clean the mess. Gravy splattered the glass of the cabinets, and lumps of succulent beef dotted the floor amidst shards of crushed pastry. Tears filled Sarah's eyes, but she quickly blinked them away.

"Let me help," Marge offered as she bustled to the sink, wet the tea towel, and elbowed the flustered Sarah out of the way. In short order, the mess was cleaned, and Sarah had managed to contain all signs of distress. Surely Marge wouldn't notice her rapidly beating heart?

"What's the matter with you, love?" asked Margery. "I haven't seen you do something this clumsy in years. Not since first form when—"

"Enough, Marge." Sarah darted furtive looks around the store, making sure no one was witness to her clumsiness. "Now explain what you meant about Connor."

Margery sent a sly smile Sarah's way. "Thought you weren't interested in gossip, chook?"

Sarah laughed. "Fine," she said. "I apologise for insulting your favourite pastime." Marge grinned. "Now tell me what you know before I combust."

"Well," Marge said as she settled herself onto the stool behind the counter. "Old man Graham plodded into the post office this morning before going to the station. Said, 'the Williams boy's back, and doesn't he look like he's survived a nightmare'." Duncan Graham loved gossip almost as much as Margery but didn't have youth as an excuse for his fascination.

Automatically concerned, Sarah asked, "What did he mean by that, do you think?"

Sarah turned back to the oven. Fortunately, there was a second tray of pies still resting in there, so profits for the day shouldn't be too badly impacted by her clumsiness.

"Well…" Marge continued. Sarah nearly snorted. If she had a penny for every time that word left Marge's mouth… "I tried asking some questions, subtly, mind you—"

Sarah laughed outright this time.

"Do you want me to finish or not, Sarah Dawson?"

Muffling the laugh, Sarah gestured for her to go on.

"Mr Graham said that when he stepped off that train, all he could think about was how broken the boy looked."

Sarah's heart stuttered in her chest. Silence reigned.

She didn't know what to say. Connor Williams had featured in her daydreams since before she could tie her own shoelaces. Two years her senior at school, the young man had sent hearts fluttering whenever he smiled.

And then his father had died. No more school for Connor. No more smiles. Except for his brother.

And, occasionally, Sarah.

"No doubt, Marge," Sarah said quietly. "Connor's tripped through hell and back out the other side, only to find everything he fought for is gone. It's no wonder they say he looks broken."

Margery stared at her intently, her clear grey eyes seeing entirely too much. "Are you going to tell him how you feel about him, now that he's back for good?"

Sarah's tongue wouldn't work. She opened and closed her mouth a few times, hoping something would come out, but was saved from answering by the tinkle of the bell above the store door.

Marge smirked as she gave her friend a quick kiss on the cheek and slipped out the back as her first customer rushed in. The young woman would be making herself busy, filling the milk cart with the bread orders for the day. Marge's Pa had volunteered to take her deliveries with his to help her while her father 'recovered.' A frown creased Sarah's brow. What would she do when Pa passed? Would Mr Cleary be happy to continue the arrangement? Lord knows, she didn't have the money to pay a delivery driver, and Isabel wouldn't be caught dead driving their old buggy to make deliveries she believed were her sister's responsibility.

With a sigh, Sarah settled herself, then turned to serve the customers quickly flocking through the doors of the bakery, eager to secure their bread and possibly a tasty morsel of a pie to share.

Those were problems for another day. She had enough to deal with in the present without borrowing trouble.

It wasn't until well after lunch when she finally had a chance to slow down again. In the wake of the Great War, local businesses throughout Australia, such as her family's, were suffering greatly. It was sheer luck that they were still operating. Despite the lack of males to operate the farms in the last few years, the women of her town had coped amazingly well on their own.

Running a plough-share system, the church matrons and their volunteers had managed to both sow and reap the wheat from every farm in the district. The silos were full and the mills still operational, if on a skeleton staff. Sarah herself, as well as the ever-chatty Margery, had signed up to help, returning home blistered and exhausted while her father ran the bakery for almost zero profit.

No one went hungry.

Every town and business in the district was still operational. All the livestock were being run on four farms, with every able-bodied man available (bar those in necessary work like her father) co-opted to manage these farms.

Their community helped its own.

And finally, the men were returning home. Granted, it was in dribs and drabs, and not all of them were whole, in body or mind, but they were home.

At least, most of them.

Sarah looked out the window, staring intently at the foundations being laid in the centre of town. It wasn't large, but when it was finished the clock tower would be a beautiful memorial to those whose lives were lost defending king and country. Hopefully, it would stand as a reminder to future generations of the consequences of war. She wondered where Caleb's name would be inscribed when the time came.

Sarah rubbed at the ache in her chest. There wasn't a day that went by when Sarah didn't think about the whippet of a boy who could always make her laugh. Though it wasn't exactly seemly, Caleb and Sarah were friends.

At least they had been before the boy became infatuated with her sister.

Before he stole away in the dead of night without telling her where he was going. Before he lost his life in a war that wasn't his to fight.

Shaking her head of the memories, Sarah looked at the antique clock mounted on the wall. Her mother's vanity. The bronze chimes ticked rhythmically in their little wooden box, counting down the few minutes left until closing time. The last of the general rush had finished an hour ago, leaving only a few stragglers to interrupt her cleaning. Sarah never left before the bakery was ready to operate the next day, so she resented any interruptions to her routine.

When the bell jingled minutes before she was due to lock the doors, Sarah could have wept in frustration. Instead, she was struck dumb when she turned.

Mr Graham had not been exaggerating when he said Connor looked broken.

The lush, dark curls he had kept closely cropped to his head had been shaved away, though a light stubble could be seen growing in. His face was all angles, jaw sharp, and though he had grown into a powerful, muscular man, his frame seemed to lean sideways. Compensating for a weakness? But it was his eyes that shattered her.

The once-laughing, blue depths were filled with anger. Shame. Pain. They chased each other across his gaze, a poisonous shadow that she was sure tainted everything he saw.

And at this moment, he was focused on her.

"Hello, Sarah," Connor said, voice nearly a whisper yet stony in its silence. Not a combination she had thought to ever hear from his lips.

"Connor," Sarah managed to force out past her leaden tongue. "Marge said you'd returned."

He chuckled softly, darkly amused by something she didn't understand. "Of course she did."

Sarah nearly bridled in defence of her friend but was too stunned by the change in Connor to find the words. Her heart ached for him, yet she didn't know how to get past the walls he reinforced with every second.

"You'll be wanting some bread then?" asked Sarah, desperate to break the tension.

"Aye," he replied, moving farther into the shop as the door closed with a *ting* behind him. "I'll need a loaf."

"I remember when your mum would take home three because between you and Caleb ..." Sarah's words trailed off into a stern silence. In her nervousness, she'd managed to do the unforgivable: remind him of both his recent losses in one sentence.

The silence stretched into infinity, and for the first time in an hour, Sarah wished that damned bell would tinkle its overly cheery hello.

"There was never enough bread in the house." Instead of lashing out, Connor appeared to be offering an olive branch. "Caleb had a weakness for it, as did our father." Those blue eyes sheared right through her. "He could always tell who was baking on any given day too—you, or your father."

Connor flashed her a wink that had *almost* all his old charm.

"Any guess whose was better?"

Sarah blushed. Everyone knew she baked better bread than her father, but no one would dare tell him that. He was as temperamental as a spirited stallion and would be as likely to blacklist you for such a comment as he was to glow with pride at his daughter's accomplishments.

"Take that talk back home with you, Connor Williams," she scolded lightly. "Or I'll tell Pa you insulted his baking."

Sarah wished that didn't feel like a lie, that her father had the strength to react the way Connor would expect. Wished he was able to react to anything.

"Where is the old man? And your sister?" His eyes turned flinty. "Shouldn't one of them be helping you lock up by now?"

She hesitated, didn't know what to say to this bear of a man who was both the same as the youth she had known four years ago and yet so very different.

"Since when is your father happy with either of his girls being here after dark?"

Since he hasn't had the strength to prevent it. That wasn't what she told Connor though.

"Oh, I suppose since Isabel got engaged last spring, Pa thought I was old enough to handle more responsibility." *All the responsibility around here.* But again, she wouldn't throw her problems at a man who clearly had the weight of the world on his shoulders. His attention sharpened at her words.

Connor stared at her, sensing the lie, waiting for her to continue.

She didn't.

Finally, he sighed. "I'll wait out front with the horse until you've finished. Then I'll walk you home." It wasn't a request, and she bristled.

"I'm more than capable of walking myself home, Connor Williams," she snapped, insulted. "I'll have you know I've been walking fine by myself for the last year. I don't need you to hold my hand and chase the darkness away."

His crooked smile held more than an echo of his former self.

"I'm sure you don't, Sarah devil-may-care Dawson," he said lightly before the smile disappeared. "But maybe I need you to help battle mine." Sarah stood stock-still, a kernel of heat rising in her chest. The tinkle of the door didn't even register as he exited, waiting for her outside.

And what was a girl to say to that? Sarah locked up, stepped out into the darkness.

Then, trembling, took the hand of the man she'd thought to marry a lifetime ago.

Chapter 2

The feel of Sarah's small hand in Connor's large, calloused one did strange things to the man's insides. Her own hand, though petite, was not soft. There was strength in the muscles, no fat around them, though her figure was deliciously curved in ways it hadn't been when he left for the front. It only took one glimpse of her lush figure in that bakery for all the blood to rush straight to his groin.

Thank God she hadn't seemed to notice.

The warmth of her hand in his was making him wish for things he couldn't have. With a little squeeze, he reluctantly let go. The reins he held in his other hand bit into Connor's skin, bringing some much-needed clarity.

Back then, all she would have had to do was crook a finger, and he would have come running. Thankfully, the young woman had been totally unaware of the effect she had on him. She'd been his brother's friend, and Connor had been regularly thrown into Sarah's company when he went searching for Caleb. There'd always been a fresh kind of innocence about her that appealed to him. It was as if she rose above the troubles of the world at large. Her company was soothing, especially to a young man plagued by loss.

Now though…

How much did she know?

Memories of the past fought with demands of the now, and for the first time in his life, Connor found himself without words. His plan demanded he get closer to her. His heart was reluctant for an entirely different reason.

She didn't deserve what would come.

"I don't know if you noticed," Sarah broke the silence. "But your farm is without its stock at the moment."

"I noticed all right," Connor said wryly. His brother's mare huffed delicately into his hair. He gave her an affectionate nudge. "It was about the first thing I noticed when we made our way around the property this morning."

"Then no doubt you've heard about the community farms?" she asked, then hastened to add, "All stock was clearly branded before being amalgamated into the larger herd. Janie Pinkton keeps the record of where each family's stock is at any given time, so you are more than welcome to ask her for the information you need to get them back."

"I've already done so." Connor smiled, the rapid delivery of her words giving him flashbacks to when she was a girl. Sarah Dawson was all sunlight and earthy goodness.

"Will you be taking them back then? Or will you continue to run them with the larger herd a while longer?"

"The sheep can stay where they are at the moment, at least until I make repairs on the fences." His mouth tightened into a frown. "There's a lot to be done. Three years with no one to see to the property... well, let's say I have my work cut out for me."

The steady clop of the horse's hooves seemed to echo in the silence. Though it was night, it was never truly dark here. Of course, there were street lamps and the glow from the various households that made up the tight-knit town. But for Connor, it was the stars that brightened the darkened world. Always would be.

The heavens weighed heavily on their small town at the foot of the Warrumbungles. Stars seemed to drip from the sky, melt into the mountains. His heart. The stars had deserted him in France. When the fog wasn't devouring them, the smoke from the artillery was a haze no light could pierce. Heaven couldn't have been farther away from Connor on that side of the world.

"Do you need some help out there?" Sarah's voice startled him. "I'm sure someone would take the time to give you a hand, Connor, after all—"

"No." The rough edge of a growl was in his voice, and he fought to temper it. "No, thank you, Sarah. It's Williams' work and it'll be done by a Williams."

Though his tone was softer by the end, Sarah was still biting her lip at the curt words. Worry swam in her eyes.

"We look after our own, Connor," Sarah said, quietly but firmly. "Don't be surprised if you find yourself with more hands than you bargained on in the next week or so."

She was right. No doubt he'd be sending many friendly faces right back home, but Connor had to do this right. For them. He had to do *something* right. Something *honest*. Because honesty was going to be hard to find in the coming months.

"And I'll deal with that when it comes to it." Sarah would know better than to argue with a Williams who'd dug his mulish hooves in. He almost smiled in the silence. By god, she knew him. If only her last name wasn't Dawson.

They walked the rest of the way in comfortable silence, her home only a few blocks away from the business. Streets that had been so familiar to him as a boy still had the comfort of youth, yet the changes over the years had given them an alien quality. There were houses where there shouldn't be. Plants taller than expected. Children's toys left discarded in yards that shouldn't have had any to begin with.

Life went on, without the redheaded whippet who loved to laugh.

Damn *life*. It broke his heart then dared to start to stitch it back together again.

Before long they reached the tidy Victorian cottage her family called home. At least some things never changed. The whitewashed picket fence shone brightly in the moonlight, English garden beds tidy and weed-free. But something about it still disturbed him. Then he realised what it was.

It was dark. The whole house was dark, and Sarah wasn't home yet.

A red wave of rage engulfed Connor, almost had him marching up to the front door to give Sarah's father a piece of his mind. Did the man have any care for his eldest at all? Sarah's hand on his arm stopped him.

"Are you all right?" Was *he* all right?

"Why is the house dark, Sarah?" Connor asked. Inside he seethed. They might live in a friendly community, but that didn't mean it didn't have its bad elements. Firstly, the girl had to walk home by herself, and now he found it was to an empty house.

She hesitated. Connor wasn't in the mood.

"Tell me now, Sarah, or tomorrow your father and I will be having words."

"For God's sake, Connor. You're not even home one day, and you think you can push me around?"

"Sarah…" His tone held a warning she'd be wise to heed.

"Fine." Sarah threw her hands in the air, shooting a glare his way. "Pa's sick. Real sick."

And the wind fled his sails. He understood the words unspoken. Should have known the only way Frank Dawson would leave his daughter alone with the business would be if he was dying. Even then…

"Does he know you're doing this by yourself?" Connor's suspicions were confirmed when her eyes flicked to the side and down. She didn't answer. "Where are the other staff? Your sister?"

He almost swallowed his tongue at having to mention the witch.

"Pa's apprentice left for Tamworth a couple of months ago. The position was better, we were barely managing to make ends meet here as it was." The truth came out in a rush. She couldn't meet his eyes,

"And Isabel?" he asked through clenched teeth. "Where is she? Why isn't she helping you when things are so dire?"

The bitter laugh that escaped her was something Connor had never thought to hear from Sarah. It twisted his insides and made him want to draw her closer. Find a way to bring the sunshine back to her voice. Just one more score on the tally against her sister.

"Since when has Isabel ever raised a finger to help anyone else?" She drew in a deep breath, then continued. "Isabel is busy organising her wedding."

"Wedding?" Connor was incredulous, any tact forgotten. "You said that before, but who'd marry that poisonous—"

Sarah snapped, "I'll thank you not to talk about my sister like that, Connor Williams. Granted she may not be the nicest of people, but she's still family. Still mine."

And there was the rub. Even though Isabel Dawson was the devil in a woman's skin, soft-hearted Sarah still loved her. Whatever he decided to do about Isabel, it was bound to hurt Sarah.

Could he live with himself if he did that?

Could he live with his ghosts if he didn't?

Connor took a step back. He still had time to figure it out, but in the meantime, he'd see Sarah safe. The silence stretched too far before he had to snap it.

"I'm sorry." And he was, ilf only for the fact that he'd hurt her. Sarah didn't deserve the heat of his anger. It belonged entirely to her sister.

"What's happened to you, Connor? The man I knew would never have spoken about anyone like that, let alone a woman. Surely war doesn't change the very nature of a man?"

"You'd be surprised what war does to a man, Sarah. What scars it leaves." He sighed, hand moving to his shoulder to scratch absently at his own half-healed wounds. "Why isn't your sister awake to make sure you arrive home safely, even if she isn't going to help you run the business?" At least that sounded reasonable. Reasonable was the best that would come out of his mouth while on the topic of Isabel Dawson.

"She's probably out with Harrison," Sarah muttered, ashamed.

"Harrison Ware?" She nodded in answer to his question.

If Connor wasn't already furious with her sister, this would have been the icing on the cake.

"So you work your fingers to the bone in the bakery while your sister spends her time dallying with her fiancé?" The deadly tone was almost a whisper. He didn't want to draw Sarah into a scandal by raising his voice in her front yard, but he was perilously close to doing something he'd regret.

"It's not like that. She's already feeling the pressure of planning the wedding and—"

"*She's* feeling the pressure," he hissed. "From where I'm standing, one sister carries the weight of the world on her shoulders while the other... I won't repeat what's going through my mind row, Sarah Dawson. You wouldn't thank me for the sentiments."

"You should go." Her tone was ice. Already he regretted his words, but he'd find a way to make it up to her. If she let him.

"I'll see you inside first," Connor said, nodding toward the dark house. "I'll wait until a light is on before I leave."

Connor watched as anger and exasperation chased each other across Sarah's face. He didn't know which won, but without a word, Sarah turned and stalked toward the house. He waited patiently until a soft glow peeked through the curtains.

Mounting up, Connor nudged the sturdy chestnut mare forward, happy for once to make the ten-mile ride in the dark. There was much to think about. Despite not being ridden for years, the mare had behaved admirably through the day. He gave her an affectionate thump on the neck. Pity he couldn't remember her name.

One more thing for his to-do list. Name a horse.

The stars lit the sky, paving the well-worn dirt road in silver. The world was a hazy blue punctuated by black silhouettes. Eerily beautiful. But Connor saw none of it. His thoughts were far away, on a battlefield in France, where a redheaded imp had been ripped to shreds in front of his eyes. An imp who should still have been home, in school, were it not for a spiteful she-devil and her carelessly given white feather.

Caleb had been no coward. Just a boy. One who hero-worshipped his big brother.

Now there was only one thing on Connor's mind: revenge.

That, and how to get it without hurting the one person left whom he cared for.

Connor looked back once toward the soft glow of town. This was going to be a fine game of chance. If there was one thing Connor Williams was good at, it was making sure the dice fell his way.

Isabel Dawson wouldn't know what had hit her when he was through with her.

Chapter 3

Sarah's heart shattered into a million pieces. Connor was leaving. He'd enlisted in Sydney, been given a week to sort out his affairs at home, and then he was shipping out. She supposed she should be grateful that he'd sought her out to say good-bye, but she couldn't shake the nagging fear that he wouldn't come home.

It was war after all.

"Sarah?" He moved closer, pulling her to his chest. Wrapped in his strong arms, she let go. The tears came out in great, shuddering gulps she desperately wanted to hide from him, but that proved impossible. "I don't want you to wait for me, but I couldn't go without at least telling you—"

"I'll wait," the words tumbled from her mouth. "I'd wait forever for you."

It was as much of a declaration of love as she could bring herself to voice. In fact, she was mortified at the few words that had already escaped her mouth. Connor was a grown man, and she hadn't even finished school.

He hesitated, then ploughed on. "I don't think you should. You're the girl I've dreamed about forever, but this war... I don't know... I have a feeling they are going to need every man they can get. And that things won't go quite as they plan."

"I don't care if it's weeks, months, or even years, Connor. I'll wait," she mumbled into his chest.

His arms tightened as he kissed her forehead. The warmth of his lips seemed to radiate through her body. An affirmation. A promise.

"Then I hope I make it home to you."

Sunday morning dawned clear and bright, bringing with it a welcome reprieve from Sarah's work. Or at least work at the bakery. She shook the fog of memory her dream had stirred from her mind and set about getting ready for the day.

"Morning, Pa." Sarah bustled brightly into his room. She opened the curtains, letting the light flood in, and unlatched the windows for some fresh air. Only then did she turn to the bed.

It broke her heart every time she looked at him. Her pa, once larger than life and full of energy, wasting away slowly in a bed he could no longer leave. A quick glance told her almost everything she needed to know.

Today would not be a good day. His hands were already trembling on top of the sheets, sweat dotted his brow, and the pain in his once clear grey eyes had her running for the laudanum. With a steady hand, she spooned the liquid gently into his trembling mouth, trying hard not to remember the times when he had been the one holding the spoon, and she the invalid in bed.

"Thank you, Sarah." Her pa's voice was reed-thin and took up no space in the almost empty bedroom.

"You right now, Pa?" she asked, her no-nonsense tone concealing the worry.

He nodded, though to Sarah it seemed shadows still danced across his eyes. Her heart squeezed in her chest. He wasn't getting any better. In fact, it seemed as if the night had stolen more of his flesh, more of his vitality. She wondered when he would cease to exist at all.

She leaned down, kissed his brow. "I'm heading off to church shortly. What would you like me to bring you in for breakfast?"

"Eggs? Bacon? A thick slice of toast?" The teasing held a dark note. Scrambled eggs he may be able to handle, but bacon and toast? His throat wouldn't work well enough to handle those. At times his frailty made him bitter; other times he could laugh it away. Mostly, it humiliated him to be seen this way.

"And shall I be getting you a cup of concrete while I'm at it? Toughen you up a bit?" Her teasing had the desired effect. A raucous laugh followed by a fit of coughing, the latter being outside the intended outcome.

"Witch," he said fondly. Once a big man, Frank Dawson still had the deep belly rumble of someone who laughed loud and long, even if it often ended on a wheeze. His eldest had inherited his propensity for spontaneous cheer. Though it wasn't much in evidence lately.

"I'll bring you some eggs in a minute, Pa. Then I'll get Isabel to help me change your linens before I go."

"You're a good girl, Sarah," Frank said. Sarah could feel the 'but' coming. Frank didn't disappoint. "But you're letting that sister of yours run roughshod all over ye."

Sarah blanched. Her pa always saw straight through to the heart of a situation. Said it was his Irish background, that they had the fair folk in their blood. She didn't know how true that was, but Sarah was glad he hadn't discovered what she was doing with the bakery.

It would break his heart if he knew how much she'd had to take upon herself.

"It's fine, Pa," she said, addressing the main concern "You know she's busy with that wedding of hers. I'm sure once she's finally settled, she'll be around to help."

Frank snorted, and Sarah found her lips twitching up in a smile she struggled to hide. She was sure Isabel would *eventually* become someone who could see the needs of others.

As if reading her mind, her father said, "And maybe pigs will grow wings and fly." He sighed. "I love the girl dearly, but it's no secret the lass could do with a firm thrashing."

Sarah raised her eyebrows and stared pointedly at the man who should have been Isabel's disciplinarian.

"Okay. I know that look. Maybe I could have been a *bit* harder on her." Sarah didn't bother to stifle the unladylike guffaw that followed his statement. "She looks so much like your mother, always has."

Sarah leaned forward and gave his hand a squeeze. The mood had turned pensive at the mention of Lucy Dawson.

A coughing fit broke the silence. Sarah handed him a handkerchief, disturbed to see it return all blood splattered.

"Won't be long now, lass, 'til I see your mother again. Think she'll have a place waiting for me next to her up there?" Frank attempted to wriggle his thin eyebrows, succeeding only in making the two wiry creatures twitch like hairy caterpillars in their death throws.

"I think she'd chew your ear off for leaving her girls alone and unwed." Sarah sat down and looked him straight in the eye, hoping the contact would emphasise her point. "Don't leave us, Pa. Not yet. We still need you." She swallowed the lump in her throat. "I need you."

"Settle down now, chook." Frank squirmed in embarrassment. Despite having raised two girls on his own since he'd lost his wife when Sarah was three, Frank still wasn't comfortable with emotions. "I'm not leaving you yet. I've still got a wedding to attend."

Neither of them stated the obvious. Frank wouldn't make it two steps from the bed, let alone the church.

"True, Pa, and don't you forget it. You still have a daughter who needs walking down the aisle." Sarah swept from the room in a flurry, mindful of the need to get everything done before church.

She was serving up the scrambled eggs when Isabel surfaced, strolling casually into the kitchen still dressed in her nightgown.

"Are those for me?" Isabel asked, drawn irresistibly to the smell. Sarah passed her the plate wordlessly, then transferred the serving that should have been hers to a plate, taking it in to her father.

"You'd best be quick. Church starts in an hour and you aren't even dressed for the walk," Sarah threw over her shoulder at Isabel.

"Harrison's picking me up," she replied dismissively, flicking her long blonde locks over her shoulder. Harrison and his blasted buggy. It seemed Isabel never walked anywhere anymore. And she never bothered to ask if her sister might like a ride as well.

By the time Sarah got back into the kitchen, Isabel had polished off the eggs and was moving back toward her bedroom.

"I'll need your help shifting Pa later so I can wash those sheets," Sarah said, her words stopping Isabel cold.

"Can't you do it yourself?" Isabel asked, the look of revulsion on her face sparking Sarah's temper.

"No, I can't do it by myself," she hissed through gritted teeth, mindful to keep her voice low enough that Pa wouldn't hear. She didn't want her father to think of himself as a burden.

Isabel had no such compunctions.

"And why not? You're going to have to do it all yourself soon anyway. Once Harrison and I are married, I won't be here to be your slave, Sarah." Her voice was shrill, and Sarah knew their father heard. Her heart broke for him anew.

Flabbergasted, her mouth opened and shut a few times, but nothing came out. Isabel used that time to withdraw, slamming the door to her room with a loud thud. Experience had taught Sarah she wouldn't win an argument with her sister. When faced with Isabel's aggression, all thought fled Sarah's mind. She couldn't reason with her, could come up with no rational arguments that would show her sister the error of her ways.

The worst thing was how all of this hurt her father.

Sarah hovered outside his bedroom door, trying to think of the words to make it better. She needn't have worried.

"Get in here, chook. Yer going to worry a hole in the floor with all that to-ing and fro-ing."

She ducked her head inside, the rest of her body dragging slowly after.

"Told yer. What're you going to do about her?" Frank shot her a pained smile.

"Me?" Sarah asked, incredulous. "When have I *ever* been able to talk to her? What about you?"

Her father laughed bitterly. "Tried last week. The witch listened until she figured out I was lecturing then turned and walked away, with me mid-sentence."

That did sound like Isabel.

Sarah sighed. "I'll talk to her tonight."

"You'll try," her pa said. "That's all either of us can do. Try."

"Lord, Pa. What does Harrison see in her? He's actually a good man." Sarah winced, biting her lip at her uncharacteristic outburst.

Frank laughed, coughed, then laughed again.

"Your sister has her moments, chook. And she is a beauty. Some men find that a trait worth overlooking other things for."

Sarah sighed, critically thinking on her own abundant curves. Even the amount of work she was doing at the bakery wasn't enough to slim down her figure.

"I can see those cogs turning, girl. Just so you know, there's many a man who appreciates a woman who's an armful." She winced. Sarah knew he meant well, but no girl wants to be told she's an 'armful.' Especially by her father. "Surely there's some young man who's come sniffing around the bakery for you?"

Sarah blushed and looked down, confused anew by her meeting with Connor again the other night.

"Oh. That's a look I didn't expect to see on your face, chook. Tell me then." Despite the teasing, Sarah knew it was an order, and she didn't have the heart to walk out on him as Isabel did.

"Connor Williams is back."

"Aahhh." The teasing had left his tone. "And you're still of a mind to have him then?" Frank Dawson had always seen too far into the heart of his eldest.

"Pa," Sarah said, horrified. "He's not an item to be bought or sold. And I said nothing of wanting him, only that he's back."

"And you set your heart at that boy's feet when you were five years old, and he pulled you out of the creek after Caleb had pushed you in." Sarah stayed silent. She wasn't going to tell him he was right. The man was insufferably smug as it was.

"Chook, everyone knows you only had eyes for him. The question is…" He stared straight into her eyes. "Is he the same man you fell in love with as a child, or has someone else come home from that damned war in Connor Williams's skin?"

Sarah didn't answer. Couldn't. Because while some trace of the old Connor still remained, she was very much afraid that a new man had taken his place.

But there was something about the darkness inside the new Connor that had her heart aching to soothe, to be the one he turned to in the night when the blackness seeped in.

"I don't know, Pa, but I think I need to find out." Sarah gave his hand a squeeze and walked out the door.

She left quietly for the church. Walked out with an empty stomach, burdened with worry about two men and one foolish young woman.

Was it too much to hope that she would find answers in a house of God?

From her experience, all it left her with was questions.

Chapter 4

"Whatta ya doin', Connor?" Thirteen-year-old Sarah bounced *eagerly on her toes, the end of her braid stuck firmly between her fingers and her mouth. When she saw where he was looking, she hastily pulled it out. He felt his own mouth twitching into a smile. "Can I help?"*

The words had left her mouth, but already she was looking beyond him, eyes focused on something in the distance. It was always the way with Sarah. Heart of gold, but her mind drifted like a bird on the wind. Granted, she was a sensible girl, but everyone who knew her understood that when she had that look in her eye, you'd get nothing more from her until whatever artistic muse that visited her had left.

"No, Little Bird," Connor said, dropping the lathe for the moment and turning her toward the house. The beams for the shed could wait—her muse wouldn't. He gave her a nudge, bringing her back to earth. "You go on in and get your charcoal. I'll be happy enough with your company later."

And he would. She would sit and draw for hours next to him in silence, but it was never uncomfortable. At fifteen, Connor knew he should be drawn more to people his own age but with her, everything was easy. No one held his attention as she did, no one offered the relief he needed when things were...difficult at home.

As Sarah strolled through her dreamland toward the house, Connor caught sight of her father. Frank had that same knowing grin on his face the man had worn when Connor had shown up, asking to help with the shed. The boy ducked his head a little, embarrassed, but then looked Sarah's father straight in the eye. Connor nodded.

With a solemn nod of his own, Frank went back to his own business, and Connor his. Nothing needed to be said. Sarah was theirs, and they'd both look after her needs before their own.

Even a fifteen-year-old boy knew the truth of that.

***

Connor didn't know why he was here, at the church. Church had never been a regular fixture of their lives before the war, and Lord knows he had too much to do to make the trip into town and back just to listen to a sermon. Perhaps it had something to do with his mother. The woman had lived for the social contact of the congregation after the isolation of the farm.

Or perhaps a feisty redhead drew him here.

Either way, he found himself hitching Caleb's still-nameless chestnut to the post outside the church. The building was a simple brick hall, the front door inset and solid oak. Nothing had changed in the years he'd been away, except maybe that the white paint around the wooden windowsills was a little more faded and peeling like a snake shedding its skin. Connor found himself hovering at the door when all he really wanted to do was turn around and ride back home. Recognising his own cowardice, he straightened his aching back and pushed through the double doors, hoping he hadn't missed the beginning.

He'd mistimed it.

The priest and the entire congregation turned as one to glare at the man who'd so rudely interrupted the sermon. They turned back to the front as he slid silently into a pew. But not without a few more pointed and curious looks his way. He fought an itch between his shoulder blades at the attention. They'd settle soon enough.

A clean-shaven youth stood at the front in his robes, like a little magpie giving the sermon. He should have been laughable, but a room full of people were hanging on his every word. The priest had a presence. A soothing aura and a commanding speaking voice. And a message that didn't include hellfire and damnation.

Just love.

What the hell had happened to this church in the years he'd been gone? Father Wilson had been an ageing tyrant more than capable at seventy-one years of striking the fear of God into what he saw as his "wayward flock." As a boy, Connor had been convinced he and his brother were going straight to hell. Wilson had seen everything as a sin and had the clout to influence anybody.

Not this priest.

Connor leaned forward, mesmerised, like everyone else.

All too soon, the young clergyman had finished and was giving communion. Connor joined the line like everyone else, then filed out into the front yard, where the church matrons had set up refreshments. This was what his mother had loved about the church. She hadn't cared for Father Wilson's fire-and-brimstone approach to scripture, but she had loved the church community.

And they had loved her. When she was herself.

The older women hovered around the tables in clusters like flocks of seagulls, only instead of being focused on the food, their sidelong glances rested on him. Connor shifted uncomfortably. He knew what they were doing, and he was going to do his damnedest to avoid any of the snares they were setting. There was only one girl he was interested in, and she wasn't anywhere near as vapid as the girls these well-meaning busybodies would foist on him.

His mother would have laughed in their faces over their scheming, then turned the conversation to something she was interested in. And they'd forgive her instantly.

Thoughts turning dark, Connor scanned the crowd for the one face he wanted to see. It was a sea of vaguely familiar faces, in dry washed-out tones. But no Sarah. Instead, he was bailed up by Duncan Graham.

"Good to see you here, lad," the stationmaster said. "Your mum would have been right pleased. She always did hate it when you and your brother would skip church."

Connor's mother had always been insecure, and she'd hated going in on her own. She'd seen her menfolk's preoccupation with the farm as a lack of interest in her and believed the whole town thought the same way. It didn't matter that half the farmers in the district didn't make church on a Sunday. Her boys not being there was an insult to her. There was so much work to do, but after their father's accident, the boys had usually taken it in turns to take her each week. Except in shearing season. Or lambing. Or any time really when the workload was too much for one, which was too often in their mother's opinion.

She'd put on her Sunday best dress, curl her hair, spend an hour applying makeup that Connor couldn't even tell was on. No one would see through the mask to the hurting woman underneath. No one had.

And then it was too late.

"That's why I'm here," Connor said politely. "I don't know how often I'll manage it, being the only one working the farm, but the new priest is worth listening to in any case."

Mr Graham laughed. "Yes, a damned sight better than that fire-and-brimstone Wilson. The new one's young, but a welcome replacement."

"What happened to Wilson?" Connor asked.

"Man was promoted to a bishopric. Can't remember where. Wish I'd paid attention because I'll stay right out of that diocese," muttered Mr Graham with a careful eye scanning for the matrons. They'd clip even the old stationmaster over the ear if they thought he was speaking ill of one of the Lord's representatives.

"Connor. Connor Williams," a voice called out.

Mr Graham used the approach of this other person to make his excuses and move on. Half his luck. Connor's own feelings about his next visitor were mixed.

The younger man who strode up to shake his hand enthusiastically was familiar. Harrison Ware had been in the grade below Connor at school and had been friendly with both Williams brothers. He was also now engaged to Isabel.

Looking at him now, Connor felt a little inadequate. The other man was dressed smartly in a crisply ironed shirt and pants, suspenders straight and clips shining. His coat was draped over one arm in deference to the heat, but Harrison Ware was still neatly put together.

In contrast, Connor couldn't stomach the thought of putting his uniform back on, even though it was by far the nicest thing he owned. He also hadn't had much time for washing, so though his clothing was clean, the work pants suspended over his singlet were not what his mother would have approved of for church.

"How are you, Harry?" Connor asked quietly.

"A damn sight better than you," Harry said, running a critical eye over Connor. Harrison had always been blunt. His eyes lingered over the scarring just visible on Connor's shoulder underneath the singlet. His eyes softened with compassion, which only served to irritate Connor. "You know if you want to talk about it, I'm—"

"Thanks, Harry, but no." Connor would sooner have died with his brother than share the horror he'd lived.

Harrison looked hurt, but Connor didn't have the energy to smooth his ruffled feathers.

"I know I wasn't in the trenches like you, Connor, but in the supply line we saw—"

"I said no." Anger sent a flush up his neck, leaving him struggling to control his tone. He didn't blame Harrison for the lot he'd been given, knew the other man had enlisted, same as him, but his poor eyesight led him into supply, rather than the front.

No, he didn't blame Harry. There were plenty of bastards to blame, but not the men who thought they were doing the right thing for their country, enlisting.

He wanted to forget.

And yet the one person he did hate with everything in him chose that moment to sidle up to them and worm her way under Harrison's arm. Connor's eyes shuttered. He wrestled with his anger.

It wouldn't do to have her wary of him because he couldn't control his emotions.

"Connor, I don't know if you remember Isabel Dawson?" Harry wrapped his arm affectionately around her, despite the disapproving gazes of the matrons, Harry's mother included. Their open affection was scandalous in a small, conservative town. Lucky for them, their engagement seemed to have stilled wagging tongues.

"I remember," he said quietly. "A tiny terror who used to follow in her older sister's shadow, making a nuisance of herself." That was the kindest thing he could say about her and was a far cry from his current feelings.

Isabel laughed, flicking her long blonde hair behind her. Harry's eyes were glued to her fondly. He always had a hand on her, no matter which way she turned.

It made Connor sick.

"That hasn't happened for years," she giggled, irritating him further. "I throw my own shadow now. And Sarah tends to follow."

Not likely. Isabel was obviously too self-centred to realise her sister measured herself against no one. That she walked to her own beat. His own heart beat a little faster in his chest at the thought of Sarah, whereas it was ringed with frost for her sister.

"Isabel and I are getting married next month," Harrison said with pride. Connor suppressed a shudder of revulsion. "Even though it's been difficult, with Mother disapproving of the match, I can't wait until we're properly wed." Harry squeezed his fiancée affectionately. She flashed him a grin in return, full of such vapid love Connor was forced to consider whether she was really that sickeningly romantic, or whether it was all an act.

He was betting on the latter.

The glimmer of an idea surfaced in Connor's mind. Harry's mother. And Isabel. Now that was full of possibilities if only he could get close enough to everyone involved. An added bonus would be saving his friend from the clutches of a harpy.

"I'm happy for you, Harry," Connor lied. "And for you too, Isabel."

Isabel beamed, and he was forced to admit she was incredibly beautiful. It was no wonder both Caleb and Harry were blinded to her true nature. With her hair of spun gold, perfect pouted lips, and flawless English rose skin, Isabel was the type of woman many men dreamed of making their own. It was a pity she was the wasp hiding behind the petals, not the gentle flower itself.

He much preferred a certain curvaceous beauty to her cold-fish sister.

With a final handshake and pat on the back, Connor extricated himself from the happy couple's company, in time to see Sarah round the corner of the church in conversation with a statuesque brunette he assumed was Sarah's best friend, Margery Cleary. The girl had certainly changed from the round butterball who used to find any excuse to get in trouble.

He had a feeling that part of her nature hadn't changed very much, even if she had lost her baby fat.

That was the moment Sarah noticed him. The smile that lit her face had his heart hammering like a drum inside his chest. Margery's curious little head twisted and turned, trying to see what had her friend so distracted. When she made the connection, her expression turned smug.

Not strong enough to resist the pull, Connor made his way inexorably to Sarah's side.

"There you are, Connor Williams," Marge said, leaning in to give him a brief hug. He shifted uneasily, not at all comfortable with the public display from someone he barely remembered. If it had been Sarah, on the other hand...

"Nice to see you here Connor," Sarah said, finally finding her voice. Her face was flushed a little. She made an awkward move to shake his hand but hesitated and withdrew, causing a hollow ache to form in his chest. No wonder. He had insulted her family at their last meeting. "I'd thought you'd be too busy with the farm to come into church for the next few weeks at least."

Her braid shone like a flame in the sunlight, daring him to stroke it, but her pale skin held a hint of grey that worried him. As did the black bags under her eyes.

"Thought I'd come and pay my respects here, for Mum," he said distractedly, trying to pinpoint the exact thing that had him worried this time about Sarah, aside from her pallor. That could be explained away by lack of sleep.

She reached up to tuck a wayward curl that had escaped its confines behind her ear. He caught the slight tremor in her hand. His heart stuttered. Was she ill? Had she injured herself since he'd seen her last?

"What's wrong with you?" As soon as the words left his mouth, he knew he'd said the wrong thing.

Marge laughed. "Still no tact, hey, Connor?" She laughed again when he turned to glare at her.

"What's *wrong* with me?" Sarah asked through gritted teeth. She might have been pleased to see him initially if that blush was anything to go by. She wasn't now though. "What's wrong with *you*? Surely your mother taught you better than to comment on a lady's appearance?"

"I didn't think—"

"That's right, you didn't think. I've seen you twice since you've returned and both times you've managed to insult me and mine. You really need a re-education in manners, Connor."

"I'm trying to tell you I'm s—"

"And another thing," Sarah continued, a freight train speeding along the tracks. "If you think—"

"That's enough out of you, sweet pea," Marge said firmly, dragging Sarah around to face her. "You're letting your temper get away with you. Haven't seen that happen since—"

"Don't you dare, Margery Anne Cleary. So help me, I'll... oh." Sarah's eyes lost focus, and she swayed a little on her feet. Words had left her. Not a good sign.

"Sarah?" Connor asked, concerned.

Marge laid a hand against Sarah's forehead. "Good Lord, girl. You're clammy as a fish. Connor, go get her a glass of water."

Connor turned to do that, but before he'd moved an inch, Sarah crumpled. Limp limbs were no longer able to support her weight. He lunged forward, managing to catch her before she hit the ground.

"Take her inside," Marge ordered. They'd already attracted too much attention with Sarah's outburst. The usually mild girl would be mortified to know she was the centre of attention. Particularly since the matrons were muttering amongst themselves and giving her the stink eye.

Connor caught the hint of a smile that crossed Marge's face. Though confused, he didn't stop. Sarah needed him, never mind the fact she probably wouldn't appreciate it. In fact, she'd probably be mortified when she woke. That was beside the point, however.

Sarah needed someone to look after her. And it was going to be him.

Though the scarring on his back tugged in warning, Connor kept a tight grip on Sarah until they were inside, and he could lay her gently on one of the pews. Already she was starting to stir, but so was his worry, and his anger.

When her eyes flicked open, he took it as a sign to let loose.

"You haven't been looking after yourself, have you?" he accused. "You've been taking care of everyone else around you and barely seeing to your own needs at all."

"I take care of myself," she muttered, though everyone knew it was a lie. "I didn't get time for breakfast this morning."

"Didn't get time for..." Connor's mouth opened and closed silently.

Margery came to the rescue.

"What are you talking about, peahen?" she asked. "You make that father of yours breakfast religiously, every morning before the sun rises. Surely you made enough for you, too?"

Sarah turned away, reluctant to continue the conversation.

"Sarah..." Connor's tone brooked no argument.

She sighed in defeat. "I *did* make enough for me."

They both looked at each other, confused. Then understanding hit Marge first, followed quickly by Connor.

"That cow of a sister you still coddle ate your breakfast, didn't she, Sarah?" Marge accused, pointing a bony finger at Sarah's chest.

Connor seethed. He'd already done enough damage with his words today, so he kept his mouth shut. It took everything in him to keep from either turning Sarah over his knee for allowing Isabel to treat her like this or doing something much worse to her sister.

Thankfully, the priest himself rescued the sisters from his rage, and most likely Margery's as well.

"I'd thank you not to speak ill of another in God's house, children." It should have sounded ridiculous coming from the mouth of someone who appeared younger than themselves, but the priest's words chastened both Marge and Connor, soothing the beasts.

"Sorry, Father," Connor mumbled, looking anywhere but at the stick-thin man in his flapping robes. "Injustice tends to get me a little angry."

"I can see that," the priest said wryly. "What is your name, soldier?"

Connor didn't ask how the priest knew. It was written in the face and body of every veteran. In the frown lines on the forehead, the sunken cheeks from malnutrition, the scars that couldn't be hidden by clothes or locked up in minds. Of course, he knew.

"Connor Williams, sir," he answered respectfully.

"Ahh... I'd wondered when I'd have the pleasure of meeting you."

Connor flicked a glance at Margery and Sarah, uncomfortable with the attention. Both women were trying to smother smiles, so he shot them a mock glare, daring them to say something. Of course, cheeky Margery didn't disappoint.

"Don't know if you'd call it a pleasure, Father. Connor's frown is a mile long these days, and it would take an act of God to get him to smile."

Connor's lips twitched at this, giving the lie to her statement, and the priest laughed.

"I'm sure he'll find something to smile about soon enough, Margery, even if it's only at your antics." The man turned to Connor, offering his hand. "I'm Father Benson, Father Ben, or just Father if you prefer."

He'd expected the man's hand to be soft, but the calluses that roughened his palm surprised Connor. The priest noticed his reaction.

"I don't always spend my time ministering to my human flock," he said, correctly addressing Connor's curiosity. "I've been helping with the community farm as much as possible, but thankfully I'm not needed as much now that the men are returning."

"Connor should be taking his stock back to his place soon," Sarah cut in. There was a sly look on her face that Connor didn't understand but was making him nervous.

"A few weeks yet, I think," said Connor, mentally tallying the list of things that needed to be done before he could safely run his stock on the farm again. "There's plenty needs to be done and only one set of hands to do it."

Sarah grinned.

Too late he realised he'd walked right into her trap.

"We can't have that. You know we help our own. Excuse me a minute." The priest flapped his way back outside again as Connor groaned. No way of escaping the interference of the matrons now.

The woman's grin turned into a pealing laugh. Marge joined in when she realised how neatly Connor had been manoeuvred. He couldn't believe it himself.

"You certainly know how to get your way, don't you, Little Bird?" Connor's use of the nickname for Sarah was automatic. He froze for a moment, wondering how it would be taken, but her smile softened, and her eyes turned wistful.

"I didn't think I'd be hearing that nickname again, what with Caleb..." Her voice trailed off as Margery clamped a soothing hand on her shoulder. He'd forgotten that Caleb had taken to using the name as well. "And yes, I've become very good at getting what I want from difficult people, with the least possible fuss."

The reference to her sister didn't go unnoticed, but he chose to ignore it in favour of keeping the peace.

"Then I'll be on the lookout in the future for your little traps, Sarah Dawson," he said, turning a blinding grin on her. "And maybe I'll set a few of my own."

Sarah sucked in a gasp, skin burning bright pink as she stared at him, dumbfounded. Connor's grin grew wider. She'd always been appealing, but the years he'd been gone had given her an aura of velvet over steel that made her stunning.

If things were different, he'd be dropping his heart at her feet and begging her to take it up. As it was, the attraction could be useful. But he'd better avoid thinking about Sarah in the long term because if everything he hoped came to pass, the woman wouldn't be speaking to someone who'd destroyed the sister she was fiercely protective of.

"All right, that's enough of those heated stares from the two of you," Marge interrupted, grinning in delight. "We'd all best get outside so Connor can battle the matrons for dominance."

"We all know who's going to win that battle," Sarah snorted as she stood gingerly, taking a few moments to steady herself. "No one's going to put their money on Connor."

Connor scowled in mock anger. "I'll have you know I've a winning way with the matrons. Give me five minutes, and I'll have convinced them it's not necessary to send everyone in the district out to the old homestead." He didn't sound convincing, even to his own ears.

The young women looked at each other for a heartbeat, then burst into gales of laughter.

"Come along then, Captain Persuasion. Let's see you work your wiles on the canniest women in the district," Marge said as she took both his arm and Sarah's.

He had a feeling he would be regretting coming to church in the next five minutes.

But he'd be damned if he didn't at least acknowledge the spark of warmth their care left in his chest.

Chapter 5

The mud of the trenches sucked at Connor's boots, almost begging him to stay where he was. Egypt, with its dry heat and shifting sands, hadn't prepared them for the horror of the mud. Or the incompetence of the generals. Please, Lord, let Caleb make it through. Let us both see each other again on the other side.

"Ready, boys?" It sounded like a question, but everyone knew it was a prelude to one of Lieutenant Colonel Norris's orders. Feet shuffled, some of the men nodded, others just stared. Resigned to their fate. The 53rd was used to the uncertainty, but it didn't stop the sinking feeling in Connor's gut.

Something was wrong.

Things weren't adding up, but it wasn't his place to question orders. He could only hope Caleb's troop were better organised. Better informed. This was starting to smell like Gallipoli all over again.

No. Connor was a survivor. And he was going to make damned sure he and his brother got out of here alive.

How he was going to do that with Caleb attacking from the other side of the Sugar Loaf was beyond him, but Connor's luck had always been good. It was why he had outlived the 1st Battalion at Gallipoli. He had to hope it had rubbed off on his brother in the sixteen years the boy had shared his life.

"Positions, lads," Norris bellowed. Connor sucked in deep breaths, shifted to his toes. The heels of his boots squelched out of the sucking mud. He raised the loaded rifle, made sure the bayonet was secure. The air seemed to still, even the shriek of British shells frozen at that moment. Then, with an enormous roar, the men of the 53rd surged over the trenches and into No-man's Land.

Into fire from an enemy who wasn't supposed to know they were coming.

Connor sat bolt upright in bed. Sweat streamed down his forehead and bare chest, mingling with the rank smell of fear that seemed to fill the room. Though his windows were bare, hardly any light filtered into the room. Dawn was only just kissing the horizon, silhouetting the mountains.

The cock crowed again.

Connor relaxed. That was what had woken him. Not the whistle of shells or the eternal drumroll of the machine guns, only a rooster greeting the morn.

Shoulders stiff and sore from too much activity the day before, he rubbed a soothing hand over the tender scarring.

Shaking the last of his dream, Connor tramped toward the kitchen and the goodness of a fried egg breakfast. Nothing could be more opposite to the bullied beef stews of the trenches than fresh eggs fried with herbs from his mother's garden. He stirred the coals in the stove, tenderly bringing the fire back to life, then organised his breakfast.

The sun was above the mountain when the first cart trundled up the drive, quickly followed by a dozen more. Connor stared in horror from the kitchen window as an army of women and men invaded his yard. An army intent on conquering both him and his problems.

First among them was Sarah Dawson, smiling unerringly at him through the kitchen window from the same seat next to Mr Graham he had claimed on that first ride back home. She lifted a saucy hand and waved at him.

Despite his annoyance, he couldn't help but smile.

The cheeky minx had done it. She'd marshalled the town into helping fix his property. Wagon after wagon filled the yard, each with its own troop of infantry ready to battle his fences, wrestle his overgrown yard and, by the looks of the women carting pots and pans, invade his kitchen.

He couldn't help but panic slightly when Mrs Ware stepped from a fashionable buggy, the delicate thing an entirely frivolous choice for the dusty roads of the northwest. Her hair was in a tight bun under a wide-brimmed straw hat, and she waved a ladle to marshal her troops. The statuesque woman was a force of nature, and age certainly hadn't dulled the formidable weapon that was her voice. The men moved immediately toward the barn, the women to the house, and a horde of children descended upon the garden, led by the portly Mrs Ware.

It was no wonder Harry was terrified of her if this was the way she had treated her son when he was a boy. Mrs Ware's voice boomed across his yard, almost seeming to echo through his house. The children ran to do her bidding, nestling in the garden and digging out the plants she directed them to, while she set up a stool in the shade. Connor hoped to God they were weeds and not his mother's prize daffodil bulbs, but he was too scared to go question his friend's mother too closely.

The screen door rattled and the hinges squeaked. The invasion had begun.

"Connor, the men will be needing you outside. I think we can manage the house." Sarah breezed into his home, bringing with her sunshine and women's laughter. Four women he didn't recognize trailed in after her, some carting kitchenware, another a laundry tub and soap. One bustled over to his threadbare curtains and threw them aside, sending sunshine streaming into the room.

Mortified, he saw the dust motes swirl around the room as the women proceeded to strip sheets from furniture he hadn't yet used. A hint of shame curled in his gut that he'd allowed his mother's fortress to remain in disrepair. She would have been horrified these women had seen it like this. Then again, maybe if she'd held on a little longer, this wouldn't have...

Connor reeled in his spiralling thoughts, trying to find the words that would send the unwanted army on their way. Instead, the woman with the laundry tub was already filling it as another put the kettle on the old stove to boil water. Someone was trooping out of the bedrooms with dusty and rumpled bedding. Including the sheets off his own bed.

His face flamed as he realised Sarah was the one exiting his room, her own smile hesitant. He understood why. The room was stark, bland. He'd removed all photographs from the walls, and his kit bag remained packed beside his bare wardrobe, despite his having been home a week.

"Do you not have anything left here, Connor? Surely, even if you have grown some, there was something in here we could let out, maybe add a bit of fabric to so you can get some more use out of it?" Sarah's words sent sorrow piercing through him.

Abruptly, he turned, striding out of the house and around the back of the chook yard. Breaths coming in short sharp pants as he struggled to control himself, Connor tried to shove memories aside before it was too late. It didn't work.

"I'm sorry you had to hear about it like this, son." As the mayor, Harrison Ware Senior had seen it as his duty to come to see Connor himself. It wasn't a conversation that should have been had with the recipient of the news in a hospital bed covered in shrapnel wounds, but it was a necessary one all the same. Hopefully, news that, if broken here, where there were people to help, would see him able to cope a little better with the situation.

Connor struggled to breathe. Not only his brother but now his mother. No one left to return home to. He was a husk. An empty shell. Everything that had meant anything to him was gone. All because of that—

"Maybe you could ask someone to help you flesh out that kit bag of yours with a few more clothes before you go? Your mother..." the mayor hesitated. Connor's gut sank. He knew what was coming, had seen it himself before when his father passed. "She wasn't herself at the end. When the ladies found her, they also found two piles of charred remains of clothes. Gave them an even bigger scare, that did. Why..."

Connor's ears buzzed, the words no longer clear. Two burning piles of clothes. If she had waited a month, she would have had the news her eldest was coming home.

Instead, she gave in to despair.

And left Connor to face it on his own.

A gentle hand on his wounded shoulder had Connor whirling, fist stopping short of the face of the last person he'd ever hurt intentionally. Remorse filled him, and shame burned a hole in his chest. Sarah didn't flinch, however, just stared boldly at him with pity in her eyes.

It was almost worse than fear.

Abruptly, anger filled him. At himself, at the do-gooders invading his space, but mostly at his mother. And here in front of him was a convenient outlet.

"I don't want your pity, Sarah, so if that's what's running through that clever little mind of yours, you can take it with you as you turn around and march your troop back through my gates," he snarled.

She didn't back away. No, the brave chit stood there, riding his anger, the pity in her eyes melting into a temper of her own. He admired the way it made her eyes flash with fire, even as it stirred his own further.

"Pity is the last thing you need. A swift kick in the behind is more like it." Her swift retort stoked his own anger.

"A swift kick in the arse you mean?" His attempt to shock her with crude language fell flat. Apparently, being friends with his brother had inured her to the effect of vulgarity.

"If that's the only thing that will get you to start acting like a man instead of a brooding thunder cloud again, then yes. A swift kick in the arse is what you need."

Frustration and anger ate at him, her words lighting a fire in him. He wasn't sure whether it came from his temper or his arousal. Trying to rein in his churning emotions, he explained, through gritted teeth, "I told you yesterday, this is a Williams' work and it'll be done by a—"

"Williams. Yes, I understand, Connor." Sarah's sarcastic eye-roll saw his temper soaring. "You're the man of the house. You'll do all the work, even if it means reopening the wound on your shoulder that still has you hunched." *Hunched. Of all the—* "Go ahead, you great, galloping fool. Ignore the fact that people care—"

When his lips crashed down on hers, Connor wasn't sure whether it was to shut her up, or because the sun turned the wispy curls that had escaped her braid into a fiery halo that drove him to taste. Either way, his hands cupped her face, touched those tantalising curls, as he took the kiss deeper with a groan.

She tasted of sunshine and summer, hope and passion. As his tongue danced with hers, he burned with it. And there was no melting from Sarah. Oh no, she met him stroke for stroke, nip for nip, as if her lips, her passion, had been made for him alone. One hand drifted from her face, down her back, pressing her closer still. His cock was rock hard between them and though he knew she was innocent, he couldn't seem to care. She was sweetness and light. Everything he'd dreamed about, surrounded in the mud and rot of the trenches, and it was beyond the limits of his self-control to let her go now.

***

Connor's lips were on hers, and it was all she could do not to beg him to take her right there behind the chook shed. In the dim recesses of her mind, Sarah knew she'd have to stop, that to go any further would be to invite ruin, but the taste of him was driving her to distraction. As were the hands that currently roamed her body in ways no man had before.

His thumb traced the curve of her breast, sending electricity straight down her spine to her core. Though she knew she should be embarrassed by her response to him, it seemed all common sense had fled at the first touch of his lips.

For a moment, those lips left hers, tracing a path lower down her neck as he backed her slowly up against the shed. She almost moaned at the loss, but they returned to her almost as soon as they had left. The hard, wooden wall was firm against her back, as was the man who pressed his body closer to hers.

She did moan against his lips when those hands traced their lightning up the inside of her thighs, drawing up her simple skirt and meeting the loose fabric of her underwear. He hesitated. Mindlessly, Sarah spread her thighs farther, granting him easier access. He didn't wait any longer, his urgency almost as great as hers, hand slipping under the confines of her underwear.

Finally, those talented fingers met her feminine core, and she became boneless, melting into him. He stroked through her damp heat, higher until he hit something that saw her eyes opening wide with pleasure. Wordlessly, she writhed against him as he rubbed gentle circles around that firm nub.

It was maddening, driving her to a frenzy, yet she couldn't seem to find release. Her hands clutched at him, drew him closer then traced lower to where she could feel the hard outline of him against her stomach. Sarah traced the waistline of his pants, searching for something to end her torment, but as she found the button, Connor flicked her nub and she exploded.

Stars danced across the back of her eyelids.

He feathered kisses across her cheeks, her eyelids, the corner of her lips, before gently taking them again with his own. A brief kiss full of tender wonder.

"You're so perfect, my Sarah. So bloody perfect," he breathed against her lips, drawing her close into the comfort of his arms.

Then he froze and pushed her away in horror.

Sarah sensed his withdrawal as if someone was tearing out a piece of her soul. He'd already stolen hers, but now he was about to tear it to shreds. The stars in her eyes disappeared and with their loss came clarity. No, she wouldn't regret it, even if it had been ill-advised. She wouldn't let him regret it either.

"Don't you dare, Connor Williams. If you say this was a mistake, you'll break my heart." Oh Lord. Her stomach sank. Knowing Connor, those words were the last thing she should have said.

The man was as stubborn as a mule, and she'd just delivered an order.

Chapter 6

The words hovered on the tip of his tongue. This *was* a mistake, but the desperate look in Sarah's eyes gave him pause.

He couldn't hurt her. Not deliberately. But this couldn't happen again.

"I won't say it," he said cautiously as he stepped back farther, putting some much-needed space between them. He couldn't think when she was close. "But this shouldn't happen again. You should probably get back inside."

She stepped forward and laid her hand on his arm, that one touch destroying the clarity he'd created with space.

"I think it *will* happen again," Sarah said, ignoring his comment. "And you'll get just as lost in it next time as you were a moment ago."

His brain was mush as she trailed her fingers up his arm, stroked his hair. No one had touched him like this in years. With gentleness. With care. And with something else he wasn't going to name. It was a comfort he was desperate to sink into, but after a brief pause, he found himself stepping away again.

"Maybe," Connor said. "But that doesn't mean I won't try my best to avoid it. You don't deserve to be shackled to the likes of me. And I'll do my damnedest to spare you that fate."

The dice were rolling in his head. Who knew what numbers they'd show when they eventually stopped. He'd always been lucky but with Sarah... Connor didn't know in this case what luck was. Should he pursue her, despite knowing he'd hurt her in the end, then hope she'd forgive him? Or was he better to let sleeping dogs lie? He turned and stalked toward the barn and the other men, leaving part of his heart silent behind the shed.

***

Sarah stared after him, at a loss as to what to do. When she'd been sixteen, the future had seemed like a perfectly straight road. Connor would return. They'd get married. Fill his house with children and live happily ever after. She shook her head at her former self.

Not with this Connor. The man was a mess of contradictions, not to mention the fact he had somehow avoided the conversation she'd come out here to start. His mother's death was a festering sore inside him that needed to be addressed. Soon, if his helplessness in his home was anything to go by. A broken man wasn't someone you built a future with. He had to want to help himself first.

Yet there was no chance she was going to let him go now, not after the man had melted her bones and remade her in an instant. She'd have to tackle him like she did everything in life—with a damned good plan. Some imagination.

And reinforcements.

Thankfully, her biggest supporter had arrived, riding astride a bay stallion who should have been too much for her to handle, skirts bunched at her knees. Mrs Ware's mouth screwed up with disapproval as Marge threw her leg over the rump of the beast, unconcerned with modesty. The older woman started to raise herself off her designated throne, became distracted by a shriek from one of the children, and thankfully, Sarah's best friend was safe.

"Sorry I'm late, chook," Marge called, leading the deceptively docile horse behind her. Sarah wasn't fooled. The animal lashed out at anyone who dared approach him. The poor farrier wouldn't go near the beast unless Marge was there with him, stroking his nose and whispering sweet nothings in his ear. Sarah couldn't blame him. As it was, Marge tended to laugh when he got snappy, only stopping him when it looked like he'd succeed in taking a chunk out of some unsuspecting fool. "Where do you think I should put him, love?"

Sarah looked around. The house yard was full of children, so that was out. A group of men, including Connor, who was currently trying his best to walk tall, were heading out with carts full of star pickets and wire into the west paddock, presumably to do some repairs. As were another group heading south, another to the east.

All that was left was the front paddock. And it wasn't empty.

Sarah sighed, weighing up the slight possibility of a foal come spring with the very real possibility of bodily harm coming to one of the volunteers. Surely Caleb's old mare couldn't be on heat? She'd be past the age where that would be a problem. Right?

Marge eyed the mare warily as Sarah led her to the gate separating the front paddock from the house yard. "Are you sure this is a good idea, chook? That mare looks pretty flirtatious to me, and Bunny here is just about chomping at the bit to get into that paddock."

Bunny. Snuggly Bunny would have to be the most ridiculous name for Marge's devil-spawn horse, but on this she was right. The mare was flicking her tail and prancing up and down the fence-line like a model at one of those new fashion shows that Marge was always talking about. Bunny himself was being bossier with Marge than she'd ever seen him. He was dragging his mistress toward the paddock.

Sarah picked up her pace to keep up.

"It'll have to do. It's either that or let him maul the volunteers."

"Righto," Marge said with a cheeky grin. "Two extremely happy horses it is."

Marge barely had a chance to remove his tack and Sarah open the gate before the stallion bolted into the yard.

Marge laughed.

"Let's go give them some privacy," she said as she took Sarah's arm, leading her toward the house. "And you can give up yours because by the state of your braid and the red in your cheeks, I'd say someone has some gossip to share."

Sarah laughed, filling her friend in briefly as they walked toward the homestead. It was no use trying to keep a secret from Marge, though in this case, she didn't want to. The only person whose secrets were safe with the notorious gossip was Sarah, and she'd need Marge's help if she was ever going to get Connor to admit he loved her.

"Are you sure this is what you want?" Marge asked quietly, stopping Sarah just out of earshot of the house. "The man has problems, Sarah. You can tell by looking at him. You sure you want to take those on?"

It was a fair question, and one Sarah had mulled over plenty in the last week. The truth was, Connor was it for her. She didn't pretend to understand it, but the man had been in her blood since the first time she met him. She'd only ever seen *him*. And after that kiss and that…

Her face flamed again.

"I'm sure." There was no doubt in Sarah's voice and Marge relaxed, nodding. "There never has and never will be anyone else for me but him."

"And it's bloody obvious he feels the same."

Sarah raised her eyebrow at the profanity. Marge blushed.

"Sorry, I've been around my brothers too much lately." That was understandable. Marge did have four of them, and Sarah had been awfully busy lately. She let it slide. "So how are we going to get that tall glass of water to admit he's head over heels for you and always has been?"

And there was the problem. Connor didn't *want* to love Sarah. And it was going to be the biggest fight of her life to get him to give in.

But it was one she wouldn't lose.

"I don't know, Marge, but I'm sure between the two of us we can come up with something."

"Of course, my little dumpling," Marge said, flicking a superior hand out. "We can do anything, you and I. But first we'd better start with fixing this place up. I can see Betty Cleary through the kitchen window burning holes in your back. Think she's trying to read our lips? Or is she willing us to get a move on?"

Sarah laughed, hooking her arm through her best friend's as they made their way to the house.

Connor didn't stand a chance with Marge on the case.

"We've already made our first move, pumpkin," Marge said as they climbed the stairs to the veranda.

"We have?" Sarah asked, perplexed.

"Well, do you really think I'm going to be able to get Bunny out of that paddock any time soon?" Sarah turned to look back at the two horses, then quickly looked back at Marge, blushing.

"You're right," Sarah stammered, blinking to try to erase the image that was seared onto her eyeballs. "I think Bunny's going to be too busy to go home."

"No way I'm walking into that paddock while that mare's on heat." Marge grinned slyly. "But I'm going to need someone to check up on him over the next few days. I have to help Ma with the carding, so I can't do it myself."

Sarah thought about all the things she had to do. Where was she going to find the time to come out here each day as well? But she'd do it if it meant seeing Connor daily when he would more than likely avoid her otherwise.

"Hurry up, girls," Betty bellowed from inside. "The first load of sheets is ready to hang on the line. And you'll need to string up some new ones. There's no way the old line will handle this many sheets in one go. Get a move on."

Grinning, the girls rushed inside.

They had a plan of attack. There was no way Sergeant Connor Williams could outmanoeuvre these two generals.

***

Connor waved farewell to the last of the volunteers, his shoulder aching fiercely. Though he'd tried to ignore the pain during the day, his mind was either flooded with agony or visions of Sarah as she came apart in his arms.

He didn't know which was worse.

Resentfully, he'd had to pass the dolly to other men, the strain of lifting it too much for his wound. Instead, he'd threaded and unwound the barbed wire, nicking himself constantly with it in the process. Too distracted. Pain and fantasies were not a good combination when you needed to keep your wits about you. It was all oddly humiliating, though no one had said anything to him about his weakness.

Despite his surliness, he'd enjoyed the company of the men, the chatter and occasional ribaldry that accompanied men hard at work. It had made him feel alive again, part of something when every other unit he'd been a part of had been destroyed around him.

The only thing that would destroy this unit was his own bad temper.

When he realised what he was doing, he tried to change his mood. Gave himself a 'swift kick in the behind,' as Sarah would say. Found himself smiling at the thought, even though he'd told himself he wouldn't think about her. At least for today.

Surprisingly, Harry hadn't come out with Mrs Ware, though his father had. Harrison Ware Senior was a good, solid man. Quiet, except when he was nervous, unlike his son or wife, with a deep sense of responsibility. Perhaps that was why Connor found it odd the son hadn't come too.

Mr Ware grunted when Connor asked him about it.

"Fool boy couldn't be found this morning when we were leaving," he growled in response to Connor's question. "Probably being led by the nose by that twit he's so set on marrying."

Connor agreed with him there, but twit wasn't the word to describe Isabel. Manipulative. Conniving. Evil. Any would do in a heartbeat, but Isabel was no twit. She was too smart for that.

Now would be a good time to start planting the seeds of his plan.

"Wouldn't be the first man she's had tied in knots," he said as he was turning away. The next he made sure was only audible for the old man as he walked away, "and he won't be the last."

Mr Ware was quiet for the rest of the day. Brooding.

Connor was filled with a sick sense of satisfaction. He knew this was going to hurt Harry. And Sarah. But it was the only way he could think of to make Isabel suffer for the pain she'd caused. The lives she'd destroyed.

The day passed so quickly that the sun sinking behind the mountains was a shock when it began. Their group had finished mending the west paddock fences. As he waved the men off gratefully, he wondered how the others had gone with the less damaged paddocks. They had already left by the time his group had returned. He started toward the front paddock, intent on saddling the still-nameless mare and riding the fence lines to check their handiwork when he pulled up short.

There was a great, bay beast in the paddock with his mare. And they were enjoying themselves immensely.

Furious, he stomped toward the paddock, intent on separating the two, when the stallion abruptly finished, dismounted his mare, and rushed directly toward Connor, teeth bared.

Whatever happened to the afterglow? thought Connor, horrified and a little frightened. He backed away from the gate just in time to avoid the teeth of the great brute, beating a hasty retreat toward the homestead. Maybe he'd find answers inside?

There were. Right on his now immaculate mahogany benchtop was a note.

Connor,

Marge rode Bunny in today and the only safe place to keep him was the front paddock. Didn't realise the mare was in heat. We tried to get him out, but he wouldn't even let Marge part him from his new lady love.

I'll drop by tomorrow to check on him. Marge won't be able to.

Don't worry, I'll try not to bother you.

Yours,

Sarah.

What the hell did she mean by 'yours'?

And how in God's name was he going to avoid her if she kept turning up on his doorstep?

She'd breached his defences and Connor wasn't sure he'd be able to shore them up again in time.

Or at all.

Did he want to?

Chapter 7

Monday morning dawned bright and clear, but Sarah didn't see it. Instead, she'd fired the ovens at the bakery well before dawn to hopefully close the shop early. She had a date with two rambunctious stallions she didn't want to miss.

Unfortunately, the morning didn't go quite as smoothly as she'd hoped. Isabel breezed into the bakery as Sarah was about to open the doors.

"Pa's asking for you," Isabel commented, breezing in and pilfering a fresh loaf of bread, raiding the cool room in the process for some of Sarah's cream she'd skimmed from the milk delivered that morning. Incredulously, she looked on.

"Why is Pa looking for me when he knows I'm here working?"

"You didn't bring him any breakfast before you left. He's hungry." Isabel flipped her golden hair behind her shoulder, loose strands flying everywhere. Why couldn't the girl put her hair up, at least to come into the kitchen?

"I left you a note, Isabel. His breakfast was waiting on the kitchen bench for him. All you had to do was take it in. What happened?" Marge often accused Sarah of having the patience of a saint with Isabel, but now, she felt ready to clobber the selfish snob.

"What note?" Isabel asked. Sarah's heart sank. Surely her sister wouldn't have— "You left my breakfast on the bench like always. There was only one plate."

"It was Pa's plate," she hissed through gritted teeth. Isabel had the gall to look confused. "You ate your bedridden father's breakfast, which you would have known was his if you had bothered to even pop in and say 'good morning' to him."

"Now wait a minute, Sarah. I'll have you know—"

"That's enough from you," she hissed, trying and failing to control her temper. "You need to take a long hard look at yourself and ask if you like the woman you are today. And to make it clear how it looks from where I'm sitting, I'm not going to sugar-coat it for you. You are possibly the most selfish human being I know."

Isabel's shocked gasp served to calm Sarah. A small, mean-spirited part of her even found it a little satisfying.

Sarah took a deep breath and continued. "You treat everyone around you as your servant, even though most around here have known you since you were in swaddling. You leave me to run the bakery single-handedly, while you go god-knows-where with your fiancé. You steal our products and profits to buy yourself trinkets when all that I earn here goes toward keeping food on our table and buying laudanum to manage Pa's pain. And by far your worst offence, you ignore our pa, who doesn't have very long left with us, and who has treated you like a princess from the day you were born."

Her chest heaved as she fought for breath. Isabel was spluttering, trying to find words and discarding sentences as she started them.

"Have you ever done something for someone that didn't benefit you in some way?" Sarah asked finally, sick of waiting for her sister to formulate a response.

The silence was endless.

"Where's Pa's apprentice?" Isabel asked.

Sarah saw red. "Get. Out."

"What? I'm just wondering why you're running the bakery al—"

"You selfish, ignorant little twit." Though she felt slightly ashamed of losing her temper, by God, it felt good to say those words. She waved the wooden spoon in her hand menacingly at her sister. "Pa's apprentice has been gone for months, which you would have known if you cared enough to help keep this place going. Get out of here now, Isabel, or so help me, I'll swat you with this wooden spoon like Pa should have done all those years ago when you started putting on your airs."

The taller girl, who had been slowly backing away from her sister, turned and fled, perhaps faster than she'd ever moved in her life. Sarah followed her out the back door.

"And make sure you cook Pa some breakfast before you leave him there alone," she screeched after Isabel, barely stopping herself from throwing the spoon after her.

A slow clap started as Isabel rounded the corner and Sarah turned to go back inside.

Great. As if the day couldn't get any worse. Now Connor had seen her screeching at her sister like a fishwife, her furious face so red there was a real possibility it would explode with the force of her anger, with her hair and apron dusted with flour.

So much for dressing nicely and surprising him that afternoon.

Now he'd seen her at her worst, there was no way he'd entertain the thought of loving her again. Or rather, enticing him to acknowledge the feelings she was sure were buried not so far beneath the surface.

She might as well take one last look at him, a long one, because he wouldn't be coming back here any time soon. Boldly, she looked him up and down, eyes tracing the broad shoulders, tanned skin, and lingering on his tapered hips. His dark hair, once military short, was starting to grow out. The loose dark curls suited him.

Sarah barely stopped herself from reaching out to touch him; only his hasty step backward saved Connor from her questing fingers. She looked down, blushing, as he cleared his throat awkwardly.

"How much of that did you hear?" she asked, shame riding her.

"Enough to know your sister had it coming." His voice was hard but the words were understanding. Sarah looked around the alley for eavesdroppers, only now realizing their conversation was very public. Thank God there were none. Or at least no obvious ones.

"Come inside," she said, resigned. At least this bit of dirty laundry could be kept from the public. Connor followed, a silent shadow, and she sighed. Having him behind her made her feel safe, like nothing in the world could touch her. Unfortunately, he was also one of the only people with the power to hurt her.

As soon as she entered the kitchen, she washed her hands, picking up the nearest batch of fully risen dough and kneading. Shaping bread was second nature to her and gave her the excuse to avoid eye contact. She didn't want to look at him as they had this conversation.

Damn Isabel. She was the only person in the world who could ignite Sarah's temper. Well... Isabel, and the man currently behind her.

She pounded the dough with her fists, rougher than needed. The loaf would be worse than useless, but it was worth it if only to help her let go of her anger.

Connor cleared his throat again.

"So why are you here at this hour, Connor? Shouldn't you be collecting your stock today?" Sarah was proud of herself. She *almost* sounded like her usual calm, collected self.

"I had intended to tell you not to bother checking on Marge's horse bu—"

"It's no bother, really," Sarah cut him off, still avoiding eye contact. "Marge loves that beast, and if anything were to happen to him, she wouldn't know what to do with herself." Her hands were moving at a furious pace, pounding until the dough resembled a flat pancake. She stared at it in silence.

A hand touched her shoulder, hesitantly.

"Do you want to talk about it?" She almost laughed. If anyone needed to talk, it was Connor, and here he was offering to let her unburden herself on him.

"Not really," she said quietly. "I'm only just managing to stay afloat in this sea of troubles I've somehow managed to acquire, but they're not your problems to solve. I'll manage by myself. I always have."

"Sarah…" He gently grabbed her shoulders, turning her to face him. She went reluctantly.

"You've already told me you don't want a repeat of yesterday, Connor. I'm not going to make a fool of myself pining after something I can't have, so there's no need for you to feel obligated to comfort a teary woman." Because, she realised with dawning horror, she was. A weeping woman.

Great, big, salty tears dribbled soundlessly down her cheeks, betraying her emotions yet again.

He tilted her chin upwards, searching for something in her eyes as she stared at him defiantly. His mouth drifted achingly close to hers, hovering just out of reach, and for a heart-stopping moment, she thought he was going to pull away.

Then his lips brushed hers. Once. Twice. So achingly gentle, more tears followed the first round. He rested his forehead on hers, eyes closed.

"I thought you didn't want to do that again?" Her voice was a breathy whisper. She barely recognized it as her own.

"Sometimes, some things are inevitable," he whispered back, pausing again to sample her lips, teasing them with his tongue. "I'm not sure I want to fight this, even though you'd be better off without me."

"Let me be the judge of that," she said, aching for him to continue. Instead, he gently pushed her back.

"The stallion is well this morning, but I had to hitch a ride in with Duncan Graham. Need to organise a few boys to help me move my stock, and that beast won't let me near my mare." Sarah thought he was changing the subject, and her heart sank, but then he continued. "Could be I'll need someone out there regularly to keep an eye on him, let me know when it's safe to rescue her."

Sarah's smile stretched wide, so bright it eclipsed the sun. It was as good as a declaration; he wanted to see her, be near her.

"Could be I know someone who'd be willing to ride out of an afternoon to help you with that." Her cheeks hurt she was smiling so hard, but the soft tilt to his own lips made her heart swell in her chest. It was the first true smile she'd seen from him. There was hope for Connor yet.

Connor brushed his lips one more time over hers, then abruptly turned, walking back outside. "I'll see you this afternoon then, Sarah Devil-may-care-Dawson," he said as he paused at the door.

She waved, then, forgetting herself, ran a hand through her hair.

The man laughed, actually laughed, a deep belly rumble that seemed to echo in the hot confines of the kitchen. It was glorious.

And worth it. Sarah looked critically at her dough-streaked hair. Even if she had to wash her hair six times to get it clean again, that laugh was worth any price.

"Off with you, Connor," she scolded teasingly. "You've stock to find and I've a bakery to run. You can laugh at me all you want this afternoon."

His laugh seemed to linger as he closed the door behind him.

Maybe this wouldn't be such a bad day.

***

As the smile faded from his face and the door closed, doubts crept in. Being with Sarah was a double-edged sword, both a blessing and a curse. He didn't know whether it would prove to be lucky or not for him, but there was no way he could deny that connection or the opportunity being with her presented him with.

The question was, had he really sunk so low that he was willing to use someone he cared about to get his revenge? He almost turned toward the Travellers, craving the familiarity of company and beer, but thought better of it. They liked to dice there in the afternoons. Play two-up in the saloon bar. The last thing Connor needed was dice in his hands.

"Roll the dice, Connor. Roll the dice." The boys' cheers spurred him on, encouraged him to rattle the dice in the cup a final time. The tension in the cramped dugout ratcheted, the air heavy with expectation and more than a little fear. Connor's dice never lied.

"What's the question this time?" Connor asked quietly, though every man heard him.

"How many of us will survive tomorrow?" asked John Blunt. The man had a young wife at home, had just found out he was a father. Poor bastard hadn't even seen action yet, and he was already aching to go home.

They made mistakes, the ones who were homesick.

He shared a meaningful glance with Smith, and the other man nodded. The seasoned soldier would keep an eye out for the green private tomorrow.

He shook the mug one final, ominous time, and upended it onto the narrow cot, hoping they would remain on it. The floor would devour the dice in an instant, the mud having encroached into even this little shelter.

No one breathed as the die rolled, finally coming to rest alongside the dugout wall.

Six. And one.

"Fifty/fifty," he breathed, fear building. His skin prickled with knowledge he wished he didn't have. The dice never lied. "Devil's number six for death, one for God and life." The story they told may not make sense to others, but it always did to him.

The men stared uneasily around them, taking in the faces of the mates they had made, memorizing features as they slipped out to begin their own rituals. No one said anything as they passed. It wasn't anger, just resignation.

Except for Blunt.

Fear had him, and for some, that translates to anger. Connor tried not to take it personally, but when the dice dealt in life or death, often he became the target.

"No doubt you'll make it out, hey, mate?" The bitterness in Blunt's voice had him sighing. There was always one. "Luck of the Irish, they say. Sure your dad was a Scot? Seems like you got a double dose of Irish luck. Maybe you should be comparing features with the milkman when you get home." It was only Smith's fingers digging into Connor's bicep that saved Blunt from a fist in the face.

That and the fact Connor recognized the anger for what it was—fear.

"You should go settle your affairs, cobber," Smith said as he ushered Blunt out of the cramped room. "And next time, if you see us on the other side, you might want to rethink insulting someone with the devil's own luck."

The greenhorn raced out as if the hounds of hell were chasing him. Smith came back to sit on the tiny cot with Connor.

"It may be me you know," Connor whispered. "One of the unlucky half."

Smith sighed. "If there's one man I know is going to see it through this war, cobber, it's you." He shifted slightly, running his hands through his hair. "You have purpose, Connor. Even the devil wouldn't be so heartless as to steal your chance of revenge from you. You'll get home. You have to, for Caleb."

Yes, for Caleb.

His mother wouldn't be best pleased when she saw the man he'd become, but surely she'd understand.

Isabel needed to pay, and he hoped he was lucky enough to see it happen.

His gut tightened, guilt swirling, when he realized he *was* lucky enough. And he had sunk low. Sarah wasn't a means to an end, but if he could use her without hurting her, he would.

There was a very real possibility he was as much in love with her as he had been before he left for the war. She was too young then, and his future uncertain. Connor wasn't going to leave a war widow behind to grieve. There'd been enough of that where his family was concerned.

Be that as it may, he'd tossed the dice. He'd have to live with the consequences.

Hopefully, Sarah would still want him when all was said and done.

Chapter 8

"Where do ya think yer going, chick?"

Sarah stopped with her hand halfway toward the door. Not quick enough. She turned a winning smile on her pa.

"Nowhere, Pa. Just out for a bit of fresh air," she said innocently.

Her pa glared disapprovingly at her. "Not at this time of night you aren't. Come on, I'll walk ya back to yer room." Sarah sighed. Maybe she could sneak out the window after Pa had gone to sleep? With heavy steps, she followed him up the corridor. "Now in ya go. And straight to bed, mind."

Dutifully, Sarah slipped back into bed, waiting until she heard her Pa's footsteps fade away as he went to stand vigil in the kitchen. She definitely wouldn't be getting out that way.

The clatter against her window had her sitting bolt upright in bed. She stared intently at the window. Nothing. And then...

Another clatter and a grinning, shaggy redhead appeared within the frame. Caleb's hair was standing up at all angles and his clothing...well, the best that could be said about it was "well-worn." Sarah had to smother a chuckle when she saw him, lest she disturb Pa. A moment later, Margery's dark hair joined him. She held up a fistful of river pebbles, smiling mischievously. A roll of the eyes was all Sarah could manage. Of course, the stones were Marge's work.

The girl in question motioned frantically for her to open the window. When she reluctantly did, both climbed in, making no effort to be quiet. She shushed them as they settled on her bed while Sarah had her ear to the door, listening for Pa.

"What are you doing here?" she hissed at them when she was finally convinced Pa hadn't heard the commotion.

"We've come to get you, my little van Gogh." Sarah wrinkled her nose at Marge comparing her to a man she privately considered a maniac.

"I can't go. Pa caught me sneaking out." Not that she'd tried too hard. The sneaking felt a lot like lying, and she'd never done that in her life.

"We figured you'd seize any excuse not to go, so we've come to take you with us to the river." Though Caleb echoed her earlier thoughts, she didn't like having it thrown back in her face.

"I'll have you know Pa's a very light sleeper. Why, only the other day he—"

Marge's hand covered Sarah's mouth, stopping her words.

"You'll come with us, chook, because," Marge leaned in to whisper in Sarah's ear, "Connor will be there. And you know you want to see him in the river, all wet and glistening in the moonli—"

"Let's go." Sarah threw off the covers and followed Caleb hastily out the window. A muffled chuckle followed her, but Sarah only had one thought—get to the river before one of the Robertson girls got her hooks into a half-naked Connor Williams.

He might not know it yet, but he was hers, as she'd always been his. Always had been, always would be.

Not even the thought of disappointing her pa would keep her in the house now.

"Tea's early tonight, Pa," Sarah said, bustling into his room with a bowl of soup and slice of bread. She ran a critical eye over him, taking in the shaking hands and loose skin, concerned. "You didn't take any of the medicine I left on your bedside table today, did you?"

"I took it, chick. Twice." Pa's voice wobbled, eyes crinkling in pain. Sarah did her best to hide her surprise and concern, bustling toward the table as she measured out a stronger dose of laudanum. He was deteriorating faster than she thought and it wouldn't be long before she wouldn't be able to use the medicine at all. Too much and it would kill him.

Frank's hand trembled as he picked up the spoon, trying to appear nonchalant as the soup sloshed onto the wooden tray. Sarah pretended not to notice.

"So why are you home so early today? Is something wrong?" He may have been fighting a losing battle with his body, but Frank's mind was sharp as a tack. Sarah put the increased dose of medicine beside him for when he'd finished his meal.

"No, Pa," she replied. "I had an early start this morning and caught a lucky break. The Robertsons are shearing and bought all the remaining loaves. Even put in an order for the next few days." A thought occurred to her. "I suppose Connor will have to make a start on his stock soon too or else miss out on the rise in the market."

"I'm sure Frannie Robertson would be happy to send her boys over to Connor's to lend a hand when they're done with hers." Her father's look turned sly. "Would probably be quite happy to send one, or both, of her girls over too. To help with the carding. And the meals. Didn't you say neither was married?"

"And neither would suit Connor," Sarah said tartly, before realizing she'd given herself away.

"So you've made your decision then?" There was no real question there, just a statement of pure and simple fact.

"I have, Pa," Sarah said, smiling. "Connor may have been broken into tiny little pieces by this war, but he's still mine. Always has been, always will be. I'll have to put him back together again."

Her father chuckled, the sound of merriment dissolving into a hacking cough. She handed him a handkerchief, but when his shaking hands couldn't quite grasp it, Sarah held it to her pa's mouth herself. When she pulled it away, it was thick with blood.

Horrified, she stared at Frank as he struggled to equalize his breathing.

"I suspect I've not long now, chick," he said matter-of-factly between coughs. "It's nice to see you happy, but remember that sometimes, when something breaks, it's easier to use the remaining pieces to make something new, rather than trying to put them together the way they once were."

She dabbed at his lips, then carefully poured the laudanum into his mouth. He screwed up his face in disgust.

"I'll remember, Pa," Sarah said quietly. "Connor's still the same man, yet so very different. Maybe what we both need is to build something new together."

His eyes started to drift shut then, as something disturbed him, popped open again. "That's not where yer going now, chick, is it?"

She laughed. "Of course I am, Pa. How else am I going to catch that man if I don't hunt him down?"

"Yer can't do that. Whaddle people fink?" Her pa's horrified words slurred as the laudanum dragged him under. She grabbed his hand, eyes twinkling.

"They won't think anything. Aside from the fact that no one knows I'm going out there, it's not the same as it was when you were young. These days—" Sarah cut herself short as she looked down at the already sleeping man. His face had lost muscle definition, was just a sad skeletal frame that housed the one thing he had left to him: his mind. The thought of losing him left a hollow feeling in her belly. But seeing him like this...

With a last kiss to his brow, she left him to his rest and made her way out the back of the house.

The small corrugated iron shed out the back had previously stored garden tools but had remained largely unused in the years after her mother died. When Sarah turned thirteen, she had appropriated it as her own. She pushed open the squeaky-hinged door, moving immediately to the louvered window, an extreme luxury in a shed, particularly with windows so large, and flipped them open so the remaining light in the day filtered in.

Unfinished canvases were strewn haphazardly around the room, sketches in all shapes, sizes, and degrees of detail fluttered in piles long since abandoned. Her dreams of painting seemed a foolish pipe dream when compared to the reality of life, but still, she couldn't help but feel as if she was home every time she stepped in here. Even if she only managed it once in a blue moon these days.

It was an enchanted world, and she a child bright and enthusiastic, with fingers that itched to pick up a brush again. Before the war, when the bakery was thriving, Sarah had spent all her free time out here. Now, she was lucky to have the chance to make a quick sketch on the run, let alone turn it into a full-size canvas. Still, she always carried a stick of charcoal in one pocket and a couple of loose leaves of paper in the other, for when inspiration struck.

She was lucky Marge was so handy with a needle and thread and had added pockets to all her clothes; otherwise, she wouldn't have even this much of her guilty pleasure left to her.

But there wasn't time to paint today. No, today she was searching for a charcoal sketch. One that she had long since turned into a glorious canvas that now hung in her room, but she had kept the paper safe as a gift for someone else.

Sarah pulled open the wooden folio box Caleb had made her for her sixteenth birthday and with trembling fingers reached for the top sketch. He'd always hated the state of her shed, calling it a "studio" and saying she should take better care of her artwork because someday, it was going to make her rich. She'd laughed at him, but the polished and precisely carved wooden box was her most prized possession.

It was the last thing she had left of the boy who had been one of her best friends.

On impulse, instead of removing the single sketch she had intended to take to Connor's, she grabbed the whole box, moving swiftly from the room in case she was tempted to pick up a brush. While there were loose leaves of paper all over the room, Caleb's gift held all her most treasured pieces. Connor would want to see them.

Daisy, the family's gentle grey mare, grazed peacefully in the small paddock behind the shed. Sarah had run through the routine motions, saddling and bridling her, securing the box behind the saddle, while the patient mare waited. She'd brought her to the mounting block when—

"What do you think you're doing?" Isabel's shrill voice vibrated through the air. Could one's ears bleed from noise at this distance? Sarah winced, then schooled her face into a stern expression. Her sister hurriedly stomped over to Sarah. She waited until the minx was in a normal speaking voice range before she replied.

"I'm heading out. Pa has had his tea and is now sleeping quite soundly. Make sure to check on him every hour or so before you go to bed." There, she was civil. And that was the best she could do after this morning.

"But I was going to meet—"

"I wouldn't finish that sentence, Isabel." Sarah's voice hardened, a threat on its own. "It's high time I had a break around here. If you want to see your fiancé, he can come to the house." Though it wouldn't be quite seemly, Isabel being to all intents and purposes unchaperoned, few knew how bad Pa was right now. Isabel's reputation should be safe, especially considering Harry was going to marry her.

She couldn't say the same about herself, however.

Her sister paused, thought about it then, without another word, turned toward the house. Presumably, Harry would turn up here when she didn't meet him at the designated location.

Perhaps Isabel was learning?

Sarah snorted. *If wishes were horses,* she thought.

From the block, she hitched up her skirt and swung her leg over the saddle, making a mental note to get Marge to use some of the new flour sacks to make her a more appropriate skirt for riding. This one was almost indecent, hitched as it was to mid-thigh. Thankfully, there were few on the road to see her as she made her way out to Connor's property. None she knew.

Whistling cheerfully, Sarah nudged the mare into a trot.

She had a stallion to check on and a man to win.

***

He knew Sarah should be chaperoned if he didn't want to ruin her reputation, but he couldn't find it in him to invite someone over and ruin their time together. He itched to go roll the dice, check if he was doing the right thing, but he'd made a promise. Connor would have to find something else to take his mind off Sarah. He'd just checked the gates and fences in the western paddock when the red dust swirling up the road heralded a visitor.

And not the one he was expecting.

"Ho, Connor," Harry called as he drew the smart little buggy to a stop out the front of the homestead. Connor was both happy to see his friend and nervous. What if Sarah arrived while her soon-to-be brother-in-law was here?

His plans to ruin Isabel wouldn't fall into place if there was any inkling of impropriety around Connor. And Sarah's reputation was more important to him than anyone. She had to live in this town still after he'd realised his plans. He rode a very thin line courting Sarah as it was.

"Brought you some supplies from Mum," Harry continued, grabbing a crate from the seat of the buggy and striding confidently toward Connor. "Even though she spends most of her time glaring at me in disapproval these days, when I said I had plans to meet with you this afternoon, she sent me out with this whole box full of goodies."

"But we didn't have any plans…" Connor racked his brain, trying to remember when he'd run into Harry and organised this.

"Of course we didn't," laughed Harry. "I was meeting Isabel, and Mum has very firm opinions on what is appropriate or not in courtship. Never mind that the world has changed. My mother is caught in the dark ages." Harry rolled his eyes at what he considered his mother's dramatics, but Conner didn't think her so misguided.

"I don't think the world has changed quite as much as you think, Harry," Connor said uneasily.

"Nonsense. You only need to take a trip to Sydney to see that. Why, just last month when we took the girls shopping," by 'the girls' Connor knew he meant his sisters, "we were confronted with all manner of women working in men's jobs."

Connor snorted. He'd seen them as well. And more, when a fellow veteran had taken him to an establishment where you could drink after six pm and dance unchaperoned. The women were beautiful, knowledgeable, sophisticated—and not the tender-hearted, no-nonsense firebrand he'd spent the war dreaming about.

While he could see the appeal of the more relaxed standards, there was only one woman he was happy to walk out with. And she was as wholesome as they come. This town was still 'stuck in the dark ages,' as Harry had so eloquently put it, so he'd make damn sure no one thought poorly of her because of her association with him.

"City folk are a different breed than out here, Harry," Connor said, taking the crate from his friend. "What's commonplace there would see you run out of this town in nothing but the shirt on your back." And he was planning to use that to his advantage.

"Well, it shouldn't be like that," Harry said, chin jutting out stubbornly as he followed Connor inside. "The rest of the world is moving on, and so should we. Why, look at how well the ladies did while the men were at war."

Connor's face clouded as he dropped the crate heavily onto the kitchen bench. His fist clenched as he fought the urge to send it through his friend's face. It wasn't the man's fault. Harry wasn't overly bright, and his mouth often opened before his mind had a chance to catch up.

Still, when Harry continued, logic left him and Connor saw red. "So many single ladies and matrons managing their own properties, or the community farms, with no complaint and positivity all around. Why when…" Harry's voice trailed off when he caught the stony look on Connor's face and realised what he'd done.

"I'm sorry, Connor. I wasn't thinking. Can I help you with that—"

"Enough, Harry. I think it's time you left."

"Come on, cobber, you know I didn't mean—"

"You never do mean it when your mouth runs away on you. But it still does." He turned and looked Harry right in the eyes. "I can't escape the memories while I'm here. My father's love of this place is in every fence, every building. And Caleb… I see him everywhere. It hurts, but at least the memories I have of them are happy. My mother is another story."

He stopped abruptly. Harry didn't need to hear this. "Just…Don't ever mention her around me again."

"Are you sure that's what you—"

"Ever. Again."

Harry nodded, taking a hesitant step toward Connor. "For what it's worth, I truly am sorry." He pauses briefly before continuing. "I know you don't want to hear this, but I'm going to say it once then I'll hold my peace."

Connor grit his teeth, reining in his temper while his friend had his say.

"Your mother was a good woman. A good woman, but a sick one." Connor started angrily but Harry held his ground. "You need to forgive her for what she did. She was broken, possibly beyond repair, and she thought she was alone."

"Get. Out." Connor stalked forward, sending Harry stumbling backward toward the door. Harry's eyes widened. He darted quick glances backward, scared to take his eyes off Connor. He'd been told he was a fearsome sight when the fury was upon him, but it wasn't until that moment, seeing the terror in the eyes of his friend, that Connor realised what a true monster the war had made him.

Chastened, he stopped.

"Please, just go," Connor said quietly.

Harrison straightened himself up, regathered his dignity, and nodded gravely at Connor before opening the screen door. He paused.

"I'll be here when you want to talk, Connor. You might be a terrifying bastard when you're angry, but you're still my friend." He strode toward the buggy, not looking behind him, and Connor watched incredulously as he drove away.

What the hell had he done to deserve such a friend? Particularly since, if his plans came to fruition, Harry would be the person most affected by his choices.

Connor's skin crawled. It was not only one, but two people he cared about whom he was prepared to break to have his revenge. Neither Sarah nor Harry deserved his anger, but they were going to bear part of it just the same.

His eyes fastened on his kit bag, memories of others he'd cared about and lost filling him. Gallipoli, Fromelles, Polygon Wood, Villers-Bretonneux. So many men lost. So many he'd cared about, despite trying to remain detached. Was it any wonder shells still screamed through his mind?

Smith was the only man who'd served with him since Gallipoli who'd managed to survive, and he was far from whole. Far from it—the man had his own demons that chased him and a missing arm to remind him of everything else he'd lost.

The dice cup stared at Connor from the bag, begging him to tempt fate again. His fingers itched to take the cup, ask his questions about Isabel. About Sarah and Harry. But he couldn't bring himself to do it.

What would he do if the dice had an answer he didn't like?

Fortunately, another smaller plume of dust was making its way down the road, distracting him from fate. Hopefully, Harry had made it back to town without seeing the woman on the distinctive grey pony; otherwise, there'd be more questions to answer the next time he saw his friend. And Harry didn't need any more ammunition on him when Connor's plans came to fruition and Harry's life imploded.

As she came closer, Connor's breath caught in his throat. Creamy white legs, bare almost to her rear, drew his eyes like a lodestone. His cock hardened. Fingers itched to trace them again, see if his memory matched reality, but he'd told himself he'd do right by her, and by God he would.

"Did you see Harry on your way out?" he asked, concerned for her reputation.

"No." She smiled down on him from atop the pony as wordlessly he lifted his arms to help her down. She didn't even hesitate before swinging her leg over, giving him a tantalizing glimpse of those loose knickers she was so fond of wearing. He could swear they'd been damp, but that was probably wishful thinking. And a direction he needed to take his mind from.

Sarah had no such high ideals, it seemed. She slid shamelessly down his body, pressing dangerously close to him, and his brain melted as she stood on tiptoe to brush her lips across his. Then she backed away from him, grinning.

"While that was lovely, Connor," she said, a devilish twinkle in her eye, "you're not the man I'm here to see."

Anger surfaced immediately at her words, then embarrassment as she laughed, turning toward the front paddock. The horse. She meant the horse, not another man. He could only blame her kiss for the way he'd reacted. It seemed his brain was still mush, minutes after she'd pulled away.

He quickly hitched her pony to the post then hurried after her.

Sarah continued as if she hadn't noticed his reaction, for which he was thankful. "He seems to be happy," she said, almost skipping toward the fence near where the two horses grazed peacefully. At their approach, Bunny raised a lazy head, baring his teeth at them.

She laughed again.

God, he loved that sound.

"I don't think he's quite ready to leave just yet," Connor added wryly. "The cranky bas... thing... has been covering my poor mare any chance he gets."

Sarah looked critically at them, particularly when the mare nickered, flicked her tail to the side, and exposed herself to the suddenly very lively stallion.

"Yes, he does seem to be very...enthusiastic, and she's a right Jezebel, isn't she?" She smiled. Connor grabbed her hand, almost dragging the curious Sarah away as the stallion got down to business. Jezebel did seem to be a good name for the flirtatious mare, though. That was one chore ticked off his endless list.

Sarah shook herself, moving over to her pony and untying a box from the rear of the saddle.

"Come along, Connor. We don't have all day, and I have something to show you before I have to leave." Her face clouded for a moment. "I have to be home after dark. Pa won't be best pleased if he wakes and finds I'm still gone."

Sarah tucked the box under her arm and strode toward the house. He walked in a daze behind her lusciously swaying rear, helpless to do anything but follow where she led. She paused at the top of the steps, staring intently at the screen door, then purposely moved toward the porch swing. It was with total bemusement that he watched her set herself up, opening the lid of the box and patting the spot next to her imperiously. He couldn't help but obey.

Particularly since that hesitation at the door said she was respecting his ghosts.

The porch swing rocked gently as he sat in it. This close to her, the fresh, citrusy scent of her soap curled around him, making him think of lazy summer mornings and crisp white sheets. He shook his head, trying to clear his thoughts of her so he could see what she brought him.

Sarah's wooden box lay between them. He ran his fingers across the rambling vines and flowers, recognizing the handiwork immediately. Caleb had made the box for her, asking Connor to carve the finishing touches. The brothers had always been good with their hands, Caleb able to see the connections between things, Connor providing the details.

It pleased him to see her still using the gift, though he doubted she knew he had anything to do with it. Connor had always watched her from afar, content to let his brother's friendship keep her close. Caleb wasn't a threat—the boy had been head over heels for Isabel.

And didn't that thought darken his mood?

Sarah was holding a single sheet of paper in her hands but gestured at the box as she said, "You'll want to have a look at these. Take what you like. I've painted the ones I value onto canvas." She sat a little rigidly, both hesitant and expectant, unsure of his reaction to what was to come.

With trembling fingers, he picked up her sketches, sifting through image after image of his brother. In the yard at their small school; under the shade of a gum tree; laughing at a joke and staring at something in the distance with longing. His heart swelled in his chest as the tears leaked, without shame, from his eyes.

At the first one that detailed his own features, he looked up, startled. She blushed.

"I may have watched you." The blush deepened. "A lot."

He put them back in the box, the blush telling him he was intruding on the personal. Warmth spread through him at the thought she had watched him as much as he had her. Sarah's face had been so etched in his memory that every time he closed his eyes on the front, she was all he could see.

"And what is that one that you have clutched to your chest like you're never going to part with it?"

Startled, she pulled it up to look at it, her heart in her eyes. Curiosity was getting the better of him. Sarah passed it hesitantly toward him.

With reverent fingers, he clutched the image, staring at it as if he could will the memory from paper into the present. She'd drawn them as they were the day before he enlisted. Connor and Caleb, arms around each other as they strode dripping from the creek. Laughing.

It was the last time he'd seen Caleb smile.

Her fingers touched his cheek, startling him, as she traced the path of his tears.

"I don't know whether these are good or bad," she said, staring at the moisture beaded on the tip of her finger. "But if this is what it takes to make you let go, then I'll bring you something of his every day."

Putting the box and its precious contents on the floor beneath them, he gathered Sarah to his chest, content in this moment to hold her. Tears trailed from both of their eyes, a silent release. It was cathartic.

Together they watched the sun set behind the mountains, in the swing his father had built with love.

For the first time since he'd come home, Connor felt at peace.

Chapter 9

When she was happy, the days seemed to slip by too quickly. Even though she knew her father was dying and it'd become more and more difficult to manage a business by herself, Sarah found herself smiling as she pored over the books to work out how they could afford to pay someone to help with the bakery.

It was looking like a pipe dream now, but that didn't mean she was going to give up. While Sarah had breath in her body, she'd keep on juggling the finances to keep them afloat. Maybe one of Marge's younger brothers would like some extra work? A chance to learn a trade that didn't involve udders and clearing droppings?

Bunny had been reluctantly dragged away from Jezebel when the mare, having finished her heat, objected to the enthusiastic stallion trying to mount her and took a chunk out of his shoulder. Sarah supposed she couldn't blame her. Five days of that behaviour would have anyone snapping. The normally even-tempered mare had had enough, it seemed.

But Sarah hadn't. She shook her head, picked up her quill, and dipped the nib again. A clear head was needed for bookwork but all she could think of was Connor.

Now there was no excuse to go out to Connor's of an evening, sit with him on the swing, and bask in his presence. Very few words were spoken between them, but both felt the comforting presence of the other in a myriad of different ways. Sarah baked in his kitchen while Connor carved all manner of details into the wooden beams of the house, the arms of the swing. A garden of wildflowers. Twirling vines. The sunset over the mountains.

And endless fields of poppies.

When Sarah saw these, she tugged him close, pressing a kiss to the back of his neck in silent support. They both missed Caleb with a searing intensity.

That day had seen her rush home and paint, long after the sun had set, only stopping when the gas lamp had run out of fuel. And Connor had been there, waiting to steal one more kiss before heading back to his farm and leaving her to her increasingly lonely bed.

The bell above the bakery door tinkled, startling her from her thoughts.

As Sarah looked up, the smile on her face stretched her mouth so wide her cheeks hurt. Connor stood in the doorway, framed by the early evening light.

"Fancy seeing you in here at this time of day," Sarah teased, happy to see him. "To what do I owe this pleasure?"

The bakery was still open, but business had slowed after lunch, giving Sarah some much needed time to balance the books. She sat at the small wooden desk behind the counter, keeping an ear out for the jingle of bells. For any excuse to put aside the numbers that were blurring in front of her eyes.

"I'll be needing to make an order, Sarah, love. The Robertson boys are coming by tomorrow to start shearing." He leaned against the counter, not an ounce of fat covering his deliciously strong body, the harsh lines of his clothing unable to disguise his appeal. She knew she shouldn't be staring in public but looking at the man had her burning with need. Sarah almost licked her lips before she realised what he said.

"You're starting shearing? Do you need my help out there?" she asked. She was desperate for another excuse to spend time with him. Her fingers ached to touch him, almost as if he was an extension of herself, a phantom limb she missed with every fibre of her being.

And they hadn't even made love yet.

"No," he said as he made his way around the corner to her. "The Robertson girls are coming to help with the carding and cooking. You have enough to handle here."

Though she knew that everything that came out of his mouth was the truth—she did have enough to handle here—that didn't mean she wasn't going to bridle when those Robertson hussies were going to have time with her man that she didn't. In what she'd come to think of as *her* kitchen, no less.

It was only yesterday they'd been in here with their mother, tittering about Connor. The girls didn't have a thought in their heads between them. And the mother…

"I think I can spare some time to make sure you don't get mauled by the wild beasts while you're out there working," Sarah said lightly, trying to disguise the hint of jealousy that had found its way into her words.

"You don't have to," Connor reiterated as he stalked closer. Sarah's heart beat a little faster. "But I wouldn't say no if you were to visit after you've finished and locked up. It is hard to avoid questing hands when some people's parents are so obviously fine with their daughters making fools of themselves."

She almost laughed, but the thought of Elsie and Elizabeth Robertson with their hands on Connor had her seeing red.

"I'll be there." Her tone was curt and Connor chuckled. He probably knew where her thoughts had roamed. Insufferable man.

He'd just reached for her with an amorous spark in his eye when the bell rang again, this time signalling an influx of customers. Drat.

"Wait right there, Connor Williams. You'll get what's coming to you when I've finished serving the *real* customers." He laughed at her challenge and Sarah's heart swelled as it always did on the few occasions she could coax mirth from him. It was only laughter that chased the shadows from those tormented eyes of his, and by God, she'd continue to work to earn every chuckle.

A steady stream of customers filed through the door, finishing with Barbara Ware. The woman had her permanent frown on her face. Sarah would swear under oath the woman was looking for grime, even though the bakery was the cleanest establishment in town. She didn't envy Isabel her future mother-in-law. For all the good she did in the community, the woman was a snoop and a harridan, which cancelled out the positive effects.

"What can I do for you today, Mrs Ware?" Sarah asked.

"Two loaves of your finest white please, young lady," Mrs Ware ordered, waving an imperious hand at the few loaves left lining the wall behind Sarah. *Finest white?* There was only one kind of white bread here, the one Sarah made with her bare hands that rose in the enormous wood-fired oven out the back. Maybe this woman was Isabel's model when she put on airs.

"Sorry, Mrs Ware, only one loaf of white left, but there are still a couple of grain loaves left. Do you want one of those instead?" The woman sniffed. Actually sniffed.

"I suppose that will have to do. Maybe you should be more prepared next time, Sarah. It isn't smart for a business to run out of product when there are customers still asking for it." It also wasn't smart in this economy to make more bread than you can sell, but there was no telling Mrs Ware that. Sarah schooled her face to politeness, used to this behaviour.

She turned to fill the order, catching the smirk that darted across Connor's face as she did so. She was tempted to shoot him a grin of her own but instead, threw him right into the deep end with Mrs Ware.

"Have you spoken to Connor since he's been back?" she asked the older woman slyly, nodding toward the man trying to remain unobtrusive in the corner. "He has big plans for his family property, don't you, Connor?"

He shot her a glare before smiling politely at the matron.

"I did come to your place a few weeks ago to oversee the cleaning of the house yard," Mrs Ware said to the noticeably uncomfortable man. "But I didn't get the chance to speak with you. How are you coping out there all by yourself?"

For all her faults, Mrs Ware did have a streak of kindness at times.

"I'm managing as well as can be expected. Getting some help with the shearing tomorrow, ma'am, from the Robertsons."

"Just be careful if those girls are out there. Shameless pair of hussies they are," Mrs Ware said bluntly. "Before you know what's hit you, you'll be caught in some compromising position and have to marry one of them." She wasn't wrong about the girls, but Mrs Ware was a little outdated in her views on marriage. Sarah was a little more…liberal. She'd like to be married, of course, but the order things went in? That could be adjusted.

"No fear, Mrs Ware," Connor said. "I only have eyes for one woman." Sarah's heart melted as he smiled gently at her.

The matron ran a critical eye between the pair of them, then nodded. "Yes, you two will do well with each other." She turned to Sarah. "But you'd better make sure you're out during shearing as often as you can. No use leaving things to chance if you can help it. You know those Robertson girls." She shook her head, clucking her tongue dramatically.

"My thoughts exactly, Mrs Ware," Sarah said, handing the wrapped loaves across the counter. "Eight pence please."

The woman handed over a shilling then said flippantly. "Keep the change."

Sarah stared at the coin in her hand, fighting her own pride. Any bit of extra cash was welcome, but it rubbed her the wrong way that in these hard times there were people who could afford to so casually hand over enough coin to feed a family for a meal.

"Thank you," she said almost pleasantly through gritted teeth. The effort wasn't wasted on the oblivious Mrs Ware.

"Not at all. We are almost family after all," she said, though her mouth pinched with distaste. Clearly, the woman did not like Isabel. Could anyone blame her?

"Have a good evening," Sarah said diplomatically.

With a regal nod, Mrs Ware sailed outside.

***

Connor watched as the old harridan swept through the door, only to linger within earshot. He almost smiled at how easy this was going to be. Still, the swirling in his gut told him his actions were wrong. It was tearing him apart, the constant battle between revenge and friendship, but if he gave up on it, everything he'd suffered in the war would be meaningless.

His revenge was the only reason he'd survived.

"So has your chat with Isabel improved things around here the last few weeks?" He needed to get the ball rolling quickly before the matron lost interest.

"A little," Sarah answered absently. "But she still hasn't set foot in the bakery. At least she's paying more attention to Pa."

"When she isn't 'entertaining,' you mean," added Connor. Sarah looked at him sharply.

"What do you mean by that?"

"Nothing really," he said, trying to nudge the conversation into calmer waters. He'd pushed too far, too fast. "Only that you said she'd seen a lot of Harry outside of the church."

Sarah looked warily around, Connor catching sight of Mrs Ware from the corner of his eye as she only just managed to duck out of sight. "He's been spending a lot of time at our house. Truth is, he's there more than I am these days, always leaving as I'm coming home. Whistling." The words were almost a whisper, Sarah's worry clear, but Connor was sure the sharp-eared matron outside would have heard.

Now I can add the final nail to the coffin.

"But didn't you say your pa was sleeping most of the time now, as sick as he is?" It wasn't hard to fake concern when he knew he was furthering Isabel's doom. Sarah nodded tightly. "So you're telling me they're alone in the house, and Harry comes out whistling?"

She nodded again.

"Well, I sure hope his mother doesn't hear about it. You know what Mrs Ware will do if she thinks Isabel isn't untouched. Sounds like he isn't very careful with his fiancée's reputation."

"We don't know that's what they're doing…" Sarah's voice was uncertain, hesitant, and filled with concern. Even she couldn't hide her fear that it was true. "And anyway, they're getting married. Surely in this day and age, that sort of thing doesn't matter?"

Yet they both knew it did. And the Dawsons lived in town, where there were many prying eyes. Connor watched as Father Ben came into view, the priest staring quizzically at Mrs Ware as she hightailed it around the corner. The woman would have made a terrible spy—her eyes kept darting back toward Father Ben before the wall hid her from view.

"*I* don't think it matters," he said quickly to Sarah. "But I'm not the one whose opinion counts in this town." He moved closer to her, briefly cradling her cheek with his palm. "I'm having a hard enough time keeping your reputation clean when all I want to do is declare to the world that you're mine." His eyes smouldered into hers.

"Then why don't you then?" asked Sarah, a little breathlessly. When he moved back at the tinkle of the doorbell, disappointment chased its way across her face.

"Because it's not time yet."

"Not time for what?" Father Ben asked as he strode cheerfully through the door. "Did you two see Barbara Ware acting strangely outside just now? When she saw me, her legs took her away faster than I've ever seen her move before."

Sarah stared, horrified, into Connor's eyes. He mimicked her fear. It nearly broke him to lie to her, even if it wasn't in word but gesture. Still, he did it. It would have been better if Father Ben hadn't arrived, sparing Sarah the worry, but if wishes were horses...

"What's going on?" Father Ben asked, his jovial tone replaced by a hint of steel. Again, Connor was amazed at the impact the young priest could have. "You look like you're about to lose your lunch, Sarah. Sit down before you fall down."

The priest was right. Connor pulled over her chair, and Sarah sank gratefully into it, hands covering her face.

"What have I done?" she mumbled, and Connor's heart bled. He'd already hurt her, manipulated her into this position.

He hoped to God Caleb's ghost would stop hounding him after this business with Isabel; otherwise, he would have hurt the woman he loved for nothing.

He almost startled with the realisation. *The woman he loved.* He shouldn't have been surprised by the thought, because hadn't he really loved her since before he went to war? But he hadn't intended it to go so far, not before she learned the truth at least.

He loved her.

And now he was going to shatter the world of a person she cared about, all for the sake of a dead man.

Would she forgive him?

Could he forgive himself?

As if reading his mind, the priest said, "The church doors are always open if you need to talk. Clear the air." His kindly blue eyes flit between the two of them, looking for a hint of weakness so he could do what he did best: fix people's problems.

"I might take you up on that, Father," Sarah whispered through her fingers. "But not today. Connor, could you serve Father Ben, give me a minute alone?" She didn't wait for an answer as she fled toward the ovens.

Without words, he leapt to her bidding, guilt riding him. The priest was staring at him with narrowed eyes, but he didn't point out the negative emotion written so clearly across his face. No, the man instead offered his own comfort. "Sometimes, our sins are washed away by the Lord. You should come to church Sunday, Connor," the man said. "Lord knows, you soldiers could all do with the comfort of the Lord." His eyes seemed to pierce into Connor's soul. "You more than most I think, Connor Williams."

Not likely. God would forsake him forever if he were privy to his plans. Then again, he surely was already. Connor's stomach churned as he served the priest.

After paying for his bread, Father Ben left, but not without casting a backwards glance at the pair still inside. Connor couldn't interpret his expression, but it smacked of pity, and if there was one thing Connor couldn't stand, it was people feeling sorry for him.

No. Connor wouldn't be attending church on Sunday.

Not now and not ever, if he had any say over it.

After all, if there was a God, surely he would have looked after a sixteen-year-old boy whose only sin was an excess of pride? And love. That thought firmed Connor's wavering resolve.

Isabel would pay, even if it cost him everything.

Unfortunately, Connor's everything was staring at him with teary eyes as he made his way out the back. He folded her into his arms and hoped like hell he'd make it through this with her still by his side.

God help him if she wasn't.

Chapter 10

"Why, Caleb? What on earth do you see in her?" Enough was enough. *After putting up with a whole afternoon of Caleb mooning over her sister, Sarah couldn't listen anymore.*

"She's perfect, Sarah. Every time I look at her, she leaves me speechless." Containing her eye roll was harder than expected. *Yes, Isabel was beautiful, but she was also selfish, ignorant, and had no desire to change either of those things.*

"Anything else?" she asked. "Something other than how she looks?"

He ignored her question. "We're meant to be together. I can feel it, Sarah, right here," he said, thumping the left side of his chest.

His impassioned speech left her cold. God help him if he couldn't let go of this. There was no way Isabel would have him. Sarah was sure her sister had much bigger fish to catch.

"I need to tell you something," Sarah blurted to her sister when she arrived home to find her cooking dinner. Her heart ached that Isabel was finally trying to help, and now Sarah was going to ruin the relationship. But she had to be honest.

The girl didn't stop stirring. "What's preying on you, Sarah?" Isabel didn't even bother to look up.

Sarah supposed that made it easier for her to share her shame than if her sister stared at her with accusing eyes. She was bound to do so when she heard what Sarah had to say.

"I may have done something that could affect your relationship with Harry."

That caught her sister's attention. Carefully, as if fighting her temper, Isabel shifted the stew from the stove to a warming tray. "No sense burning dinner," she said when she noticed where Sarah's attention was directed. Then Isabel's voice turned to steel. "Now explain how you've ruined my wedding?"

"I didn't say I'd ruined your wedding," Sarah hedged. "Just that I may have affected your relationship with Harry. Negatively."

Under her sister's disapproving glare, the whole story came out, from the start of the conversation with Connor to the end when Father Ben arrived. Sarah's stomach was in knots, but then her sister did the unexpected. She snorted, then let out a great guffaw.

Isabel was laughing so hard, tears fell down her cheeks.

"Oh Lord, Sarah. You had me worried there for a bit." And she wasn't worried now?

Finally noticing the look of horror in her sister's eyes, Isabel calmed herself. "Even if she listened to that whole conversation, Sarah, the only conclusion she would come to was one she'd reached herself ages ago."

"What do you mean?" Sarah asked indignantly. "Surely you're worried that your mother-in-law-to-be thinks you're a common hussy?"

Isabel laughed more. Sarah's face flamed, first with embarrassment, then with anger. She'd beaten herself up over her slip-up all afternoon, and here was Isabel, laughing it off like it meant nothing.

"She's thought that of me since she met me, Sarah. Harry and I don't care." And from her blasé tone, Sarah was inclined to believe her. "In fact, we've often thought we might skip this wedding ordeal that his mother's so intent on having and drive to Sydney for a quiet wedding in a nondescript chapel."

This was news to Sarah, though she supposed she hadn't really had time to talk to her sister since their pa had been unwell. She'd always assumed the big wedding was Isabel's idea. Being the centre of attention was her sister's style. A hint of shame lingered at the back of her mind. Maybe she should have tried to get to know her sister better over the last few years.

"Are you sure that Harry doesn't care what his family thinks?" Isabel hesitated at the question, cluing Sarah in that there was more to the situation than she believed.

"Harry doesn't care, but that doesn't mean he's not eager to make sure he keeps his inheritance," she replied. "After all, he does have two younger sisters who, theoretically, could now inherit instead of him."

Sarah looked at her, aghast. Was money that important to the two of them?

"What?" Isabel defended herself. "Just because we love each other doesn't mean we want to live in poverty."

"You know, Isabel," Sarah said as she pondered her sister's words, "I think this is the first time you've said you love Harry. At least in my hearing."

"You haven't been too interested in my life, Sarah," Isabel replied, a hint of censure in her tone. "Between the bakery and Pa, you've barely had two words for me."

Sarah bristled. "If you'd bothered to help me a little, we would have had time to talk."

"You made me feel useless."

She froze in her tracks. "What?"

Isabel's voice increased in volume. "You made me feel like nothing I did was good enough, because you could already do it better and more efficiently. Do you have any idea what it's like, competing with that?"

Sarah's mouth open and shut, fish-like. Isabel looked at her with such an angrily earnest expression she didn't know what to say.

Her sister's face fell, her shoulders slumping when she didn't get a response.

"I knew it was silly to try to talk to you about this, but Harry insisted." Isabel sighed. "I told him you wouldn't give me the time of day, but he thought I needed to give you a chance.'

Suddenly Sarah found words. "You talk to Harry about us?" She was a little indignant, though she didn't know why. At least Harry was giving Isabel sound advice. Sarah had always thought he was a little dim, but apparently, his cheerful attitude masked a thoughtful mind. Shame coursed through her, not an emotion she was used to experiencing.

"Of course, I talk to Harry. About everything. As I'm sure you do with Connor." Sarah blushed at Isabel's words and her arched eyebrow. Had they been that obvious? "You don't keep things from the person you love, even if they're things that embarrass and hurt you."

"And what did Harry have to say about our conversation the other day?" Sarah asked, still a bit miffed.

Isabel snorted. "Conversation? Tongue lashing more like."

"Well, you deserved it." Sarah drew herself up, glaring at her sister.

Isabel looked down, ashamed. "That's what Harry said when I stormed around the house ranting about it. He didn't know things were so bad between us. Otherwise, he would have encouraged me to do something sooner." Sarah's younger sister was looking everywhere but at her. "It's taken me a while to let that settle, but I hope you've noticed I've been trying recently."

And she had. It was the little things that stood out. Isabel hadn't been to the bakery, but tea had been on the table or in the pan by the time she got home every day this week. Sarah still had to manage Pa's medicine, but she'd found Isabel feeding him lunch the last few days when she'd come home to do the job herself.

"I should have thanked you," Sarah mused. Praise and soft words worked better than the lash when you trained an animal. Why should her wayward sister have been any different?

Isabel laughed. "I'm not one of your pets, Sarah," she said. "I don't need thanks for something I should have been doing all along. Hopefully, it's taken some of the weight off you though."

Sarah hesitated, then reached for her sister's hand. She couldn't remember the last time she'd touched her voluntarily, and with friendship at that. "I have something in my room that's to be yours, now that you're getting married."

It was an olive branch. Fortunately, Isabel saw it as such, too.

Sarah hurried down the corridor, her sister following. It felt good, as if an invisible band had relaxed its grip around them. They could breathe again.

She went to her dresser, taking out the small box of jewellery that had belonged to her mother. There wasn't much of it, because even in the best of times they'd never been rich, but there was one thing in here Isabel needed.

"You miss him a lot, don't you?" Isabel said suddenly from her perch on the bed. Sarah's eyes were instantly drawn to the painting of the Williams boys that held pride of place on her wall. She knew Isabel was talking about Caleb, but her eyes were drawn to the image of Connor. Connor, who carried the weight of both his brother's and mother's deaths as a load on his shoulders.

Sarah's eyes welled with tears.

"Yes. I do. Very much." Caleb had so much to live for, but Connor was now suffering for his loss.

Isabel hesitated. "I'm afraid I didn't treat him very well."

That was an understatement. Caleb had worn his heart on his sleeve when it came to Isabel. Her sister continued. "I can only blame it on the fact I was fifteen and had no idea how to shake his interest. I still don't know how I could have done it gently." Sarah almost snorted in disbelief but caught it in time. She didn't want to lose the little ground they'd gained with one ill-timed sound. "Even then, it was all about Harry."

"Of course, it was." Sarah rolled her eyes. "It was all about Harry for every girl in the district. He's funny, handsome, rich— what's not to like?"

"But I bet you didn't know that we were already seeing each other secretly," Isabel bridled, tone heated. Sarah's eyes widened— she'd never had any clue.

"You were only fifteen. Surely Harry was a little more cautious than that?"

"We were careful," she replied. "We only saw each other around school or social functions. Then he went off to war when your Connor did." Sarah felt a silent thrill at having Connor referred to as hers. "Luckily his father managed to pull some strings and get him a commission that was less...deadly. But I was a wreck the entire time he was gone. And his battalion returned earlier than expected."

But Connor's hadn't. And Caleb hadn't returned at all. She couldn't help but feel the injustice of it, the rich boy returning home when others hadn't.

"I don't understand why you're telling me this," Sarah admitted.

"My point is, I know you blame me for Caleb running away, and maybe I blame myself a little, but I was a stupid little girl and people make their own choices. Things are different now. Can we move beyond this?"

Was this the same Isabel who'd eaten her own father's meal a couple of weeks ago? Sarah stared suspiciously at her before voicing her thoughts. "Is that little speech Harry's work, too?"

"No." Isabel's face darkened with anger. "And thank you for thinking the worst of me, yet again." She jumped stiffly from the bed and stormed toward the door.

"Wait," Sarah cried, desperate to regain the comradery of a moment before. Isabel paused, but still didn't turn to face Sarah. "I'm sorry. Sit back down, please. I'd like to give you something of our mother's."

Isabel returned reluctantly to the bed, back ramrod straight as she battled with her anger. Isabel may have been justified in her anger, but Sarah had every right to question the motives of the girl who only thought of herself. Sarah rifled through the meagre contents of the jewellery box until she found it, grasping the piece in loving fingers. She handed it to Isabel.

Dangling from her sister's delicate fingers, the fragile necklace looked perfect. A single stone, almost navy blue in colour, dangled from a fine gold chain. All the colours of the rainbow swirled in its depths.

"It's an opal," Isabel whispered. "But look at that colour."

"Pa found it when he was working the mines in Queensland before he met our mother," Sarah shared. "He should have sold it, but something told him he'd need it. He met our mother a year later and everything made sense."

"Why aren't you keeping this? You're the eldest." Isabel couldn't take her eyes away from the stone. Sarah laughed self-deprecatingly.

"It's just too delicate for me," she said, indicating her fuller curves. "The ring Pa had made with another of his opal finds suits me much better. No, this one was meant to be yours."

Sarah took it gently from her sister's grasp, unclasped it, and helped to settle it around Isabel's neck. "I hope, as does Pa, that you'll wear this on your wedding day. Your something blue."

Isabel was looking down, still riveted by the colours in the stone. "Of course," she replied, almost reverently. "Thank you so much for this, Sarah." She finally looked up at her sister, tears in her eyes. The girl turned and rushed up the corridor. Sarah could hear her talking quietly in their pa's room. She smiled.

Isabel hadn't had the chance to get to know their mother the way Sarah had. At times Sarah felt as if she were the mother figure in her younger sibling's life. It was a terrifying thought. Somehow, she'd found herself styled the 'responsible one,' when she felt anything but. It was moments like these that helped her see that sometimes, she could do something right. Particularly when it was time for giving.

Not that there'd been much chance of doing that recently.

Still, this was perfect. Isabel had the piece of their mother's jewellery that was always meant to be hers, and Sarah had a fragile new relationship with her sister.

With any luck, things would only continue to improve in the future, particularly when Sarah told Connor the outcome of their slip-up with Mrs Ware.

She was sure he'd be just as thrilled as she that no lasting damage had been inflicted on her sister and Harry.

Chapter 11

The morning the new troops arrived fresh from Australia was free from the usual whine of shells in the distance. Being in town usually meant a few days' freedom, but Connor felt an ominous pull in his gut as he searched the faces of the new recruits for anyone familiar. Everyone searched as he did. It was a ritual learned by all veterans. Sometimes news from home was spare, and new recruits had been there more recently.

Connor never expected to see his younger brother standing at attention in his shiny new uniform when the men arrived.

His sixteen-year-old, under-the-age-of-enlistment brother.

His heart fell.

When the troops were finally dismissed with orders to eat then report back in three hours, Connor took the opportunity he'd been given. Darting through the chatty men with their fresh, innocent faces, still rounded from good food and rest, he made a beeline for where he'd seen Caleb.

His brother found him first.

"Connor. Ho, Connor." Caleb's voice rose above the crowds and Connor followed the sound to see him standing on a boulder, frantically waving. The idiot. Making a target of himself.

Connor strode over, grabbed his brother's arm, and marched him to a relatively private area. At least they were a bit behind the lines, Connor having been sent as security for the men collecting their rations and Caleb having just arrived.

"What are you doing here?" Connor hissed. He was beyond angry. Caleb was supposed to be home, making sure the farm still ran, and nothing happened to their mother. Especially at her own hands.

"I think that's obvious," Caleb said, false bravado lacing his words. The young man's eyes darted everywhere, taking in the pockmarked walls of the buildings, evidence of shell and machine

gunfire. Caleb's body seemed to tremble, a battle occurring within between fear and excitement. The front was constantly shifting. Tomorrow, this village could be under German control again. And now Connor had to worry about his brother as well as himself.

"I can see you enlisted, Caleb," Connor said through gritted teeth. "What I want to know is why you signed yourself up for a death sentence when you shouldn't have even made it past the registration desk?" His words had increased in volume and intensity, shocking both himself and his brother. Connor had always been the quiet one.

"I'm no coward, Connor. What made you think I was content to remain home with the women while you got all the glory?" Caleb's jaw was set in a stubborn line and Connor groaned. The fool had been paying attention to those ridiculous enlistment posters.

Then Caleb's first words penetrated. Connor's interest sharpened.

"Who called you a coward?" He knew that was the key to this mess. Caleb wasn't that naïve that he would parrot propaganda. Someone had put a bee in his bonnet and Connor wanted to know who.

"No one," the young man hedged. "I just wanted to see a little of the world." The tone was light, but it was the mechanical recital of the words that had Connor's hackles raised. So far, Caleb had repeated every slogan on those damn posters and the only thing that rang true in anything he'd said so far was, "I'm not a coward."

"I'll ask you one more time, little brother, before I beat it out of you like I did when we were kids. Who. Called. You. A. Coward?" Caleb swallowed as Connor stared at him with haunted eyes that didn't belong in the head of his big brother. Ashamed, the young man hung his head.

"I was sent a white feather." Connor sucked in a harsh breath at Caleb's words. Whoever had done that was the scum of the earth. All men cursed the rotten British admiral, Charles Fitzgerald, for that revolting idea. No man should be shamed into going to war by women with a little feather. Coward? No, smart man. Connor wished he'd never left home, every single day.

"Sent it by post? Or were you given it?" If Caleb was sent it, there was a chance it was anonymous. If it was delivered by hand...

"Isabel gave it to me," Caleb said, his broken heart in the eyes that stared up at Connor.

The words lingered in the silence, Connor's anger building to an inferno then receding as he looked at his younger brother.

He couldn't decide who he was most mad at: the stupid, selfish girl who'd given that nightmarish "gift" or the stupid boy who'd allowed it to send him to hell. He sighed, resigned to the fact he'd have to write his mother and tell her he'd found her youngest boy.

"Come on, I'll find you a nice, hot meal. It's only iron rations from here on out," Connor said, referring to the tinned food used on the front.

Connor clapped a hand on Caleb's shoulder and led him to the mess hall.

God willing, they'd both survive.

Connor rolled slowly to wakefulness, the dream still lingering. It had been the last time he'd seen his brother alive, and it was hard to shake the fear and anger that had lingered over the entire meeting.

At least he *knew* what had happened to Caleb. His mother had known nothing. His idiot brother had left quietly in the night without telling her a thing, probably guessing she'd convince him to stay. And he'd have been right. Their mother had always been as good at laying on the guilt as she was the love.

Then the mail had been delayed, so even Connor's regular letters had stopped.

He rubbed at his chest as he got out of bed, heart aching as he thought of his family. It was like a Shakespearean tragedy, the whole sorry story, but it was his life. Now Sarah was the one light he had to guide him.

The room around him was small, a remnant of his childhood, but he couldn't bring himself to move into his parents' room. Connor paused on his way to the kitchen and stared into their room across the corridor. It had possibilities, but was he ready to clean the room of everything that had been his mother's? His father's?

If he was going to marry Sarah, he couldn't continue to stay in his old room, and this was the only room in the small homestead built for two. Inching into the room, he ran his fingers over the simple wooden frame his father had made for their bed, the bare timber of the wardrobe, the simple woven rug that covered the floor.

It looked a lot smaller to him as an adult, but it was still bigger than the shoebox he was sleeping in.

It wouldn't be hard to make this place his own. Well, his and Sarah's.

The question was, would she even have him, when the truth finally came out?

With determination, Connor set about clearing the room of anything that reminded him of his parents. Thinking quickly as he worked, Connor concluded he'd need a little help with this project. While he could handle the woodwork, coordinating colours and fabrics was not on his list of skills. Thank God he knew just the tricky little stallion saboteur to enlist in his assault.

Fortune favoured the bold, and he'd always been lucky. Dice rattled in his head as he leapt into action.

***

"Marge," Sarah called as she rode around the back of her friend's home then pulled abruptly at Daisy's reins.

Jezebel was hitched to the post, pointedly ignoring Bunny, who was tossing his mane, strutting along the fence line, and generally making a fool of himself in front of the disinterested mare. If Jezebel was here that meant—

The back door swung open and Connor exited, laughing, followed by Marge. The green-eyed monster rose in Sarah's chest, threatening to overwhelm her at the sight of Connor smiling at Marge when those smiles and his laughter belonged to her.

Still smiling, Marge called, "Hey ya, pumpkin. Come to get some butter from the coolroom? Isabel been eating you out of house and home again?" Sarah's jealousy vanished in an instant. Marge was an open book, except when it came to Sarah's secrets. There was no way she'd ever be able to steal Connor away from her; it wasn't in her nature.

No, there was another reason for Connor's presence, and she'd have to get to the bottom of it. Right after she got over her shame for thinking so poorly of her friend, even if she did discard the thought moments later.

"Got it in one," she joked, ogling Connor from the corner of her eye. She could see Marge's mother in the kitchen window, keeping a close eye on proceedings. It wouldn't do to let gossiping tongues wag about them. Mrs Cleary was almost as bad as Marge at keeping things to herself.

Sarah gave her a little wave, which was returned enthusiastically by the woman smiling in the window. In fact...was Mrs Cleary fanning herself as she pointed at Connor? Mortified, Sarah turned back to her friend and...beau? Clearly, Connor and Sarah were beyond friendship, but what did she mean to him exactly?

"Well, you've come to the right place," Marge said to her, then turned abruptly to Connor. "Off you go, handsome. You've got work to do."

Connor's mouth kicked up again at the edges as he put his wide-brimmed hat back on, tipping it mockingly at Marge. "Yes, miss. I'll be off then, shall I?" Sarah's heart doubled its pace at the sight of his grin. Even if it was directed at Marge.

Marge flicked an imperious hand to shoo him away, her mock dignity ruined by her laughter. "I'll see you again soon, Connor. Try not to get into any mischief before we're finished." Before Sarah could question them on that, Marge plowed on. "And tell your mare to stop teasing my Bunny. She'll give him a heart attack and then I'll have to find a new best friend." She flicked a quick apologetic look at Sarah. "Present company excluded of course. I was referring to the four-legged kind."

Connor laughed again, shot Sarah a heated look that sent tingles to places that had no business tingling when she was here to talk to Marge, then turned to go. As he unhitched Jezebel, he smiled at Sarah. "I'll stop by the bakery tomorrow to see you." Without waiting for a response, the infuriating man swung into the saddle and nudged the mare into a casual trot.

Sarah only stopped staring at his behind when someone delivered a stinging flick to her ear.

She whirled on her friend. "Ouch. What was that for?"

"Just a reminder that you need to close your mouth. You have a little bit of drool, right here," Marge said, pointing to the corner of her own mouth. Sarah whipped her hand upwards and swiped at it, coming away with nothing. She glared at her friend.

"I'll remind you of this when you find a man you can't live without," she threatened her friend. Marge only laughed again. This was getting old.

"Never happen," she retorted. "We both know I'm going to become a famous fashion designer, move to Sydney, and live comfortably in spinsterhood, while I horrify my mother with a string of lovers that goes on for miles." Her eyes widened theatrically. "Perhaps I'll even be disinherited. Oh, shock and horror."

Sarah laughed at her ridiculous friend. The only true thing in that speech was Marge's desire to be a fashion designer. The young woman would never leave town; the mountains and plains were in her blood. And as for lovers...

"Surely there's someone in town who interests you, Marge?"

"No." Marge was flippant, but Sarah could sense the underlying sadness behind the teasing. "I'll have to wait for a handsome stranger to ride into town and sweep me off my feet."

"I hope it happens soon," Sarah said seriously. "You deserve to be happy, with children of your own." Marge had two older brothers, both living at home with their families, and the woman doted on her young nephews. Four of them so far with Rachel, her brother Simon's wife, due to pop out another any day now.

"We'll see, chick. Things will turn out the way they should in the end." Marge's response was enigmatic.

Sarah changed the subject. "To the buttery?" she asked Marge as she grabbed her saddlebags.

"Of course," Marge replied, already heading toward the small, thick-walled building near the barn. The little hut disguised the cellar where the Clearys kept the products that needed to be chilled and doubled as space where Marge and her mother made butter and cheese. Ice was too hard to come by on a large scale, it was only useful for the small household iceboxes, so the cool cellar was a necessity.

"Pa took the milk cart out early this morning, so feel free to raid what he left behind," Marge continued.

Mr Cleary had already stopped by the bakery with his daily delivery and to pick up Sarah's deliveries, so she wouldn't need milk, but the thick butter and cheese the Cleary women made had Sarah's mouth watering.

"I've meant to ask you to make me something I can ride astride in," Sarah said while filling her saddlebags with some butter and a large round of cheese.

Marge's eyes lit up. "You have some flour sacks I can use?"

"Of course," Sarah replied. "Draw up your designs and let me know how many you need. I'll even let you select the pattern." This was a big concession. The two had nearly come to blows over some fabrics, though in the end, Marge was always right when it came to fashion.

"Done. Now, when are you going to do that portrait of Bunny you've promised me?"

Sarah smiled. "Isabel's been helping around the house lately, so I've a little more time on my hands. If you like, I can make some sketches today and get started by the end of next week?"

"Leave your bags in here," Marge said as she hurried Sarah out. "I know you've got a nub of charcoal in that pocket of yours, and a piece of paper. You can start now."

Sarah laughed at Marge's eagerness.

"All right. Get me a seat and I'll make a few sketches." It seemed almost instantaneously the stool appeared, along with a flat piece of wood. Sarah looked up quizzically at her best friend.

Marge shrugged. "Don't have a table out here I can move. You'll have to make do with that."

Without further ado, Sarah bent her head to the task. Her fingers flew across the page, bringing to life tiny portraits of the feisty stallion while Marge hovered over her shoulders. It didn't take long—the initial sketches never did for Sarah—but even she was surprised by the spirit she'd captured in so few strokes when she put the stick of charcoal down.

"You have such talent," Margery breathed. "It's such a waste that no one ever sees it. Tell me you'll do something with it when things with your pa are…settled." This was an old argument, but one that was a more immediate possibility now that her father was so poorly.

Sarah's heart ached at the thought of life without Pa, but it seemed death would come and claim him sooner rather than later. And she had to think about the future.

The silence lingered.

"Surely you don't want to keep running the bakery by yourself?" Marge asked.

Sarah hesitated before answering. "I'll think about it." That was the best she could do under the circumstances.

Wisely, Marge left it alone and fetched Sarah's saddlebags as Sarah unhitched Daisy from the post. She swung herself up into the saddle as Marge fastened the bags over Daisy's rump, carefully draping them either side of the mare so she didn't startle.

Marge grabbed the reins, looking up at her best friend before she left. "Don't you let that man go, Sarah Dawson," Marge scolded. "You both need each other, so don't disappoint me."

Sarah smiled. "No chance of that, Marge."

She clucked her tongue and Daisy started toward home.

***

Marge waved from the gate of the house yard, giving a secretive smile. Sarah hadn't remembered to quiz her on Connor's presence, a well-timed manipulation on her part.

She'd always believed the two of them should be together, and then that ridiculous war had stolen Connor from their midst, right when she thought the young man was going to make his move. At least he had the sense to realise Sarah was meant for him. The man was making every effort to make up for lost time, and Marge was determined to help him.

Yes, Marge thought. Sarah wouldn't know what had hit her when Connor was through courting her.

Thankfully, Marge had a front-row seat.

Chapter 12

*"Lift yer head up, chook. Let me get some of this soup into ya."
Sarah lifted her weak head, mindlessly obedient. The fever had
raged for three days and showed no sign of stopping.*

*"Come on, Pa. You need to get to the bakery, and I need to get to
school," Isabel yelled from the front porch.*

*"Can't handle Sarah being the centre of attention," Frank
muttered to himself, then turned to call, "I'll be out to see you off in
a minute, lamb, but then I'll be heading back in to look after your
sister."*

*Isabel finally ducked her head inside Sarah's room, refusing to
even look at where her sister wallowed on the bed. Heaven forbid
she move her whole body into the room. It might be contagious.*

*"What about the bakery?" Isabel was aghast. Their pa never
missed work, except for Sundays.*

*"The bakery can wait," he said, levelling his youngest with a
hard stare. "Your sister's more important than a pile of bricks."*

Cornflower blue eyes stared into Sarah's with no recognition of time
or place.

"Open up, Pa," Sarah coaxed. The man complied, a baby bird
opening its mouth for its mother. It broke her heart to see her pa like
this, but what else could she do? He was still capable of eating, even
though he couldn't communicate with them anymore.

Hacking coughs racked his fragile body, sending bloody spittle
dribbling out of his mouth. Sarah wiped at it gently while the
shadow of her loving pa gasped air into his dying lungs. She tried to
dribble the laudanum into his mouth, but another cough tormented
him, the precious liquid flying over the coverlet.

"Come on, Pa. Just a little bit, then you can get some rest." And
rest was the only thing that was helping him these days, the
laudanum only serving to send him into the land of dreams, not

deaden the pain. They were past the point where the medicine was safe. Any higher dose and her pa wouldn't wake from his sleep.

And hadn't she thought about helping him on his way…

Every time he looked at her with those pain-riddled eyes, she was tempted to slip a little when measuring his doses. If she hadn't been terrified of what would wait for her in heaven, she would have done it months ago and spared him this pain.

Did that make her selfish? That she would let her own father suffer because she was afraid of the state of her own soul?

"He's getting worse," Isabel said from the doorway, fighting her own tears as she stared at Frank Dawson. "How does he keep holding on when every breath must be agony?"

Isabel hovered at the threshold a few moments longer, watching as Sarah tried, again and again, to get their pa to swallow the medicine. She turned away in disgust. "I can't watch this anymore."

And there was the selfish Isabel Sarah had thought gone in the last month or so. It didn't matter that Sarah liked this even less than Isabel did; their pa needed care, and they were the only ones around to give it.

Didn't he deserve their devotion after all he'd sacrificed to raise them on his own?

Finally, Sarah managed to spoon enough of the mixture into his mouth to let Frank slip into a comforting sleep. It didn't stop the coughing, but at least it didn't disrupt his rest. Careful not to disturb him while he slept, Sarah shifted her father, removing the blood-speckled sheets and pillow slip and putting a new one on. It was backbreaking work by herself, but as Frank faded a little more each day, so too did it get easier to shift him around on the small bed he had shared with their mother.

Sarah had removed the worn patchwork blanket her mother had made from the flour sacks in the bakery in the first year of their marriage, knowing her pa would be mortified if he ruined it. Even in the state he was currently in.

His skin was paperbark thin, dry as those trees as well. Where before it had been an effort to move him, now he was so frail she wondered, if she used too much force, whether her pa would snap like a twig. Bones seemed to lurk just below the surface, waiting to break through.

She dropped her usual kiss to his forehead and went to the kitchen to see Isabel. Sarah was in time to see Harry's back disappear into her sister's room and hear the giggles of her sister as the door closed. She couldn't decide whether the flush that stole up her neck was in response to what she was sure was happening in the bedroom right under her father's nose, or in her fury, that it was happening at this time at all. She almost barged in to give them a piece of her mind. The only thing that held her back was that if she started, she wasn't sure she could be stopped. And that might wake Pa.

The fire in the stove beckoned her with the promise of warmth and comfort. Sarah drew up a stool next to it. With the season turning slowly to autumn, the cold air bit at you when dark came. She inched closer to the big iron stove, but no matter how close she got, Sarah couldn't seem to shake the chill. A bowl of stew sat steaming on the benchtop, obviously left there by Isabel for her, but she doubted she'd be able to force it past the lump in her throat. Her bed was looking like a promising option to the heartsick Sarah.

A knock seemed to echo around the empty room.

Sarah lifted her achy body off the stool and answered the door.

Like a dark angel, Connor stood framed in the doorway silhouetted by the now flaming street lamps. That lump in Sarah's throat swelled further before the young woman burst into great gasping sobs.

The relief at seeing him when she needed him most was overwhelming.

Connor gathered her into his arms, hustling her from the chilly doorway into the warmth of the kitchen. Sarah found herself deposited on the kitchen table as he stepped closer, wrapping his arms around her as she sniffled into his homespun shirt.

"What is it, love? What has you weeping at the very sight of me?" She sobbed harder. The dam had finally burst. "Surely I'm not that horrifying?"

She hiccupped a laugh through her tears at the bad joke, as he'd no doubt intended. Sarah took a few deep breaths, struggling to control her emotions. He didn't need to see her like this. Connor gently wiped at her tears with a handkerchief he pulled from his pocket. It was covered in flowers and so incongruous with his roughened workwear it shocked her out of her tears.

Still, it seemed an age before she was confident enough to speak. Connor beat her to it.

"Do you want to talk about it?" he asked, dropping a kiss to her forehead. The warmth of the gesture almost undid her again. Sarah opened her mouth to reply when a moan of pleasure from her sister's room seemed to echo around the whole house. Thank God her pa was sound asleep.

"Or perhaps we could go for a ride, and talk about it on the way?" Connor's eyebrows were raised at the shameless display from her sister and her fiancé.

"I think that'd be best," Sarah replied, hustling Connor out the front door before the noise became unbearable.

As if it wasn't already on a mortifying level.

They quickly exited her pa's home, Connor grabbing a blanket from near the hearth as he went. His leggy chestnut mare, Jezebel, waited patiently for her master. She didn't even flinch when Connor gave Sarah a leg up into the saddle then vaulted up to settle almost on her rump. He wrapped the blanket securely around Sarah, gathered the reins in front of her, and clucked for the mare to move.

Sarah finally relaxed. This was what she'd needed. Connor and the peace of the night. He wrapped his left arm around her and drew her to him as he shifted the reins to his right hand.

Yes, this was bliss.

***

Sarah was wound tight as a bowstring yet as they plodded forward, she softened against him with a sigh that had him hard at the most inopportune time. He shifted back slightly on the mare's rump, making sure his erection was well away from the innocent temptress.

This wasn't the time or the place.

They moved away from the town, following the Castlereagh River as it wound past the station and out into the bush.

"Where are we going?" Sarah asked him quietly.

"You'll see when we get there." Connor nudged the mare into an ambling trot, eager to get out of the saddle. The night was full of noise—the hoot of an owl, possums scurrying through the eucalypts—but the two on the horse were silent. Connor could feel the heat of her body against his own, but he knew what the woman needed most was to escape. She needed that more than he needed to touch her.

Connor hadn't been able to stay away from Sarah any longer, though both were so busy it was almost impossible to find time to visit the town.

It had been more than a week since he'd seen his girl. Shearing was over and the lambs had dropped, but Connor was busy preparing the property to make sure all was ready for breeding. He'd organised for the Robertsons' ram to service his ewes in exchange for them using his. After the war, his stock was depleted, so he'd need to have a good few seasons to build it up again. This season was particularly important, as the lambs born next spring in time would form his new breeding stock.

He'd have to have a new ram by then, as the Robertsons couldn't service the young ewes. For obvious reasons. And that would be another expense.

Perhaps he could leave one of the young bucks intact and stud him out...

Plans whirred through Connor's mind, its activity counterpoint to how relaxed his body was at present. Sarah had that effect on him. Everything worked better when she was around. His project with Margery was coming along nicely. Sarah's outgoing best friend had somehow managed to turn his mother's old-fashioned bedroom into a feast for the senses.

When he finished making his own touches on the space, he'd ask Sarah the one question he'd been burning to ask since he realised it was fruitless to fight fate.

As they finally rode into the clearing, Sarah gasped. "I had no idea this place was here." Her eyes shone as she took in her surroundings.

Connor had taken them to a natural clearing by the side of the river, a place where his brother had loved to come after their father had died. Caleb couldn't handle the depression his mother had sunk into when the heart attack had claimed their fun-loving father, and Connor had often found himself unerringly drawn here when looking for the young man. People had always said they were closer than twins and it seemed that wherever Caleb was, Connor had a string attached to the young man that drew them together.

He supposed that was why he found what remained of his brother on the battlefield even though the face was unrecognisable.

The flies covered everything. At first, Connor had vomited every few steps as he made his way through the field of bodies. Most were unrecognisable, but every now and again... It was the ring he noticed first. Their father's wedding band, worn on his brother's right middle finger. And it wasn't Caleb's face, because that was such a mess of blood and flesh that Connor turned hastily away and dry retched. No, the thing that confirmed it for Connor was the tip of the white feather, somehow still pristine, which peeked from the pocket of his—

Connor shook himself free of the memory. He didn't want the past spoiling this time with Sarah.

The clearing itself was small, barely ten feet by ten feet, and heavily shaded by trees. In the summer, it was the perfect spot to bathe in the river after a long day's work. But that wasn't what made Caleb's spot special. It was the night that truly transformed the place.

The ground was blanketed with flannel flowers, their delicate white petals with green hearts a soft carpet he hadn't seen anywhere else. And under the moonlight...they shone. The whole clearing seemed to glow as the flowers reflected the glow of the moon.

"I don't want to get off the horse and damage them," Sarah said in awe.

Connor laughed softly. "You won't. They may look fragile, and they certainly feel like velvet, but the flannel flower is hardy as they come." He swung down from the horse then held up his hands for Sarah. As soon as she was on the ground, she reached down to touch the petals.

"So soft," she murmured. The way she was stroking those plants had him wishing that it was him she was stroking with those strong fingers instead. He almost groaned aloud when she picked one and rubbed it against her lips.

Surely this was too much torment for any man to handle?

Clearing his throat, Connor led Sarah toward the roots of one of the larger gum trees that formed a convenient seat. "Caleb would come out here to find peace when things at home were too hard," he said matter-of-factly. Though home had been hard for Connor too.

He didn't resent his brother for leaving him to deal with their mother. He was glad someone had managed to avoid that nightmare.

"It certainly is peaceful," she replied.

Connor didn't want to break the peace with a question, but some things needed to be asked. "Do you want to tell me what had you in tears in my arms the moment you opened the door?"

Sarah's stare held weight and she stared at him for so long that he started to fidget. Maybe he'd misread the situation and she didn't need his support?

Finally, she spoke, breaking the tension. "I'm watching him die, Connor. And I feel like I'm doing it by myself." She sighed, about breaking his heart along with hers. "Isabel is *trying* to be better around the home, but I still have to do the majority of the work with Pa, and of course the bakery won't run itself."

"It's hard to be around death, particularly when you know it's inevitable," Connor said.

Smith and Connor dragged the screaming heap that had once been Phillips through the mud back to the dugout. Half his face was unrecognizable but the thing that had sealed his fate was the shrapnel buried in his gut. The two able-bodied men shared a look. The dice never lied. Fifty/fifty, they'd said. If Connor and Smith were here whole, who else wasn't coming home?

Sarah's voice drew him back to the present.

"I know I've had time to get used to the idea by now, but losing a parent... It's so much closer to home than anything I've had to deal with before. My mother's death was so sudden, and I wasn't witness to it, but even when we found..." Her voice trailed off into nothingness.

Connor's interest sharpened.

"You've been around death before?" he asked. His stomach sank like lead into his shoes.

Please don't let it be her. Please don't let her have been the one who had to see it first.

Sarah met his eyes. "I found your mother, Connor." His grip on her hand tightened briefly before he forced himself to calm. He didn't want this for her, would never have wanted this for her. Still...

"Why did they tell me the matrons found her?" he asked, confused.

"Not many people know it was me," she replied. "Marge is as good at misdirection through gossip as she is at spreading the rumours in the first place." She paused briefly, then forged on. "I didn't want to be the centre of attention, the one who everyone asked for the gory details of the death of a woman I cared about."

Of course she wouldn't. Sarah wasn't like that. She'd loved Connor's mother as if she were her own.

"It makes sense." Though it didn't explain why she hadn't told him herself. Honestly, he was a little put out that she hadn't. But then, knowing Sarah, she would have had good reason.

As if reading his mind, Sarah said, "I wasn't sure whether to tell you or not." She swallowed, gathering her courage. "Do you want me to tell you what happened, or would you rather be left in the dark?"

He didn't know. At the moment, the fuzziness of his mother's last act of despair allowed him to keep some distance from the act itself. Up 'til now, he hadn't even been able to ask where she was buried. He was so torn between anger and heartache that until he sorted out how he felt, he didn't want to see any memorial.

But if Sarah had the courage to relive those memories for him, surely he should have the courage to face it with her?

Before he could talk himself out of it, he jerked a nod.

After a short pause to gather her words, Sarah launched right into her story. "After Caleb left without any warning, your mother was heartbroken."

He hadn't thought she'd start there, but it seemed as logical a place as any.

Sarah continued, "She stopped going to church, the only outside contact she instigated was her daily trip to the station to see if Duncan Graham had received any news on Caleb's whereabouts."

But not about Connor. She knew where he was and Connor knew he wasn't her favourite. She would have been out of her mind about the disappearance of her baby.

Caleb wouldn't have even spared her health a thought when he left, too concerned with his own ego. Too young to know any better.

"Pa was still managing the bakery by himself then. I'd drive out and take her to town and back. She... well, she wasn't looking after herself, Connor." Her eyes searched Connor's face, looking for signs of distress.

He gave her none.

Connor well knew the state his mother was capable of getting herself into. After all, he was the one who'd had to pick up the pieces when their father had died. And now, so had Sarah.

He motioned her to continue.

"Then two letters came, within days of each other." Sarah's voice was full of grief. He could well imagine the contents of those letters. He'd penned one himself and had seen plenty of the other to know what it contained. "The first was a letter, handwritten by you. When I rode up to your place that day, she was all smiles and tears. 'Connor has found my baby,' she said to me, though I doubt you'd even known he was missing when you saw him."

His heart ached at the memories. Losing so many of his friends at Gallipoli, already having lost mates on the front, and then turning a corner to find his baby brother had put himself in the firing line.

Such a god-damned waste.

"Mail was notoriously erratic on the front. Later, it was almost non-existent. Everyone wrote home, but it seemed as if only a few letters made it." Shellfire wasn't the best background music for writing either, nor was it easy to write when one slip would see your paper devoured by the ravenous mud.

"Your mother treasured that letter. She went to church the next day, Sunday, and prayed for both of your safe return. She seemed almost her old self." Sarah's grip on his hand had turned to steel. His stomach dropped. He wasn't going to like what came next. "You have no idea how much I regret not checking in on her over the next couple of days. My only excuse is she'd seemed so happy, I thought there was nothing to worry about." Tears stream unabashedly down her face.

"We think the telegram arrived the next day," she continued.

Connor took her chin in his hand, tilting her head gently upward so her eyes met his. "Please don't blame yourself," he said. "She made her own choices, and I know more than most how hard it was to gauge her moods."

Her eyes were still filled with the horror of it but at least she leaned in to him for comfort before continuing.

"Thank God it was winter. As it was, the state I found her in… She'd sat in the cast-iron bath when she'd cut herself." Sarah shuddered and he clutched her closer. He didn't need an imagination like hers to see that image clearly in his mind.

"And you found her like that?"

Sarah nodded, lips pressed firmly together, trying to blink back tears.

Connor pulled her into his lap, wrapping his arms around her and resting his head on her head. Tears streamed silently down his own face.

"I can't believe you had to—" Connor choked on his own words. The horror of what Sarah had walked into was now etched in his mind. Maybe it would have been better for his own sanity if he had remained ignorant, but for Sarah to suffer alone... that was something he wasn't ready to shoulder. She was battling demons that should have been his—the ones he'd avoided seven years ago.

"I hightailed it into town as fast as Daisy could carry me," Sarah mumbled into his shirt. "Brought out the mortician and a few of the more sensible matrons to help me get her out..." Connor could feel her heart racing with the terror of the remembered moment. Sarah choked out a bitter laugh. "She was proud right to the end, your ma. Dressed in her Sunday best before she took her own life."

He could almost see it, the images on repeat in his own head. Of course, his mother's best dress would weigh a tonne, even if his mother weighed barely anything toward the end. The men would have taken care of the evidence, the women of the body. A horrific task, all in an attempt to preserve the modesty of someone who couldn't appreciate it anymore.

"Mum was always too concerned with appearances for her own good." He thought of the stained-glass window in the front door she'd begged his father for, just because Barbara Ware had one. Connor cleared his throat, wiping tears from his eyes one-handed. He wasn't taking the other one from Sarah, needed the contact like he needed air to breathe.

"The image of her weighed down by her dress in that crimson bath... I'll never forget it, Connor. Never."

"You never do. No matter how many deaths you see, those moments are imprinted on your mind." He stroked her hair to calm both her racing heart, and his own. The blanket had slipped a little from her shoulders, so Conner rearranged it while he thought how best to share his own stories.

"Did you know I was with my father when he died?" Connor asked a more relaxed Sarah.

"No. I'd always thought he'd been out on the property," Sarah said.

"We'd just finished breakfast and were heading out to do the morning chores before I got ready for school." His voice clouded as he thought back on the moment. "Dad collapsed, right there in the doorway. He hit the screen door on his way down, sending it swinging open. He'd hit his head on the doorframe on the way down, so he wasn't moving, stuck between the door and the jamb while I watched, frozen."

Her little gasp of horror woke him from his reverie. She didn't need to hear the rest—his mother's incessant screams, his brother trying to shake the still man awake and the blood... Even though they'd scrubbed that floor 'til they'd worn a dip in the timber, Connor could still see phantom blood every time he used that door. Could still hear his dad's laugh.

That ghost followed him everywhere now, a feeling of warmth when riding the property he didn't want to shake. It was only when faced with the screen door that Connor turned cold. The memories were too strong.

"Caleb never spoke about it," Sarah confessed. "He couldn't stand to relive the details, struggled to make it through the school day, so I didn't push him."

"Oh yes, *he* struggled," Connor said bitterly, hands tightening on her. "I wasn't allowed to. But that's what comes with being the man of the house, right?"

"What do you mean?" Sarah's voice was small, a sure indicator he'd frightened her. His gut churned in response, but he needed to get this all out.

"Caleb carried on as if everything was the same—the routine, the chores, nothing varied. Meanwhile, Mum had fallen into a hole I wasn't sure I could pull her out of, and all of Dad's workload had to be shouldered."

"No more school for you," Sarah whispered.

"No more school, or social life at all." His tone turned matter-of-fact. "It's probably why I enlisted. I jumped at the chance to get away from the weight of Dad's death for a while. All of it was too much to handle after two years. Even though by then it had been getting better."

Sarah turned around in his arms, slipping carelessly from the blanket. He reached for it but she stopped him with a touch of her hand. Gently, she leaned forward and pressed a kiss to his forehead. She hovered over his lips for an instant before feathering hers against his, a soft whisper of comfort. Connor felt tears pricking his eyes again.

She ran a gentle hand down his face, before resting her forehead against his, both breathing in the quiet.

"You are the strongest person I know, Connor Williams," she breathed in awe. Connor shifted self-consciously, but she held him steady with the lodestones of her eyes. "The strongest, most loyal and big-hearted man in my world."

"I'm not—"

"Hush." She stopped him with a finger to his lips and a small smile. "You're not supposed to interrupt me when I'm trying to tell you that I love you."

And there it was. The one declaration he'd been desperate to hear from her, but coming on the heels of that little speech, it left a sour taste in his mouth.

Could he truly say the words back to her when he'd decided he was wicked enough to brush aside her feelings for the sake of his revenge?

Almost angrily he took her lips with his, resolving that if he couldn't tell her, he'd have to show her. She gave a little moan into his mouth, pressing herself against him in the most tempting manner. Blanket now completely discarded, Sarah wrapped her legs shamelessly around Connor's waist, her core flush against him.

His cock throbbed in response and he broke the kiss with a gasp, trying to find sense. It was becoming increasingly difficult to think with her hot hands roaming freely over his body, having somehow made their way under his shirt.

Her fingers were stroking his nipple when he abandoned all reason. To hell with the consequences. He was willing to take this as far as she would let him. Connor let the weight of her take him down to the ground, her mouth never once leaving his.

Her lips moved feverishly on his and he parted her lips with his tongue, eagerly seeking hers. She startled a little, then moaned into his mouth and embraced the experience, teasing his tongue with her own. Connor nipped at Sarah's plump bottom lip, and she ground herself against him, desperate for relief. He grasped her hips, pulling her firmly against him.

That shook her from her pleasure-induced haze.

"Dear God, Connor. That thing is huge. What am I supposed to do with it?" The horror in her tone had him laughing, the mood broken.

He gave her a quick kiss and nudged her to stand, straightening their clothes as he replied. "I think the question you should have asked is: do *I* know what to do with it."

She looked at him askance. "Well, do you?"

This had him laughing, light-hearted again. The saucy little minx knew just what to say to stir him up.

"You'll find out someday, I'm sure," he said as she pouted, the worry of a moment ago gone completely.

They turned and walked back toward the horse, hand in hand. He noticed she didn't mention the fact that he hadn't returned the three little words. Hopefully, he'd either kissed her insensible or she'd forgotten she'd said it. Either way, he needed to do something about this soon.

At some point, he had to tell the woman he loved about his feelings. He wanted to do it at a time when he didn't feel like the world's biggest hypocrite.

But would he ever feel like a good person again?

Chapter 13

"Mrs Williams?" Sarah called as she hitched Daisy to the post and untied the saddlebags. Normally, Eliza Williams was waiting for her on the porch, eager for a chat and the bread and milk she brought with her. Recent days had seen the woman retreat inside her shell, and it didn't surprise Sarah that she wasn't waiting for her. Eliza was probably inside one of the boys' bedrooms, where Sarah had found her last time she visited.

She frowned at the thought. Maybe she should come more often? But the bakery was becoming more of a challenge since Pa's apprentice had handed in his resignation last week, and every third day was all she could manage. At least Barbara Ware had offered to come out a couple of times a week as well. She should really investigate enlisting some of the other matrons to help as well.

The first hint something wasn't right came when she opened the stained-glass door to a cool house, despite the frosty weather. Sarah opened the stove door and checked the coals. They were completely cold.

Her gut churned.

The next place she checked was Caleb's room, then Connor's. Both were ransacked, wardrobes flung open wide with not a stitch of clothing inside them, personal belongings completely stripped. Nothing was left on the walls or shelves.

A chill ran up Sarah's spine, the ache in her gut rising to a burn.

When she finally found Eliza, the bright red bath water was cold. So was the hand that hung limply over the side.

Sarah ran outside and found herself retching into the charred remains of Eliza's memories.

The morning had a bite to it Sarah didn't like, particularly since the cold sweat brought on by her nightmare still clung to her body. Her conversation with Connor still swirled in her head, but right then she had more pressing matters to address. Fortunately, she didn't have to wake Isabel to speak her mind. Her sister was in the kitchen, whistling cheerfully. While she didn't want to ruin the peace of the moment, some things needed to be said.

"Isabel," she began, but her sister jumped a mile in the air.

"Lord, Sarah. Don't sneak up on me like that." Isabel glared at Sarah, getting back to the eggs she was currently cooking.

"I wasn't trying to scare you," Sarah said, annoyed. "Perhaps you were whistling a bit too enthusiastically to hear me coming?"

"Either way," Isabel replied, "you gave me a fright. Off to the bakery this morning?"

It was just polite conversation—Isabel knew damned well where her sister was going. She grit her teeth and forged on.

"Yes, of course. I wanted to talk about last night."

"What about last night?" Her sister had the gall to look quizzical.

"About the fact that you thought it was all right to do…that, under Pa's roof, when he lies sick in the next room," she hissed at her sister, even as her face flamed.

"Oh that," Isabel said, dismissing her concern with a snort. "You told me to, don't you remember?"

"What?" She almost shouted but remembered just in time that her pa could wake. Even if he wasn't lucid anymore, it wasn't a conversation she wanted him to hear. "I most certainly did not."

"You did, don't you remember?" Isabel said earnestly. "You said he could come into the house."

"Yes, come into the house, not fling your skirts over your head and have his wicked way with you right under Pa's nose." She sighed in exasperation.

"I don't understand what's made you so upset. I'm home much more often now. This way we're all happy."

"We are NOT all happy, Isabel May Dawson." Sarah's use of her sister's full name should have been a clue to her that her fury was rising. "Did it ever occur to you that it's disrespectful to do something Pa wouldn't approve of under his roof? Especially since there's nothing he can do to stop it?"

Isabel's mouth opened and closed like a fish. Clearly, it *hadn't* occurred to her selfish sister.

"Do with your fiancé what you will, but *don't* do it under this roof. Don't disrespect him that way." Sarah sank with a sigh into the stool by the stove. This was becoming a habit, taking comfort from the warmth. "Do you understand now?"

"Okay," Isabel said with a swallow. "Do you want to eat, or will you get something at the bakery?" It was a great excuse to change the subject.

Satisfied her message had made it across to Isabel, she gave a quick nod. "I'll eat at the bakery, thanks. I'm running late as it is." Sarah threw a shawl around her shoulders to ward off the chill on the walk, then called to her sister over her shoulder on the way out, "Please take some time to sit with Pa today. I don't think we have much longer with him and I'd rather he wasn't alone when that happened."

She didn't wait for Isabel's reply, but trotted out into the gloom before dawn to shoulder the weight of the world. Or in this case, a struggling business.

Would that all her problems could be dismissed so easily.

***

Most men would be unhappy to wake up to a one-armed man at their hospital bedside. Not Connor. When he opened his eyes to see Smith relatively whole in front of him his heart gave a happy lurch in his chest. He hadn't been sure the other man would make it after the mine had exploded and the shrapnel sent them scattering.

No one had been able to tell him a thing about the whereabouts of his friend in all the chaos before departure, and Connor himself had been fading in and out of the world as the meds struggled to keep him under.

Connor smiled up at the man, even as Ben Smith turned dead eyes toward him. His heart plummeted. What had gone wrong to leave his friend looking like this? It couldn't be the arm—they'd both said they'd happily be one-armed (or -legged) bandits than dead. That sentiment hadn't changed even after all they'd seen. All they'd done.

"Do you remember when I had you roll the dice for me, Connor?" Smith asked.

Connor hesitated. The man's voice was as dead as his eyes. This was not the Smith he knew, the pillar of strength who'd somehow managed to see him through the worst of the war. There was only one day he could remember tossing the dice for his friend, and the results hadn't been anything that would leave this look in his friend's eyes.

"I'd asked you if I'd live to see her married." He laughed bitterly. "If I'd live to see my pregnant fiancée married. Guess I didn't choose my words carefully enough, hah?"

This story had the nasty ring of fate about it. Connor didn't want to hear it, didn't want to hear what Smith had walked into when he'd been sent to his family home in Sydney to recover, the hospitals too full for them to keep everyone. There was no stopping his friend, however.

"Walked right into a wedding reception in her parents' backyard." Smith's eyes were a little wild, and his phantom limb seemed to be gesticulating as animatedly in his agitation as the whole one was, if the way his stump was moving was anything to go by. "She'd lost the baby. Hadn't bothered to tell me, just up and married the first man to ask her when she figured I wasn't coming back like so many others before me."

"I'm so sorry, mate. If I had known…"

"Those bloody dice, hey?" The falsely jovial tone of his friend's voice was like nails down Connor's spine. "The thought of marrying Carla kept me going through all of that shit we went through over there, had me fighting through even when they sawed my bloody arm off. That little positive from those damned dice… Do me a favour, Connor?"

"Anything," he said to his mate.

"Don't use those dice again. Leave the future to play out as it will without any help from the Fates. They don't play by the same rules we do." Smith gave Connor's hand a squeeze as the bedridden man nodded, then he moved quickly from the bed toward the door.

"Will I see you again, brother?" For that's what the other man had become, a brother through choice, rather than birth. It would tear his heart out if he never saw him again.

Smith turned back and gave Connor a brief smile that didn't touch his eyes. "You can't shake me that easily. Coonabarabran, right?"

Connor nodded, heart in his throat.

"I'll be there before the end of this year. Or the spring of the next. Don't wait for me. You do what you have to do and don't look back."

With that, the one man who had been with him from the beginning left.

And Connor was a rudderless ship at sea.

The seasons were slowing and there was still no sign of Smith. Connor wasn't sure whether he was happy about that or not. On the one hand, he missed his friend almost as much as he was sure Smith missed his left arm. On the other, he didn't want his friend to see the depths he'd sunk to, even if he knew Smith would be the only one who would understand.

A case in point was the deed he was doing now.

As he'd passed by the Dawson house this morning, he'd caught a glimpse of Harry slinking away like a thief in the predawn light. The sight was only going to add fuel to the fire he was sure to start today. Nothing he'd said so far had been a lie. He'd tried to avoid that as much as possible, perhaps subconsciously unable to spread a lie that might affect Sarah.

Even today would be no exception, though it was both more cunning and more cowardly than he thought himself capable.

He needed a gossip—and fortunately, there was one person (other than Margery) who would suit nicely.

Every time he rode past the station, a wave of longing swept over him for his old life. When that station was a symbol of new beginnings, not endings. Of hope, not loss. It took all Connor had to force himself to dismount Jezebel and walk up those stairs again.

"Post hasn't been yet, young Williams," Duncan Graham greeted him. He supposed he would always be 'young' Williams to the old stationmaster, even if he was the only Williams left in these parts now. The older man was polishing the banisters and benches with his own personal blend of beeswax polish. He swore the shine lasted longer than anything bought in the general store.

"That's fine," he replied. "I'll wait a little to see if anything turns up and keep you company."

The older man gestured toward a broom and Connor gave a wry smile. No idle hands or minds in this place. It was comforting to know it was that way even now when his world had crashed down around his ears. The broom was a solid weight in his hands, the soothing rhythm of the task bolstering him for the conversation to come.

Even though he felt oily doing it.

"You know," Mr Graham said. "I hear talk you've set your sights on the Dawson girl." When Connor remained silent, the old man continued. "Not the pretty, selfish one, the one who runs that bakery all by herself. A strong woman, that one. Could be just what a man like you needs."

Connor almost laughed. "And what does a 'man like me' need, Duncan Graham? And for that matter, what's a 'man like me'?" Couldn't the man see that Sarah was the pretty one, both inside and out? Everyone always commented on the looks of her sister, but Sarah was a beauty in her own right. The fiery river of hair that fell down her back when unbound, the tiny freckles on her nose that only served to highlight her pale skin, the lush curves of her body... Yes, his Sarah was a beauty. Why did she seem to get lost in the shadow of her sister?

"A man like you," continued Mr Graham, "is someone searching for something beyond the norm. Whose experience in the world has been so harsh, made him so jaded that it would take something, or someone, extraordinary to lift him from the muck." The old man's eyes seemed to pierce right through him. "You'll never be satisfied with a normal wife, Connor. You need someone as strong, or stronger, than you. Someone with the capacity for forgiveness, because for sure, someone as headstrong as you will make mistakes."

He saw too much, yet not enough. Connor continued to sweep as he plotted how best to get around to the subject he really wanted to speak about.

"I'll give her some time to see how broken I am, Mr Graham. The girl needs to know what she's getting. If she still wants me when she's seen all I have to give, then I'll proudly make her my wife."

His words were true too. If Sarah still wanted him when she knew everything he'd done, he'd rush her to the altar and marry the woman on the spot. Connor wouldn't blame her if she refused to ever see him again.

"Those are fine sentiments, lad, but give a headstrong girl too much lead, and she'll run away on you. Keep her nice and close and she'll be yours for life." Mr Graham's words of wisdom had Connor snorting.

"You sound like you're gentling a horse," Connor said with a smile.

"A spirited woman's not so different from a horse." That sounded vaguely offensive to women, but he'd give the old man the benefit of the doubt. He had been happily married for thirty-five years. "If you don't treat her nice, speak softly to her, she'll buck you off when you want to mount her."

Connor let out an incredulous snort, eyes shooting quickly to the old man. The devil had a twinkle in his eye that said he knew exactly what he'd implied.

"Thank God I haven't tried to mount her yet." The old man's roar of laughter echoed from the high rafters at Connor's reply.

"Ahh boy, you have the same sense of humour as your father." He wiped tears from his eyes, still chuckling. Then turned serious. "You try to mount that girl before you've married her and you'll have hell to pay. Just because her pa's sick doesn't mean she doesn't have people watching out for her."

"You have nothing to worry about there, sir," Connor said respectfully. "Sarah means more to me than anything. I'd never compromise her reputation." *At least,* he thought, *not where anyone will see.* He didn't know if he'd be able to stay away from her before marriage, but he'd at least try to keep her reputation safe in the meantime. Particularly since she might leave him in the end.

He wouldn't blame her if she did. And he didn't want her reputation tarnished if she'd eventually choose someone else.

"Keep it that way, son, and we'll have no problems."

It was now or never.

"There is one thing that worries me though, sir," Connor said. He looked around cautiously as if to make sure they were alone, though it wouldn't matter if they weren't; the more who knew the better, in his opinion.

Duncan Graham leaned in closer and he knew he'd hooked the old gossip. There was nothing he liked more than a secret.

"I'm worried about what Isabel's doing. I don't think she cares for her reputation, or her sister's," he continued.

"In what way?" Mr Graham's interest had sharpened. It always did when there was a scandal in the works.

Connor managed to pull off a remarkably concerned face, maybe because it wasn't all a lie. He *was* concerned that Isabel's behaviour would affect Sarah. Only he was more concerned that Isabel would get away scot-free and happy while his brother lay buried six feet under in a field in France.

"When I've come to town of a morning to resupply, riding in before dawn, I've seen, on several occasions, a man exiting their house." Mr Graham's nose wrinkled in disgust at Connor's words.

"Surely even Isabel wouldn't be so brazen as to have men stay overnight in her father's home?" the stationmaster asked, aghast. "Even if the man is her fiancé, it's plain wrong."

Connor took a breath, stealing himself for the half-truth he was about to tell. "The worst thing is, I only clearly saw Harry once."

Mr Graham blanched, his faith in the youngest Dawson sibling weak.

"You must be mistaken. Why," the old man continued in a rush, "your own Sarah would put a stop to that in an instant. She's a good girl, even if the other is too vain to behave."

"I don't think Sarah knows," Connor said quietly. At least she didn't before last night. He wondered what the conversation had been like this morning when Sarah got around to berating her sister. He would have liked to be a fly on the wall for that dressing-down. "You know she's at the bakery 'til all hours of the night, then off again early in the morning. I'd say when the girl is home, she's likely sleeping so soundly a siren wouldn't wake her."

"Have you told her?" Mr Graham asked. "It would break her heart if she knew what her sister was up to. Maybe we can handle it on our own, spare the lass some pain? She does love the twit, despite her obvious faults."

God knows Connor wanted to spare Sarah everything he could, but Isabel needed to suffer. She needed to understand a fraction of the pain she'd put his brother through.

He took a moment to ponder his response. What would best get him what he wanted—Isabel humiliated and defeated?

"You must have some idea, lad, otherwise you wouldn't have come to me."

"Maybe you could talk to the Wares? Talk to them about their son's behaviour, see if they can get him to stop." He paused, allowed it to sink in before continuing. "As for Isabel, I don't think there's much we can do if she's so far gone she's inviting men into her house while her pa and sister sleep. Hopefully, Harry's parents can fix the problem."

Connor knew they couldn't. In fact, after his conversation with Harry the other day, he was reasonably certain Harry would continue to visit Isabel despite being warned. The man was besotted with both Isabel and the idea of more sexual freedom that seemed to have come in the wake of the war.

Never mind that the concept hadn't taken root in their little town yet.

The old man nodded, convinced this course of action was the right one. Duncan Graham was all too eager to be persuaded of the power parents hold over their offspring.

No, Harry would continue to visit Isabel, and Duncan Graham, being the busybody he was, would be keeping watch. He'd see a man enter or exit the Dawson house, though with his failing eyesight he wouldn't recognize Harry, and he'd most likely report back to the older Wares that Isabel was unfaithful. He would have been convinced Harry's parents would keep him away.

Connor knew no man but Harry and Connor himself had crossed that threshold in months, but he was willing to perpetuate the scandal. The truth wouldn't be leaving his lips until the whole scenario had unfolded. Hopefully, by then it would be too late for Isabel Dawson.

Her life would be in shambles once the older Mrs Ware was through with her. Isabel's hopes of living an easy life as the wife of a wealthy landholder would be shattered, and when the rumours started to spread, no other man would have her.

And when it was all done, she'd live with the knowledge that she'd brought her fate on herself. That the white feather she'd so carelessly given was the cause of her own ruin.

Connor continued to sweep for several minutes more until the train rolled in and it was clear there was no mail for him.

"I'll be off then," he said to the old man, tipping his hat in farewell.

"And I have an unenviable task to do, so I'd best start to lock up. No more trains coming through today." He looked world-weary, and Connor almost rethought his whole plan in that instant. It hadn't registered how many people he'd be hurting with his plan.

Then he steeled himself.

"I wish you well, sir. Hopefully, it sorts itself out before Sarah's embroiled in the whole mess." It was with a heavy heart that he mounted the chestnut mare who stood waiting for him at the hitching post.

It wouldn't be long now until the whole house of cards came crashing down.

Hopefully, he wouldn't be inside when it did.

Chapter 14

The bakery had taken everything from Sarah today. Not only had she had to bake, sell, and clean up on her own, she'd also had to spend a good few hours after dark had fallen with her head full of numbers as she tried to balance the books.

Things weren't looking good. If something didn't change soon, they'd have to look at closing. Sarah didn't know what to think about that. They needed the money, that was true, but soon Isabel would be gone, and it would only be Sarah and their pa. And sooner than she would like, just Sarah.

It was darker than Sarah had realised when she'd made the earlier decision to stay late tonight. As she walked home, the clouds rolling in from the north hung heavy in the sky. She picked up the pace, eager to avoid a drenching from the rain that threatened. This time of year the rain stung, tiny forceful drops that seemed to pierce you to the bone and chilled you in ways you never expected.

Each shadow seemed to hold a secret threat, the street lamps concealing more than they illuminated. Even the rustle of a young animal in the neighbour's hedge had Sarah startling. The street had been her home all her life, but suddenly it was a nightmare waiting to happen.

It was with a sigh of relief that she made it to the front door, slipping quietly inside and making sure everything was latched before she turned and faced the room.

She wasn't sure what she had expected, but it wasn't this. Nothing.

The hearth remained cold, the fire obviously spluttered out hours ago. There wasn't even the glow of coals to give some indication of life. Nothing was cooking on the stove, no lamps were lit, a fact that she would have noticed from the street if she hadn't been so terrified of her own shadow. Her breath frosted in front of her face, much as it had on the walk home.

The silence was deafening.

"Isabel?" No answer. Dread stirred in her stomach as she quickly lit a lamp and raced toward her pa's room.

When she threw open the door, she could almost convince herself that all was well. Her pa lay as he always did, propped up slightly by pillows in the middle of the bed and facing away from the door. A glass of water and the bottle of laudanum sat neatly on the bedside table, waiting for her to administer it to him.

It was the curtains fluttering in the night breeze that gave Sarah the first hint that all was not well.

Curtains that hung over a window that should have been closed before dark to ward off the night's chill. The blanket on her Pa's bed was still folded down neatly around his ankles as she'd left it this morning. With the chill in the air, Isabel should have at least pulled it up if she went anywhere. Instead, it looked like the house hadn't been inhabited for hours.

Terror chased trepidation around her body. She didn't want to take those last few steps, didn't want to round the bed to see what was on the other side. In her heart, she already knew what was waiting for her—if she didn't see it, would it still be real?

But, as always, Sarah was the sensible one. The responsible one. Her feet were lead attached to her legs, dragging reluctantly across the floor, but move they did. They took her inexorably onward despite the protest of her heart.

She held the lamp closer.

Her pa lay with his head toward the window, eyes staring sightlessly into the night as if searching for what waited beyond. Those eyes weren't peaceful. They stared wide and seemed filled with agony, even now that his soul had fled his body. The sheets and the pillow on that side of the bed were covered with reddish-brown splotches, some of which still glistened in the lamplight.

Sarah's stomach heaved, but she forced herself to make sure, to check for a heartbeat even though she knew he was gone. There was no way anything inhabited the shell on the bed. Her fingers trembled as she clutched his wrist, feeling desperately for a pulse.

When seconds turned into minutes and still no beat rose up to meet her questing fingers, Sarah dropped to her knees. Her fist rose to her mouth as she tried to stifle the wail that threatened to rise from her lungs. She was only partially successful. Pitiful whimpers still escaped.

What was she to do without her pa? The man who'd given everything to raise two stubborn girls hell-bent on going their own way?

Even though she'd known it was coming, had thought she had prepared herself for this as best she could, grief still hit like a kick from a draught horse, hot and hard. The silence of the house seemed to press in around her, the weight of her grief pushing her to the floor, held up only by a hand that no longer seemed to be quite under her control. As she stared at it, the trembling increased, a physical representation of her heartache.

She didn't know how long she sat like that. Had it only been on the walk home that she was wondering what she would do when left on her own? Now here she was—prophecy fulfilled. No Isabel in sight and Pa lying cold and empty on the bed before her.

A stray lock of hair tickled her face, breaking her from her reverie. Sarah raised her hand to wipe it away and was startled when her fingers, wet fingers, brushed her face. When she realised what was coating them, she scrambled to her feet and raced out the back door, making it just in time to heave her snatched lunch into the dying bushes. Stomach empty, she stumbled blindly to the pump, desperate to be rid of the blood her father had hacked up in his dying moments.

With frantic movements, she filled the pail underneath then scrubbed and scrubbed at her fingers. Tears trailed down her cheeks, leaving them splotchy and red, but Sarah didn't care. Couldn't. Guilt rose to claim her. The moment was full of echoes of Lady Macbeth. If Sarah had come home straight after the shop had closed, would she have been here? Would she have been able to save him?

She scrubbed until her hands were raw but even that didn't feel like enough to get rid of the stain. The guilt. And where was Isabel? Where was her sister when she'd specifically told her this morning to stay with their pa, that he didn't have much time left?

The thoughts whirled inside her head, pounding a rhythm she was desperate to escape. The water had long since stopped, her hands were undeniably clean, yet she still stood before the pump. Slowly, Sarah turned back toward the house. The lamp had long since burned out, leaving her home almost sinisterly dark, even though it was haloed by the street lamp.

She couldn't go back in there.

Feet that couldn't move a second ago suddenly had wings. In what seemed like moments she'd caught and saddled Daisy and thrown herself into the saddle. Her father wasn't going anywhere, and the mortician didn't make house calls at this hour of the night, except in summer. Sarah couldn't be here alone anymore.

There wasn't any need for deliberation. She only had one place to go. Sarah gave Daisy her head as she kicked her into motion. The little mare didn't disappoint. The wind caught Sarah's hair as they galloped out of town.

Anyone who saw the young woman quickly closed curtains again. The pale girl with flaming red hair and bedraggled clothing on the even paler horse was enough to make one think of spirits—both the ghostly and the liquid gold. But Sarah was unaware.

When all was said and done, there was only one place she could find comfort on this night and nothing was going to stop her getting there.

***

Anticipation thrummed through Connor's body, though he knew he should be relaxing. The day had been a long one. After his conversation with Duncan Graham, he'd pushed himself to see to the sheep, even though the heat of the sun sapped his strength. Despite the days getting cooler, the paddocks were still no place to be in the midday heat—the Australian sun was still as deadly as he remembered. Sometimes he thought he'd imagined that heat when the days in France seemed to be wreathed in shadows.

Or perhaps that was just being stuck in trenches.

Either way, nothing natural burned like the Aussie sun, and it had only taken one day out in the heat for Connor to remember to be wary of it. He'd taken the slouch hat the army had issued him, turned the upturned side down, and used it for farm work instead. A fitting use for it. He was even thinking of adding corks to keep away the flies, but he hadn't yet reached the point he would disrespect it that much.

As the sun set, he made himself cook dinner, a simple pot stew and a bit of damper on a stick, which he opened the stove to cook. His meals never took long—he didn't have the patience for it. Still, he made sure there was enough for tea the next day. If he left it on the stove and allowed the fire to burn down low, the barely cooked stew from tonight would be tender when he needed it tomorrow.

He'd just taken his bowl to the sink when the dog barking heralded a visitor. Slightly alarmed, Connor went out to greet the unexpected guest. He picked up his rifle on the way. *Always expect the worst,* Connor's father used to say, *and you'll always be happy when it's not.* He couldn't argue with that advice—it had proven invaluable in the trenches.

The visitor, when she finally arrived, was not the worst he'd been expecting, but on second glance perhaps she was. Sarah looked like something out of a nightmare, a banshee come to claim a soul. Her hair was a wild tangle, dress dusty and stained, and she rode the horse at a speed that suggested the devil clung to her back.

She reined in at the hitching post, the poor mare's head drooping with exhaustion when Sarah finally slid free of her back. Connor looked with concern at both the lathered mare and the filthy woman, wondering which he should take care of first. He wanted to go to Sarah, but the mare... she needed attention or Sarah wouldn't be riding anywhere soon. Though by the looks of her, maybe that was a good thing.

Sarah took the decision from him. "Connor, can you see to Daisy? I... I need a moment to myself."

He swallowed, nodding his head in the affirmative. "If you want to draw a bath, I've got the donkey going." He'd put the water on to heat, thinking to have a bath himself, but Sarah was more important.

"You've got a chip heater?" she asked, distracted from her worries. "When I was here last, we were still boiling water on the stove." There was a hint of a question in her voice that Connor willingly answered.

"Made it myself last week," he said. "Found most of the materials in the barn amongst the 'treasures' my father always seemed to accumulate. But I needed to pay the Clearys for one of their old drums. Much more efficient use of my time if I can fill the tank and have it for my bath and the dishes and the washing, rather than having to boil multiple pots just to wash a few measly dishes."

She smiled a watery smile at Connor, and he started forward, intending to comfort her. Sarah raised a hand to stop him.

"Don't," she said. "If you touch me right now, I think I'll break. See to the horse, then meet me inside."

He was all for giving a woman what she wanted, but Sarah looked like she'd blow away like a puff of smoke. He'd never seen her look so fragile and it hurt his heart in ways unexpected. His Sarah wasn't supposed to be like this. She was the strong one, the rock everyone else leaned on. For her to be like this...about to blow away in the wind...it hurt his heart in ways he hadn't thought possible.

Connor picked up the discarded reins as Sarah dragged her feet toward the house. The mare came willingly when he clucked his tongue, plodding as heavily as her mistress behind him. He'd take her to the barn, wash the lather from her and rub her dry, then she could stay the night in the stall there. Jezebel was out in the front paddock tonight, so Daisy wouldn't have to worry about making nice with another horse.

Work always helped Connor think through a problem. What was he to do about Sarah? She was obviously distressed, to turn up on his doorstep looking the way she did. Had his plans come to fruition earlier than he expected? Or was there something else going on? The only thing he could think of that would have Sarah in such a state was—his hand stilled on the mare's back.

Who had died? Her pa was the more likely option, but what if it was...

Connor almost started toward the house, but then remembered that Sarah was having a bath. If he walked through that door and she was still naked in the small tub that didn't conceal anything, he didn't think he could stop himself from touching her. And now certainly wasn't the time for desire. Especially if what he feared was the truth.

That in mind, Connor turned back to the mare, making sure he did a thorough job of cleaning her up and settling her in. When he was absolutely certain the water would have chilled and Sarah would be finished, he made his way inside.

This time, he didn't hesitate at the screen door, needing to comfort his girl too badly to worry about ghosts. Sarah was waiting for him, needed him, and he wasn't going to disappoint.

He should have come in sooner.

She sat with knees to chest, pale skin almost blue as the cooling water sapped the heat from her body. Her hair lay in wet, heavy waves down her back, floating dark in the water as if they had a life of their own. Shivers racked her body. Finally, Connor stirred to action.

He didn't even seem to notice her nudity as he ran for a towel she'd forgotten to get herself. His own breaths were coming in terrified rasps, skin clammy. Even as the screen door had slammed behind him, she hadn't stirred. Hadn't once looked at him. That indifference scared him more than anything he'd seen to date. Connor grabbed three towels before rushing back out again.

Sarah was exactly the way he'd left her. He didn't know what he'd expected to find when he'd come back, but he felt foolish for thinking five seconds would change anything. When he reached out and put a hand to her, she still didn't stir. Gently, he hitched a hand under her knee, the other behind her back, and lifted her dripping form from the bath.

He'd laid one of the towels beside the still-warm stove and hastily he lowered her onto it. With deft movements, Connor wrapped her body with another, the same with her hair, then proceeded to frantically dry her. His throat was so tight he thought he'd never speak again. How the fuck was he supposed to help her out of this?

"Connor?" Sarah's voice was a confused thread but music to his ears.

"Yes, love?"

"I lost him."

Aha. So it was her pa. Though it felt a little wrong, Connor was relieved it wasn't Isabel. He didn't think he could live with the guilt of that. He may want her to suffer, but Isabel's death would hurt many more people than just herself.

Shaking himself from his thoughts, he gathered the still-trembling woman into his arms, where she promptly burst into tears. Connor's hand rubbed soothing circles on her back. He was content to let her continue to cry but somehow, he thought she'd be more comfortable in clothes.

Connor lifted her as if she weighed nothing. Indeed, she was a shadow of the girl she'd been even a month ago, the shapeless dresses that were currently the fashion disguising how lean she'd become. Too busy taking care of others to take care of herself. He frowned. She'd be eating properly in no time if he had anything to say about it.

He took her to the newly renovated room, uncaring that his surprise would be spoiled. At this point in time, she was beyond noticing anything about it anyway. He lay her reverently on the bed while he quickly fetched one of his shirts. When he helped her put it on, he was dismayed to find it barely reached mid-thigh. But it would have to do. He didn't have anything else.

He pulled the covers away from one side of the bed, urging her to climb in. This time she moved of her own accord. Sarah curled into a ball as he slid the blankets up around her shoulders, tucking her in.

The tears had all but stopped, so Connor asked, "Do you want to talk about it?"

For a moment there was no sound from the bed. Then, in fits and starts, the sorry saga came out. His heart bled for her, even as he knew he was in some way responsible for her tears. It wouldn't be a coincidence that Duncan Graham had been to see the Wares this morning and Isabel was absent in the afternoon. And night.

No. Connor tried to swallow past the lump in his throat that threatened to choke him. He'd done something that had indirectly hurt his girl, and he couldn't do anything about it.

"Am I a horrible person, Connor?" The heartbreaking question knocked him from his thoughts.

"God, no. What makes you ask something like that?" Connor was truly horrified Sarah would think of herself that way, especially when he had helped cause her misery.

"It's just, he was hurting so much. In the beginning, I'd pray for him to get better but when we realised there was no hope...well. Those prayers turned to my hoping he'd pass. That there'd be no more pain." Silent tears streamed down Sarah's face. She didn't seem to notice. Her hand didn't even twitch toward her face to wipe them away.

"And now he has, you feel responsible." It was a statement, not a question. He knew the deep drain of guilt, had experienced it himself too many times to count on the battlefield and in the field hospitals. Sarah wasn't alone in wishing a kinder fate for someone in agony.

"He's much happier now, love," Connor continued gently. "It's not bad that you wished that for him. It's a kindness."

He lay down on the other side of the bed and she rolled toward him, curled into his side like she was meant to be there. His hands stroked her hair, her face, her back. It was all meant to soothe but part of him stirred that he didn't want wakened at this point in time. He shifted uncomfortably, then sat back up abruptly.

"I'll leave you here now. Look in on you in the morning to check how you're doing." He would be leaving early to see to her pa. It was the least he could do for the man who had raised the one person he had left to care about.

"Don't go," she cried out as he turned to leave. Connor hesitated at the door. "I'm still cold and—" The tears started to fall again. "I don't want to be alone. I need you."

Those three little words were all she needed to have him doing anything she wanted.

As Connor stripped down to his undergarments and crawled into bed beside her, he cursed himself for a fool. It was going to be a long, sleepless night. She laid her head on his shoulder, curling back into her spot at his side, before almost instantly falling asleep.

Though he was convinced his own thoughts would plague him, Connor too drifted away. The warmth of a body next to his, the comfort of her presence, gave him his first dreamless sleep since he'd come home.

Even the ghosts let him rest in peace.

Chapter 15

"And what would yer be doing in here again, when ye've already been in this morning, Eliza?" Sarah's ears pricked up at the mention of Eliza Williams. Maybe she brought the boys in with her? Or even one of them? Though which she'd want to see most, Sarah wasn't sure. Caleb was her friend, but Connor...

"I swear those boys of mine are bottomless pits, Frank." Eliza laughed as she scanned the display to check what was still available. No boys. Sarah slumped a little in her disappointment. "They've already finished the bread I picked up this morning. I'll have to take more home now. You know they can't stand my own efforts."

"Our Sarah makes the best bread this side of the Warrumbungles," boasted her pa, and Sarah's chest swelled with pride. He was sparing with compliments, so when one came, you treasured it.

"That she does." Eliza smiled her way as Sarah blushed. "She also seems to be awfully good at keeping both *my boys out of trouble."*

Sarah wouldn't go that far. Caleb still managed to find plenty of trouble. He was lucky that both Sarah and Connor were good at pulling him out of it.

"Most sensible lass I've ever met, and I thank my lucky stars for her. The last thing I need is more trouble like her sister." Sarah frowned, even as her pa swept her up in a brief hug. Was she truly that boring?

"Thank you for the bread," Eliza said as she handed her coins over. "Sarah, could you walk out to the buggy with me, please?"

With a nod, a curious Sarah followed her. Mrs Williams stopped beside her buggy, turning to face the girl.

"Sarah, I've got something to say to you, and I want you to remember it, do you hear me?" The serious tone made Sarah nervous, but she nodded. Of course, she'd remember. She was

Sensible Sarah. She raised her chin and shook off her uncharacteristic bitterness.

"People will always talk about your sister, Sarah. Unfortunately, that's the way of the world, to make much of physical beauty and little of anything that matters." Sarah found herself nodding, though she wondered where Connor's mother was going with her speech.

"Beautiful people who only focus on their beauty rarely end up happy. You, Sarah, are the lucky one." Sarah couldn't see how that was the case when she was regularly overlooked in favour of her younger sister. "Not only are you pretty in your own right, but you have something she doesn't—compassion. Over time people will be more drawn to you than your sister because kindness matters more than beauty. Remember that."

A hint of pride unfurled within her. For so long, people had sung praises to her sister's beauty, often forgetting Sarah stood right next to them. This was the first time Sarah felt...important.

Eliza Williams had swung herself onto the seat of the buggy and clucked the horse on its way before Sarah had a chance to thank her.

But her words would stay with the young woman over the years.

And she'd always regret not letting Eliza know how much she'd meant to her before it was too late.

Sarah woke to the sun streaming in through the open window and a warm weight beside her in the bed. Connor lay still, more relaxed than she'd seen him since he'd been home. He'd obviously forgotten to shave over the last few days, so stubble dusted his face. His hair too was slightly longer than usual, giving him a rugged look.

In the sleep-soaked dreaminess of the morning, she reached out tentative fingers. Ran them through Connor's hair, traced a path down his face, careful not to wake him. Finally, her hand rested on his heart and she started to doze again.

But then reality intruded.

She tensed as image after image of her pa raced through her mind at record speed. Most of them of those last few months when nothing seemed to be going right when it was a struggle to see him live another day.

While her hands hadn't woken Connor, Sarah's silent agony may have. He'd always been sensitive like that. He rolled over and drew her closer, wrapping his long frame around her as she battled with memories. His lips pressed tenderly to her forehead, smoothing the frown lines that felt permanent.

"Tell me about the good times," Connor ordered. His voice was husky with sleep, but she knew he was awake, alert. The man had never slept in past cock's crow in his life. She'd even hazard a guess he'd already been up and about and come back to bed again to be with her.

His words stopped the mad swirl of negative thoughts. Instead, she was forced to focus on the positive, to see Pa's life for what it truly was: a blessing. She started out slowly, but eventually, the words came out in a rush.

"My pa loved my mother so much, Connor. She was his shining light and no other woman could ever compare to her. My earliest memories are of lying between my parents on their bed, Pa's arms around both of us and Isabel in the bassinet beside the bed." Sarah found herself smiling as she spoke. The echo of their love filled her still. "Though Ma was his light, he had so much love to give. Each of his girls felt the warmth of it."

"We were both born lucky in that sense," Connor surmised. "My dad was the giving sort as well. Would do anything to make his family smile. Mum loved to take advantage of that." His tone was wry. "She loved beautiful things, and he could never resist her requests. Even when it was more than he could afford." Much as he was with Sarah. Though she would never ask for something out of their reach. It wasn't in her to be frivolous.

"Even after we lost Ma and our little brother as he was born, Pa was a rock. He tried to smile for us even when his heart was shattered. Though we couldn't understand it at the time, I appreciate it now."

She understood now how hard it had been. Loss sucked at you, tried to drown you in your own tears. All that mattered when you were its victim was yourself, and your pain. For her pa to function beyond that pain… He was an amazing man.

"I was thirteen when he started to build my shed."

"Studio," Connor corrected, reminding her so much of his brother at that moment that her pain almost doubled. The boy never could stand her making light of her talent and calling her studio a shed was one thing he always chipped her for.

"Studio," she amended. "He found my sketches scattered around the bedroom and was horrified that I was treating them so poorly." A wistful smile tilted the corners of her mouth. "I thought he was going to tear me to shreds for making a mess of my room but instead he started planning, then building."

"He had help," Connor said quietly.

"Yes, he did." Sarah's heart was in her eyes when she looked up at him. "You were fifteen and so earnest, doing exactly as Pa said without complaint. Even though you were handier with the tools than Pa was."

"It's easy to be handy when you've had to fix things your whole life," he said. "Your pa wasn't stupid or blind. He knew I was already halfway in love with his little firebrand and had no idea how to deal with the uncomfortable emotions I had for someone so young. He also knew I had skills he didn't, so the man listened as much as he gave orders. He was patient and kind. Gave me an excuse to be around you without feeling awkward."

"He did know how to read people, my pa," Sarah said. He also had very strong opinions on what was right for his daughters. Obviously, he had decided that Connor was right for Sarah well before the young man had come back from France.

"Pa didn't take any of Isabel's nonsense either," she said. "When she was too old for a spanking, he took to hiding her trinkets." Again, she found herself smiling at the memory. "Isabel was always vain, so when she said or did something horrible, somehow her ribbons and jewellery would mysteriously disappear. It didn't take long for her to cotton on to the fact they were always gone after she'd upset someone. Life was suddenly very calm and pleasant in the house afterwards, though not at school. It didn't vary much for a while after that until Pa was too weak to work in the bakery anymore."

Sarah sighed. Her heart felt a little lighter, but she knew she had a big day ahead of her. First port of call would be the mortician. Then she had to find Isabel. Sarah dragged herself reluctantly upright, looking for her discarded dress from last night. She didn't relish the thought of getting back into the thing, but in her rush, she hadn't brought anything else. However, it was nowhere to be found.

"Where are you off to in such a hurry?" Connor said from the bed.

"I've got to see to Pa and find Isabel. Organise a funeral. See to the legal side of things." Sensible, practical Sarah was talking, but all she really wanted to do was curl back up on that bed and feel safe and loved.

"No. You don't," he said.

She sighed with exasperation. "Yes, I do. These things won't wait on me." This time as she searched for her dress the details of the room finally registered. She was stunned, amazed, and uplifted, all at the same time.

This wasn't his parents' room anymore. Nothing remained of the room she'd prepared his mother's body in; not the wardrobe, not the bed, and certainly not the linen and curtains. Everything was fresh, vibrant with colour. Not too masculine, not too feminine. A promising place for a couple. On closer inspection, she realised the bed frame was the same, as was the wardrobe, but they'd been transformed. Vines and flowers had been carved into the woodwork, mirroring his work on the veranda that she loved so much. Her heart swelled. If this wasn't a declaration of love from Connor, she wasn't sure what would be.

His words suddenly intruded on her thoughts.

"...I said I've already taken care of it. Sarah, have you heard a word I've been saying?" He looked so adorably concerned she couldn't help herself. She leaned down and dropped a lingering kiss on his lips. "What was that for? Not that I minded," he hastened to add. "You can do that any time. But why?"

"For this." She threw a hand out, indicating the whole room. "Don't think I don't see Marge's hand in this either, you sneaky man. Now," she pressed another kiss to his lips then reluctantly stood. "Tell me where my clothes are so I can get into town."

"I said I've already done most of what you need to do there already. You don't need to leave right away."

"What?" Sarah was confused. It was barely first light. What could he have done overnight?

"Well," he said reluctantly. "I may have made a visit to the mortician's house a little before sunrise this morning." More than a little, if that guilty look on his face was speaking the truth. "And I may have already helped him see to your pa. I also left a note for Isabel—she still hadn't arrived by the time we left."

She let out her breath in a huff. Though she resented the fact he'd done this behind her back, she really hadn't relished the idea of setting foot back inside their house and having to see her pa in that state again. She also didn't know what she'd do or say if forced to confront Isabel today.

He looked up at her, the picture of innocence. Sarah snorted, then lowered herself back onto the bed. "So I really don't have anything to do this morning. I'll still need to go home this afternoon to organise the funeral and the paperwork and—" He stopped her mouth with a finger. When had he gotten so close?

"You don't need to do anything until this afternoon, or today at all. Rest, draw, do whatever it is that makes you happy." He was so earnest she couldn't help but smile.

"All right, you win," she said. "What do you want for breakfast?" His eyes lit up but just as quickly he frowned.

"You don't have to cook. You've just had... What I mean is, you're supposed to be resting. You don't need to be doing anything for me. Besides," he continued, "I must go and check on the stock. The ram I borrowed from the Robertsons is looking a little worse for wear and I should separate him from the ewes for a while."

She shifted closer on the bed, dropping another kiss to his lips, because she could. Sarah knew she shouldn't really be here, but her reputation was probably beyond shattered by now. She'd spent the night with a man alone at his house, and even though nothing had happened, no one would believe that, even under the circumstances.

"I'll have your breakfast ready when you come in, so don't be too long," she whispered against his lips. He gulped, lost for words. She got up and left him like that, tossing him a satisfied smirk. The man was putty in her hands. Who knew she, Sarah-no-nonsense-Dawson, would ever have someone look at her like their world shone in her eyes?

Especially since it was Connor.

Behind her, she could hear him fumbling with his boots. She smiled.

Wasn't it always the case that the rainbow followed the storm?

Her heart eased a little with the knowledge that he loved her. He may not have said it outright, but it was in everything he'd done since he'd walked into her life again. And that love was something well worth fighting for.

***

She'd floored him this morning. As he rode a lazy Jezebel back to the homestead, he thanked his lucky stars she was still in his life. Connor had woken early that morning, well before sunrise. He'd gone to her house, wanting to spare her some of the heartache, and figured the mortician could get up at that time as well.

The portly, middle-aged man hadn't appreciated being woken well before sunrise, but he'd changed his tune soon enough when Connor explained the circumstances. Everyone loved Sarah, and her pa was very well respected. Of course the man would want to help. He'd said as much to Connor when the story came out, admonishing him for not coming sooner and letting a young, unmarried lady sleep in his house.

It didn't seem right to throw into the man's face the fact he himself had given strict instructions he wasn't to be disturbed at night. That it was this alone that had sent Sarah running to him. He had no doubt the story would be halfway across town by dinner. By tea time, everyone would know. There was nothing to be done about it, however. It would have been worse if she'd ridden into town in the filthy dress she'd arrived at his house in.

As it was, her name would be linked with his so thoroughly, she'd be hard-pressed to do anything but marry him. He shouldn't be so happy about that, especially at a time like this, but he liked the idea that Sarah could be his. Even if it felt a little like she had no choice in the matter. And especially since he hadn't come clean about his agenda with Isabel.

It had only taken Connor a little while to separate the ram from the ewes. The poor fella was so exhausted it'd taken very little persuading to move him into the west paddock. Unlike Margery's devil stallion. It seemed the ewes were glad to be rid of him too, a few baaing mockingly as he passed. Or so it seemed to Connor. The ram had hung his head in disgrace.

Who knew what the lambing would be like next season? Hopefully, the old man had covered enough of the ewes that he'd at least make some profit to see him through the year. And that the ones he decided to keep proved to be fertile. At this stage, it was all a gamble. But playing with fate was what he did best.

This morning he'd been tempted to roll the dice. Only one question really mattered now: would Sarah still stay with him after she knew the truth? The cup had called to him with a power almost impossible to resist, daring him to question the Fates. He'd always been lucky. What would one more roll hurt? But then the anguished eyes of his friend, Smith, flashed through his mind and he remembered his promise. Remembered that it was better to live your life than trust in the Fates.

***

"Connor, come here." He joined his father on the porch swing. Padraic Williams' voice held a note of seriousness that was rarely there. When it was, he listened. They all did.

"What is it, Dad?"

His father held a small wooden box. Though his hands shook, his grip on the box was strong as he handed it to Connor. So strong, in fact, that when Connor grabbed it Paddy seemed reluctant to let go. His father fought to open his fingers, but when he did, he slid back wearily on the swing.

"Open it," Paddy said. Rather than questioning his dad, Connor did as he was told.

In the box was a cup. A simple dice cup, like those the Roman soldiers had carried with them in times of war. The tips of Connor's fingers tingled as he reached toward it. Instead of touching it he lingered over it, savouring the feeling.

"These dice have been in my family since your great-grandmother's time," his father said. "She was said to be a fortune teller, a witch." He laughed a little in disbelief. "I don't know if that's true, but she did have a way with herbs, my grandmother, and could tell you an uncanny amount of what waited in your future. She's the reason why I tried my luck in Australia."

Connor finally took the plunge. Grasping the cup was familiar, like coming home. His fingers curled around it in comforting warmth. When he gave it an experimental rattle, dice seemed to roll in his head. And continued to do so even as his dad kept talking.

"Your great-grandmother knew things. Said the dice helped her sort it out in her head." When Connor rolled the dice into his palm, Paddy's eyes seemed drawn to them like magnets. "She gave them to

my mother, who passed them to me when I came of age and said I was coming to Australia." The dice in Connor's head continued its endless drumroll, only gaining in volume as his father spoke. "And now I'm passing them to you."

"Why, Dad? Why do I need them?" He was finding it hard to think through the noise in his head. "And what's happening to me? What is all this rattling?" His fingers were pressed to his temple but that didn't stop it.

His father nodded his understanding. "You have the gift, Connor, just like your great-grandmother, and my mother. Think of a question and roll the dice." Surely it wasn't that simple?

He paused. "Not you, Dad?"

Paddy shook his head sadly. "No. Not me. I think the dice were waiting for you."

Connor once more rattled the dice in the cup, the echo in his head deafening. "Will the new spring lambs all survive? Or will we have losses this year?" He took a minute to form the question in his mind, then let the dice fly. When they stopped, so did the rattle in his head.

And he knew. Somehow, he knew. One and four.

"Be prepared to lose one in four, Dad," Connor said in a daze. "One in four." His father's face paled, but he nodded his understanding.

And both went out to prepare for a season they knew would be the hardest they'd faced yet.

Connor felt the familiar warmth of his father's presence as he always did when he rode into the house yard. For the first time since he'd been back, it seemed to wash out the memories of pain and frustration, leaving him with a feeling of peace when looking at his home. He no longer saw the screen door as the portal to a nightmare. Instead, inside was his one shot at a second chance.

Sarah was framed by the kitchen window. He watched her lips move as she sang to herself while she worked, a habit no doubt learned at her father's knee. The baker had always said singing while you worked made the time pass faster. Connor didn't sing. Time might pass faster for others, but for Connor, singing made others pass him by.

It was still early, not yet smoko, but the tantalizing smell of bacon and eggs drew him onward. He quickly untacked Jezebel and set her loose in the front paddock. There was no way he was letting her have free rein of the house yard, particularly when he was sure the fence around the veggie garden wouldn't survive her determined efforts to have spinach for dinner. He'd seen that horse devour a sprawling sweet potato plant in an afternoon—or at least he'd seen what was left of it. His garden couldn't take much more of Jezebel's appetite.

Connor was too impatient to take the stairs one at a time, leaping the three in one bound to get to the seductive smells coming from the kitchen. He felt a little disloyal thinking it, but though his mother's cooking had been good, Sarah's was better. The woman was a magician in the kitchen. Her baked goods would have any man begging on his knees to have one. Or her. Connor wasn't quite sure why she was still single, but he thanked his lucky stars she was. That she'd waited for him.

"That smells wonderful," he said as he walked through the door, taking his shoes off at the door. He wasn't much of a cleaner, so he needed to make sure he avoided anything that would make the house dirtier than regular wear and tear. Dusty farm boots were number one on his list.

"Good timing. I just finished the eggs." Sarah took the frypan off the stove, lifting the eggs onto two plates. She handed one to him before taking the other herself and joining him at the kitchen table. It was sturdy and wooden but small, a fact his mother had often bemoaned. His father had loved it, however, loved having the whole family close and loud together.

Connor had loved it too, which was why the same table still sat there six years after his father's death.

He hoped it would be that way again.

They ate together in comfortable silence. Most of what needed to be said had been already, so neither felt the need to break the mood. When they'd both finished, Sarah went to collect the dishes, but Connor stopped her with a hand on her arm.

"I'll do that. You cooked." He'd learned what was fair at his mother's knee, her wooden spoon and sharp tongue providing the necessary instruction. The woman had a heart of gold and been more likely to cuddle than scold, so her boys listened when she spoke. Much like the woman in front of him.

He took the dishes to the sink as she went to the donkey for hot water. The woman couldn't sit still. Connor's heart swelled. He was proud of her, of her strength, her ability to roll with the punches. And because she'd crumbled last night didn't mean she wasn't strong. If you couldn't lose yourself in emotion, even pain, then there wasn't much point in living. We'd be soulless beings without any joy.

There had to be balance.

She'd just finished filling the bucket when he came back in, stopping to stare for a minute, taking her in. The luscious flames of her hair slid over her rear as she knelt, the sight of it unbound stirring him. It didn't help that she was still in his shirt, Connor having forgotten to tell her he'd brought some of her things with him from her home. No. Though it was selfish, the primitive side of him was beating his chest at her wearing his things, so in them, she'd stay. He almost groaned as she leaned down to pick up the now-full bucket before he came to his senses and deftly snatched it from under her fingers. Electricity sparked at the light brush of his hand over hers, a positive charge that went directly to his groin.

Fuck.

Hastily, he took the bucket to the kitchen, leaving a startled Sarah in his wake. Connor subtly adjusted himself in his pants, trying to make room for the raging hard-on that was currently trying to make itself known to anyone in the vicinity. This wasn't the time, but the thing seemed to have a mind of its own where Sarah was concerned. She was vulnerable, and he was still a cad who hadn't told her the truth. Would maybe never tell her the truth. He didn't deserve to be happy.

"Connor?" Sarah's fingers brushed his back, lingered there, only making the problem worse. If he looked at her, they'd be doomed.

"I'm fine, just need to get these done quickly." He kept his eyes resolutely on the sink, even though everything in him urged him to turn around and take her.

She didn't back away, only moved closer, and lifted his arm away from the dishes as she slipped between him and the sink. There was no way she could avoid the evidence of his desire now.

She stood on tiptoes while his heart jackhammered in his chest, as she wound her fingers through his hair and then fused her lips to his. What started out soft and sweet soon deepened as she teased his lips with her tongue, a mimicry of what he'd done to her the other night. But she didn't stop there. Oh no, not his Sarah. All the breath left his body as she drew his bottom lip into her mouth, giving it a teasing nip as she released it.

His control snapped.

Connor crushed his mouth to hers, plundered and devoured even as his own hands roamed freely over her body. The thin cotton of his shirt was no barrier for his questing hands. When his fingers met the silken skin of her bare arse, he dragged her closer.

"No underwear," Connor groaned, tracing the fleshy mounds of her arse. He gripped both cheeks firmly and lifted, seating her on the kitchen bench so they were eye to eye.

She gave him a saucy grin. "Didn't feel the need this morning. My others needed washing." He tried to pull away at the reminder of her loss, but Sarah was having none of it. She wrapped her legs around him, drawing him in close enough that he could feel the heat of her arousal even through his pants.

"Don't you dare back away now, Connor Williams, from some misguided sense of honour," she whispered urgently, driving him to distraction as her fingers deftly undid the buttons on his shirt. Her lips soon followed their path as his skin was exposed, burning a path down his chest. "I want this. Want you. Don't deny me now."

How the fuck was he to refuse that? His shirt lay discarded on the floor, so turnabout was fair play. He set to unbuttoning the shirt he'd been so eager for her to wear moments ago but now seemed to belong firmly on the floor. Only his fingers didn't seem to be working properly.

Her soft laugh gave him all the motivation he needed. Buttons popped as he grabbed either side of the shirt and yanked. The treads, worn and thin, gave almost instantly and he had the satisfaction of seeing Sarah exposed.

Her nipples were a dusky pink, full on the heavy roundness of her breasts. He feathered kisses down her neck, lingering on her collarbone when she groaned, and down to the underside of her breast. He hesitated momentarily as he reached her nipple, but the greedy woman arched toward him and he couldn't wait any longer.

Connor's tongue traced the outline of her peak, flicking the tip firmly as he sucked it into his mouth. Sarah's guttural cry had him thrusting forward, his cock so hard he thought he was going to come in his pants. But it was her first time, and by God, he'd make sure she was ready for him.

He lowered his hands to her legs, spreading her wider as he followed the silk path up toward her cleft. She was so ready for him, wet and willing, but he'd see stars shine first in her eyes before he took her.

Kneeling, he feasted his eyes on her plump folds. Her hands hovered, almost as if she would cover herself, but Sarah abandoned any self-consciousness in a moment, reaching back to grab the benchtop. She glistened, so he did what he'd been dying to do since he saw her again in that bakery.

He drew his tongue slowly up those soft thighs and between her cleft, tasting her sweet cream.

***

Sarah exploded. Within moments of his tongue touching her most private place, she shattered into a million pieces. Nothing had ever felt this good. Was this kind of pleasure really allowed?

When the stars had lifted from her eyes, she reached for him, eager to do for him what he'd done for her.

"Not yet," he said, voice strained. He gathered her into his arms, carrying her into the bedroom as if she weighed nothing. "I want to be here, in *our* space, when we become one."

Sarah's heart leapt in her chest. "I love you, Connor." She said it with no hope of hearing it in return, but instead of silence, he surprised her.

"I love you too, Sarah-devil-may-care-Dawson. More than you'll ever know."

Tears slipped from her eyes, but she quickly wiped them away as he laid her gently on the edge of the bed, not wanting to give him the wrong impression. Instead, she drew him closer and captured his lips with hers, eager to taste him. All of him. His shirt was gone but she quickly found the button on his trousers and undid it as deftly as she'd done his shirt. His manhood thrust up proudly when released and she had another moment of trepidation at the sight of its girth.

Then it twitched eagerly and she smiled, reminded of her power. She looked up at him through thick eyelashes as she lowered herself to the floor, desperate to taste. He stopped her with a hand on her head.

"You don't have to do this," he said, but his eyes shone with hunger. Sarah didn't bother to respond, just lowered her mouth over him as far as she could go. The hand on her head fisted in her hair as he gave a guttural groan, sending satisfaction racing through her. *She had done this to him.* Plump little Sarah Dawson, whose sister always outshone her, had made a man groan in ecstasy.

The thought was heady.

She experimented some more, releasing it from her mouth with a little pop, gently licking up the sides before she sucked it back in again. This time a little farther, watching to see his reaction. His head was thrown backward, and he gave an involuntary little thrust in her mouth. She wrapped her hand around the base of his shaft and bobbed up and down again.

"Just like that, love. Suck in for more pressure as you move." She did as he asked and was rewarded in spades. Though she felt her technique was sorely lacking, she supposed her enthusiasm must have made up for it. Connor fisted her hair as he gently thrust into her mouth. With one hand on his cock, she stroked his balls with the other until he pulled out abruptly.

"That's not the way I want to finish tonight." She knew what he was talking about, was as eager for it by now as he was. Hell, she was so ready she was almost embarrassed. Almost.

He laid her back on the mattress, moving again to her breasts and sucking the nipples in, one at a time. She writhed underneath him. Every time he drew a nipple in it seemed as if he had a direct line to her core. He kissed his way leisurely down her body, swooping in and sucking her little nub without preamble.

She wept for him as she exploded, shamelessly grinding down on his face as she reached her peak a second time.

She was still riding it when she felt him nudging at her entrance. Sarah lay pliant, but Connor didn't move.

"Are you sure you want this?" he asked, the strain of holding himself back causing sweat to bead on his forehead. "Last chance, love. You can still walk away."

Looking into his eyes, she brought his head down for a long kiss. Then she reached down and fisted his cock, bringing him to her. "I want to be yours, Connor. I've always wanted to be yours."

He thrust into her gently, slowly, working himself in and out until he hit her barrier. Though she felt stretched, there was no pain yet. He'd prepared her too well.

"Are you ready?"

She nodded frantically, anticipation rising. He drew back a fraction and thrust, harder than before until he'd passed the barrier and seated himself fully inside her, stilling as he dropped his head to hers, fighting for control. The pain was brief, gone almost instantly, but the stretch was uncomfortable. She couldn't decide whether it was painful or pleasurable.

Sarah wriggled experimentally under him and Connor groaned. "Give me a second, love. Get used to the feel of it so it's more pleasure than pain. I don't want to hurt you."

"You haven't so far, and I want to *move*." She thrust her hips upward, daring him to lose control.

And lose control he did.

He pulled back and pushed into her again, each thrust rubbing against Sarah's walls in a way that had her tension ratcheting higher. She grabbed his arse, encouraging him to move faster.

"Harder," she cried, searching for that release from earlier but knowing this was going to be bigger. Better.

At her words he pulled out, Sarah let out a mewl of protest, but it was forgotten when he flipped her onto her stomach and raised her arse in the air. Without ceremony he thrust into her from behind, the new position allowing him to go so much deeper.

In one, two, three strokes, Sarah found herself crying out in ecstasy, her chest dropping limply to the bed while her arse remained in the air. Connor wasn't far behind her, spilling inside her within seconds of her release. He came down beside her, rolling them onto their sides so he could stay lodged within her.

He kissed her back, her neck, as their breathing slowed. Then those strong arms wrapped her tight and pulled her in closer.

"Don't let me go," she whispered.

"Never," he replied.

Then sleep took them both.

Chapter 16

As had been the case often in the last week, Sarah found herself dreaming of Connor in the funeral director's—a stalwart gentleman called Alfred Green—office while he droned on about the details of the service. As long as her pa was buried beside her mother, anything else was secondary. They didn't have the money for fancy fripperies and as soon as she'd walked in the door, Sarah had told Mr Green so. He'd nodded in understanding, no doubt used to that as things had been tight both during the war and now after.

She hadn't been back home in the week since, preferring to stay at Connor's where she felt safe and loved. Sarah knew it was causing quite the scandal, but she couldn't seem to bring herself to care. She hadn't opened the bakery in that time either. That might make her a selfish person, but surely people could go that long without her bread? Most of the women hereabouts knew how to make their own—if not bread, then definitely damper.

Isabel hadn't been home either. Sarah hadn't seen hide nor hair of her, and she was starting to get worried, though rumour had it that Mrs Ware had driven her buggy to town in a rage when she found Harry was missing as well. Did Isabel even know their pa had died? She'd tried to hold off on the funeral a little longer, but a body would only wait so long before it was indecent to have it aboveground.

The door crashed open, admitting one very flustered young priest. It startled her out of her reverie.

"Sorry I'm late," Father Ben said in a rush. "Mrs Ware cornered me as I was leaving, demanding I let her know where her son is." He threw his hands up in exasperation. "As if I'd have any better idea than her. It's not as if I have a reputation for performing shotgun weddings that would cause her to think I'd…" His train of thought petered out as he seemed to realise his words may be a bit indiscreet with Sarah and the mortician in the room.

"It's fine, Father Ben," Sarah said. "Though I'm worried too, with a fair helping of angry thrown in there for good measure. What was Isabel thinking?"

"I must say this is a mite selfish of Harry, though I would expect it from Isabel." The priest gave her a knowing glance that Sarah acknowledged with a grimace.

"You're right, selfishness isn't out of character for my sister." It shamed her to say it, but it was true. "I've yet to conclude whether she was born with the trait or if we nurtured it. A little of both, I expect," she said candidly.

"Anyway," Mr Green interrupted. "I must be off to see to the details of this funeral. Shall I call you when I'm ready for you?"

"Yes," the other two said in unison. The portly gent left them quickly.

Father Ben shuffled to the small settee the mortician had set up for his guests while Sarah remained where she was sitting at the desk.

"Do you want to go over the details of the service one more time?" asked Father Ben.

"I'd rather we didn't," Sarah countered. The talk of death was beginning to weary her. It dragged her spirit down and made her worry more about her sister. "I've been over the details so many times now I think my head's about to explode."

"As you will," he said. "Did you know that since I've been a priest in this parish, I've only performed one wedding?"

"Only one?" Sarah was horrified. A wedding was a huge festive event in these parts, a chance for the community to come together and support the new couple with best wishes for their future. It was also the time when mothers took to scanning for likely prospects for their children who weren't so young anymore. For there to have been so few weddings meant— "How many funerals with no one to bury?"

"Five," he replied, shoulders hunching as he seemed to shrink in on himself. "Five young men who should have come home, all buried in Turkey or France with no hope of recovering the bodies."

That could have been Connor. One of those was Caleb. Sarah suddenly felt ill.

"Fortunately, or perhaps unfortunately for some, there were plenty of christenings."

"And the ones with only one parent present broke your heart further," Sarah surmised.

"The worst was the girl whose fiancé went off to fight in '15. Seemed they'd been friendlier than they should have been before he went away."

"And Angela's man never came home." Angela Currie had been in the same year as her at school, her fiancé a man from the neighbouring town of Baradine. Sarah remembered seeing the two of them together at church. They'd been so in love...

"No, he didn't." Father Ben cleared his throat awkwardly, looking anywhere but at her. There was obviously something he wanted to say, so Sarah gave him a nudge. She had a feeling she knew where this conversation was going.

"Out with it, Father. You can't say or do anything at this point that would embarrass me any more than I have been already." And she had been, by both the gossip of the townsfolk and the idiocy of her sister.

"I'm not one to listen to gossip usually," he began nervously, "but some things you hear and you just—"

"You heard I've been staying at Connor's?" The statement lingered in the room as the young man went bright red and let out a strangled squawk.

"You don't deny it?" His tone was incredulous.

Sarah sighed. "Why would I? The man is taking care of me, as I do him. When I needed someone, he was there, an angel in my time of need. Why would I deny that?"

The priest's mouth opened and closed. Sarah almost smiled. It was the first time she'd seen the priest gobsmacked.

"But you aren't married. It's improper." She nearly smiled. Apparently, Father Ben wasn't as progressive as she thought.

"No, we aren't married. But just because I'm staying out there doesn't mean we're doing what you think we're doing, either." They were, but that wasn't any of his business.

"You're not, then? There's no cause for alarm?"

She answered his last question so she could remain truthful. "No, Father. No cause for alarm." It was a beautiful and honest expression of their feelings for each other at a time when she thought she had nothing left. Thank god she had Connor, or the events of the last few days could have broken her.

146

Having to bury her pa, Isabel missing, her future was uncertain as it had ever been.

He let out a relieved sigh. "Great. Fantastic. I'll be outside with Mr Green, coordinating our efforts, so to speak." The man practically flew back out the door, their awkward conversation behind him.

She leaned back into the seat, closing her eyes briefly to try to relieve the strain of the last few days. She'd been to the police to report Isabel missing, but they said they wouldn't interfere in anything that looked to be some sort of elopement. Particularly since Mr Graham had said they'd boarded a train bound for Sydney. No, the police said, Isabel had run off on her own and, as an adult, should be trusted to return (or not) in her own sweet time. When Sarah had told them about her pa and that Isabel didn't know, they were compassionate, but still firm in their belief that it was none of their business. She couldn't say she blamed them, despite her worry.

At least they'd promised to wire through a message to the Manly office in Sydney, in case anyone had seen them there. Connor had told her that Harry's family had stayed there shopping on occasion, and even though Harry's father refused to have anything to do with the hunt for the two, it was at least a clue as to where they could find them.

And then there was Connor. The man was an open book about his family, but when it came to the war, he clammed up tight. Each morning before he woke, she traced the scars that littered his torso. An enormous knotted mess of tissue almost covered his left shoulder. It must have been paining him still when he arrived home. There were tiny slices and two puckered scars on his left arm, from bullets, she was guessing, and a large scar on his side that stretched almost from his nipple to his hip.

She didn't know how her man was still alive. It broke her heart that he wouldn't share the burden, talk to her about his experiences over there, about Caleb. But maybe some hurts were too great to share.

This morning when he'd woken up, she'd gathered the courage to ask him about them, but instead of answering, he'd rolled closer and proceeded to make love to her until her world started to spin. All questions were forgotten in the heady madness of the moment.

As he'd no doubt intended.

The grandfather clock on the far wall chimed the hour, reminding Sarah the service was about to start. A cold sweat broke out on her forehead just as there was a knock at the door.

Think of the devil...

Connor peered into the room, relief on his handsome face when he saw her. He came all the way in, and she smiled to see he'd made the effort, despite his obvious reluctance, to wear his best clothes: his uniform. Though he looked rather dashing in the khaki, she felt a little ill seeing it on him. It reminded her too much that she could have lost him; that any one of the scars that littered his body could have been the wound that ended him.

They'd given him a new uniform before he left the hospital, the old one obviously not able to be used again. She didn't want to think of the state it must have been in for Connor's shoulder to look the way it did.

"Are you ready, love?" A warm glow filled her. He'd called her 'love' almost since he'd been home, but she hadn't thought anything of it. After all, it was a common term of affection between friends here. She hadn't realised then that he said it to no one but her. That every time he said it, he really meant 'I love you.'

"Am ready as I'll ever be, I suppose," she said, taking his hand.

He looked down at their linked hands, then up at her with a quirked brow. "You sure you want to do that—walk out like this? In the interest of full disclosure, I should tell you there are already people waiting out there."

She smiled up at him. "You know there's no one I'd rather be there with than you."

His smile brightened her spirit, lifting it when the circumstances would have otherwise dragged her down. Sarah looked down at their linked hands, took a deep breath, and led him out through the door.

The mortician's office was conveniently located next door to the church, no doubt an intentional choice. His house was above the cold cellar he used to house the bodies. To be honest, it was no wonder he was still unmarried. Who would want to live there, above the dead and next to God's house? You would always be wondering who, or what, was looking over your shoulder.

They crossed the lawn at the front of the church together and into the clutch of the mourners, including the slightly menacing figure of Mrs Ware. Sarah had no idea what she'd done to the woman to make her glower so, but she was too afraid to ask. Instead, she mechanically kissed cheeks, accepted condolences and disapproving frowns in equal measure as Connor led her toward the doors of the church. His palm was warm and solid in her own, whereas Sarah's was slick with sweat. Then Marge was in front of her.

"You okay, chook? Do I need to get the broom out and beat back the old biddies so you can get your breath back?"

A little bit of Marge love was what she needed right now.

"That's right, people, move on off for a bit. Give the peahen a bit of space. That includes you too, Nancy Biddle. I see you hiding behind the bush over there hoping for a nice bit of gossip." Sarah's lips quirked in a small smile at her best friend's words, as she'd no doubt intended.

"There," Marge said, turning back to run a critical eye over Sarah. "I've enough space now to do what I've wanted to do for the last week." Without any fanfare, she ripped Sarah free of Connor's grip and enveloped her in an all-encompassing hug. It was the last straw—Sarah burst out in undignified sobs she couldn't seem to stifle. "You cry it out, my little pumpkin. No one here to see you but me and that big lump who won't let you out of his sight. Did I ever tell you about the time that—" Sarah guffawed at the typical Marge statement, a great undignified snort that had snot shooting straight from her nose onto Marge's black dress.

She looked up at her best friend, horrified.

Then, calm as you please, Marge pulled out a handkerchief from her pocket and wiped herself clean, the piece of material disappearing back to where it came from.

"Next time you want to blow your nose, Sarah, ask for my hankie. I have dozens of the bloody things." She gave Sarah a wink then turned to Connor. "Come here, my little dumpling, and take this clearly deranged little muffin inside. She's leaking body fluids everywhere, and it won't seem to stop, so maybe being in the house of God will cure her."

Connor was smiling too when he retrieved her hand, his other resting in the small of her back. Marge fell in step behind them, nattering on about nothing as they took the last few paces toward the front door of the church. But with each move forward, the cloud that Marge's presence seemed to dispel for a brief time built above

Sarah's head again, urging her to panic. When they took the final journey through the doors, she ended up stopping outright.

I don't want to do this.

Sarah took a hasty step backward, shaking her head in denial. The plain wooden coffin seemed to loom over the already seated mourners. They were too many to count, suffocating her, stealing the air from her lungs as she struggled to breathe past her grief. If she kept walking, she'd have to look. To make it a reality.

She'd half convinced herself over the last sun-filled week that everything had been a figment of her imagination. That it was a nightmare induced by too much hard work and not enough rest. Now reality was intruding, and she didn't want to face it.

It was only Connor's hand in hers that kept her from turning and bolting back the way she had come. He waited while she collected herself, shared understanding in his eyes, then tugged her gently forward. Sarah came, her will ceded to his. Just 'til this ended. Until she could be strong again.

Though she knew she was moving, it seemed only moments before the casket sat in front of her, the lid opened to the world. What was inside was not her pa, even if they'd dressed him in his Sunday best. The cloth seemed to swallow him, a vivid reminder of the shell her pa had become. A reminder of all his illness had stolen from him. From them.

Frank Dawson should have stood with his daughters on their wedding days, should have been there to spoil his grandchildren as he had his own children. He should have been able to interrogate Connor about his intentions, berate Harry for his foolish beliefs.

Fate was a fickle thing.

"Can you close it?" Sarah asked. "He wouldn't want people to see him like this."

The mortician looked for clarification from the priest, which stirred Sarah's anger, but the latter was already moving. The lid closed with a respectful thud on the courageous man who'd raised two headstrong girls on his own.

Sarah and Connor moved to the front pew, a sturdy wooden thing, completely unadorned. Their church was one of simplicity— God didn't need beautiful things to hear prayers in his house. Sarah knew her pa rested with the angels because a man as good as he was could be nowhere else.

When Father Ben cleared his throat, she tried to pay attention, she really did, but her head felt like it was full of fog. She knew because he'd asked her what verses she'd like read, that the sermon wasn't full of fire and brimstone, like the last funeral she'd attended. And that was fine by Sarah. So instead of listening, she did what felt natural, and let the tears flow.

All too soon it seemed as if it were over.

"Is there anyone who would like to say some words about the deceased?" The deceased. He had a name, for God's sake. In shame, she put aside her anger. Pa would have hated for her to be cross with someone trying to help.

Father Ben stared very pointedly at her, but Sarah's legs suddenly wouldn't work. Her throat was dry, almost as if the tears had sucked all the moisture from her body when they fell in a torrent. In a panic, she turned to Connor. There was no way she could do this.

God bless the man. He stood, providing much fodder for the gossips, no doubt.

"Frank Dawson was a man that every man should aspire to be. He was one of two men who I hold responsible for making me the man I am today." He cleared his throat awkwardly, shuffling his feet as all eyes turned his way. "Though my father taught me everything about farming, and how to be a man, Frank taught me what it was to be a friend, a good human being. I watched him give loaves of bread to widows who couldn't afford the expense when he thought others weren't looking. Heard how he left his bakery in the hands of his daughter and apprentice so he could help run the community farm." There were many nods and murmurs at his words.

"Frank was also the one who took a heartsick young man under his wing and showed him what it was to carry on for someone else when you think your heart is breaking." More murmurs, but Connor seemed to be lost in his memories and didn't appear to hear them. "He was a survivor, a lover not a fighter, though I hear he had a mean right hook in his day." A quickly strangled whoop from the back had everyone smiling. "But most importantly, he was the father I want to be. The one who put his family above everything else, did anything he could to make them happy. I was blessed because I had two men to show me how to be a good man. A good person." The expression on his face was a strange one Sarah couldn't quite interpret. It seemed to be a mix of sadness, anguish, and a hefty dose of regret, though what cause he had for regret, Sarah didn't know.

"So, thank you, Frank," he continued, looking back at the coffin. "Thank you for the years you stood as an example for all men." He sat back down to a chorus of 'amens.' He leaned into Sarah and whispered, "And thank you too, Frank, for shaping the one person I can't live without."

Sarah's heart beat erratically in her chest, even as the tears continued to fall. By God, she loved this man.

"Is there anyone else who wishes to address the congregation?" asked Father Ben as Sarah shuffled closer to Connor, unashamed. No hands were raised. Connor had said what everyone had been thinking.

The pallbearers loaded the coffin into the cart to take it out to the cemetery a short drive from town. Some of the mourners got ready to follow, while others would return home, respects paid. Sarah swung up onto the front seat of the cart beside Mr Green while Connor went to get Jezebel. As they started to roll out of the gate, a small, familiar buggy hurtled around the corner, stopping abruptly in a spray of dust.

What in hell did Mr Graham think he was doing? The old stationmaster had effectively blocked the road. There was no way anyone was getting through unless he got a move on.

"Have we missed it? My God, Sarah, where are you? Where's Pa?" A frantic Isabel leapt out the back of the buggy, followed by a very rumpled-looking Harry. Isabel was dressed to the nines in a red tasseled and sequined dress, completely inappropriate for the occasion. Her hat sat jauntily on her head and the feather on top only served to inflame Sarah's temper. How dare she turn up to their father's funeral looking like some kind of...of...hussy.

Eager to avoid making more of a scene, Sarah tipped her head toward the church and said through gritted teeth, "Inside. We'll continue this inside, now."

Wringing her hands, Isabel followed, Harry on her heels. Connor had just rounded the corner with Jezebel and, when she indicated for him to follow, handed the reins to Mr Graham and quick-stepped after them.

The church was empty except for Father Ben, who was tidying quickly. "I'll just be a moment then I'll join you on the cart, Sar—

oh." The priest had finally caught sight of Isabel and Harry. "Isabel. I suppose it's better late than never in circumstances like these, hey?" He laughed nervously.

Sarah turned to her sister and spoke over him as if he didn't exist.

"Where have you been? And what did you think you were doing, riding in here like that? Dressed like that?"

"We've been in Sydney," Isabel replied quickly. "We were out in Manly when a local policeman spotted us, gave us a message we needed to come home immediately. So we did."

She stopped there as if those brief words explained all.

"And?" Sarah asked incredulously. "Don't you have anything else to say? Ask?"

"Well, Mr Graham filled us in on the way from the station. About...about Pa and all." Isabel swallowed visibly. "We came straight here, hoping we'd at least catch some of the service." She looked accusingly at Sarah. "Why didn't you wait?"

Up until then, Sarah had kept her temper remarkably under control. Not so now. "Why didn't I wait?" Her voice raised an octave, a sure indicator someone was going to cop the rough edge of her tongue. Father Ben flapped uselessly at her to try to get her to lower her voice. She ignored him again. "I'll tell you why I didn't wait until you came back from your little holiday. Our father had died, Isabel. Died alone because you left him there to go jaunting about."

"I didn't just—"

"Save it. What happens to bodies over time, Isabel?"

Her sister's face blanched. "Oh..."

"Yes, 'oh' might be an accurate description, if by 'oh' you mean they slowly start to—"

"Enough, Sarah," Harry said firmly, taking Isabel's hand. The man had suddenly grown a backbone. "We had reasons for not being there when you needed us, when he needed us, but that's irrelevant now. The fact that we weren't here breaks both our hearts."

Indeed, Isabel was sobbing, genuinely it seemed, into his shirt as he rubbed circles over her back. A twinge of guilt pierced through Sarah's anger. Maybe she should hear them out.

"Do you want to tell me why you left in the first place, considering I'd already told Isabel we needed to keep a close eye on

Pa? And with no note, nothing to tell me where you'd gone?" Connor shifted uneasily at her back, but she was so focused on her sister she dismissed it.

"Well, it's somewhat private," Harry said, looking pointedly at the priest.

Father Ben couched uncomfortably. "I'll give you all a moment, shall I? See what I can do about the mourners out front who no doubt have their greedy ears pressed against the door?" He exited quickly out the side door, perhaps keen to use the element of surprise.

Harry took a deep breath and continued, the hand on Isabel's back never slowing. The sequins on her dress shone distractingly but Sarah tried to ignore it. Otherwise, the red scrap of material would be like a flag to a bull. "The day we left someone had been to see my parents spreading nasty rumours, both about Isabel and me and Isabel herself."

Sarah gave a little gasp. Though the town could be so supportive when it came to gossip, they were quick to censure. She didn't want that for Isabel.

"Someone had seen me coming out of your house of a morning." He had the grace to blush at this, while Sarah quirked an eyebrow pointedly at him.

"And whose fault is that, Harrison Ware?" Sarah's words were tart.

"Well, yes." He coughed. "Be that as it may, they hadn't seen my face so, by the time the rumours reached my parents, Isabel's reputation…"

"Who cares about my reputation, Harry? If I've told you once, I'll tell you a—"

"I know, darling," Harry said, pulling Isabel up short. He locked back at Sarah. "We don't care," he continued. "But my family do. They care a great deal."

Isabel's tear-streaked face lifted, eyes puffy and nose dripping. Thank God she was at least somewhat normal and was ugly when she cried. The expression on her face, however, was that of a mother dingo defending her pups. Feral. "Then we'll leave, go back to Sydney where no one cares about what's proper or not. Where no one knows us from a bar of soap."

Harry shushed her, patting her back absentmindedly. "They threatened to disown me. We left for Sydney to give them some space to rethink the situation."

"Did neither of you think it might be a good idea to *tell* your family what was happening?" Connor's words were sharp. "Or were you too busy thinking about yourselves?" The tips of his ears were red, a sure sign of either anger or embarrassment. Sarah was betting on the latter.

"I don't see what you have to do with this, Connor," Harry said, chin upturned haughtily.

"He's here because he's the only one who was here for me this last week. The only one to help when things got tough. For God's sake, Connor was the one who helped the mortician get our pa out of the house and to the mortuary." Sarah was shaking with the force of her rage. "Much as I sympathise with your plight, being the focus of some lovely rumours myself, the fact remains you left while Pa was on his deathbed, without telling me so I could be with him, and you didn't leave any way to contact you." Her throat closed up, but Sarah managed to choke out, "He died alone, and I don't know if I can forgive you for that."

The silence in the church was deafening. Harry and Isabel hung their heads, ashamed, as did Connor, though he had no reason to.

"Now," she continued. "Let's get out there and give Pa the burial he should have, with all his family there."

There was no further argument as they all took their respective forms of transportation out to the cemetery. The other mourners' whispers followed them everywhere they walked, but none had the audacity to approach them while the priest still had words to say.

There had been no choice where to bury him, but the plot was lovely regardless. Flannel flowers guarded the roots of the silver gum trees, watching warriors protecting their final resting place. Pa had picked out his plot years before when they had buried her mother. Reserved the one next door, so he'd always be with his love.

Though the wind whistled through the gum trees and Father Ben's voice drifted in and out of her consciousness as he said some last words before the coffin was lowered, the one thing that registered was the smells. Though by rights the cemetery should smell of decay instead, the rich scent of eucalypt and freshly turned earth comforted her. The mourners stood in respectful silence as the last few shovels of earth were tossed back into the hole, sealing her pa away from her forever.

The tears rolled unchecked down her cheeks while Connor stood, a silent sentinel, at her back. Isabel and Harry stood respectfully on the other side of the grave. Her pa was really, truly gone. And here they were, the two people he'd continued to love despite losing his heart, and they were fighting. Remorse settled like a stone in her gut. Nothing she said or did was going to bring him back, so why waste angry words with Isabel when the outcome would remain the same?

She walked around the grave and took her sister's hand.

Tears of gratitude were in Isabel's eyes as she smiled tentatively at Sarah. With a light tug, Sarah led the way to where the waiting mourners had set up refreshments. The scent of fresh bread sent new tears running down both girls' faces. This was what he would have wanted, people coming together over what had become his main source of pride—the ability to care for others through filling their stomachs.

But a relaxing morning was not to be.

Mrs Ware stomped toward them, long skirt scattering flowers with the force of her motion. She stopped in front of Isabel, fists clenched, and face pinched with loathing, before she turned to her son.

"I have only two things to say to you, Harrison Ware," Mrs Ware said. "First, if you ever want to inherit Coolabah, you'll get rid of this...harlot." She stared fury at Isabel's dress. "And secondly, you'll think long and hard about associating with either of them, in any capacity, in the future."

She turned to storm away without a backward glance, but Sarah stopped her.

"Mrs Ware," she called, the fury lacing her voice enough to stop the woman in her tracks. "Despite the fact you have gone out of your way to make my pa's funeral as unpleasant for everyone involved as possible, I'm going to give you some advice." She took a deep breath, struggling to control her temper. "You'd do well to think about what it is that would make Harry stay with her, despite being threatened with disinheritance. It'd also do you good to take a long look in the mirror and ask yourself, who am I hurting with this action? Because, sure as night becomes day, Harry and Isabel will do what they want, despite your ultimatums. Do you really want to be on the outside when your son continues to live his life, grow his family? Or do you want to continue to be loved into your dotage?"

The woman sneered at her before stalking off, but Sarah could see by the tears in her eyes that the barbs had hit home. Barbara Ware was not a nasty person. Just too proud for her own good.

Connor wrapped his arms around her, and Sarah soaked it up, then deliberately moved away. He shot her a questioning look, but she ignored him for the moment.

All she wanted was to go home. Her old home. With her sister. They needed to grieve together and they needed to do it on their own. At least for tonight. She knew he'd understand.

She turned to Isabel, who was looking at her with something akin to pride. It stirred within Sarah, golden and good. "Come on, little chicken," she said, using her pa's nickname for Isabel. "Let's head home, just you and me." When Isabel hesitated, she continued, "I'm sure these boys can look after themselves for tonight."

Isabel turned to Harry who, in all fairness, looked a little uneasy. Or was that unsure? He had just been threatened with disinheritance, after all. Isabel tried to stare into his eyes, but Harry's kept flicking back and forth between Isabel and his mother. She frowned and turned to Sarah anyway.

"You're right, it's time to go home." Isabel's voice held the tears her eyes didn't. Harry didn't say anything to stop her as she walked away from him toward Sarah, or to tell her he'd see her soon. Sarah's heart broke anew for her sister. Isabel had to be hurting. She'd found out their pa was dead, and here was her fiancé, wavering in his devotion. Sarah shot him a glare that promised retribution, but Harry only hung his head in shame.

She led Isabel over to the cart, ignoring the stares of the mourners still there, and snaffled Mr Green from the refreshments table. They needed to go. Now.

Sarah gave Connor an apologetic smile. He looked a little nervous but mouthed *tomorrow* at her as the cart lurched forward toward town. She nodded then slumped farther into the uncomfortable bench seat.

Finally, Sarah and Isabel could rest and reflect, away from the drama of the day.

Her heart couldn't take any more surprises today.

Chapter 17

Sarah groaned a little in her head as Caleb started complaining again. The walks from school to her house were starting to get a little frustrating. The walk was one they'd done companionably every afternoon since they were six years old and had never been a hardship. Until now.

She didn't talk about Connor in front of him, so it was doubly frustrating when Caleb continued to whine about Isabel every afternoon, all the way home. She kicked a stone and tuned back in when Caleb mentioned his brother.

"And Connor says I should forget about her. But I can't, Sarah. I know she loves me too. I always catch her looking at me from across the classroom and when..."

She resumed her daydreaming. Privately, she thought Caleb was very wrong. Isabel didn't talk to her about anything, but Sarah was convinced the only being her sister was capable of loving was herself.

"...there's no reason for it. And now I'm going to be left alone to manage the property and Connor will be winning the hearts of every girl he comes across in his uniform."

Sarah stopped short. "Sorry, what?"

"That's what I said when I found out," Caleb continued, Sarah's renewed interest in the conversation unnoticed by him. "I asked him what he expected me to do while he went off to war to gain glory fighting for our country, and do you know what he said to me?"

Sarah didn't know what Connor had said, but she knew what words she would have chosen if Isabel had spoken like that to her. And they weren't very polite.

"He said it would be good for me." Caleb's lips curled in a sneer. "That taking responsibility for everything around the farm, like he had when Dad died, would make a better man of me."

Sarah winced. The words were a little harsh, but the sentiments were right. It would do Caleb good to have responsibility for something other than himself. But what was this about war?

"I don't think it's as bad as you're making it sound, Caleb," she said soothingly. "But what's this about Connor going to war?"

"He enlisted when the recruiters came to town yesterday." Sarah's heart lurched in her chest. *"We've always done everything together. Why would he go without me?"*

Sarah didn't know. Didn't want to think about what Caleb was feeling. A hole had opened up in her chest. War was an ugly thing, no one surviving unscarred.

And her Connor had signed up to go into the thick of it.

The morning dawned cold and bright, with the bite of frost on the wind. Sarah hadn't thought she'd sleep beyond dawn, but the drama of the day before had seen her fall into her childhood bed and sink into an exhausted slumber. It was only the clatter of Isabel in the kitchen that woke her.

She yawned, threw on one of the pretty, colourful dresses Marge had made her, and went to join her sister. Wearing something her friend made with love always managed to make her feel better. The kitchen was warm, unlike the last few times she'd been home. Sarah hadn't been able to stay in the house long, particularly by herself when Connor had to work the farm, so there was no point in lighting the fire or the stove for warmth. It would have been wasted on an empty house. However, the familiar action of drawing a chair up to sit beside the stove while her sister cooked was soothing.

"Eggs this morning, and leftover bread that one of the nosy old biddies brought round last night after you went to bed."

Sarah started. When was the last time she'd heard Isabel voice something sensible, and not inherently selfish? Her sister's movements were short, sharp, and economical. A far cry from her usual graceful motion. In fact, this moment would be one of the few where an observer would see they were sisters.

"What's wrong, chook?" Sarah asked. Isabel choked out a laugh, bringing the pan down a little too hard on the stove. Eggs flew all over the benchtop and down the cupboard doors.

"Shit." And that wasn't like her sister either. Neither the clumsiness nor the curse.

Sarah grabbed a rag from under the sink and started cleaning the mess, being very careful not to look Isabel in the eye. Like any wild animal, it was a sure way to send her sister into fight-or-flight mode. If Sarah was patient, Isabel would work up to it on her own.

"I can't stop thinking about it." Case in point. Thoughts never stayed buried in her sister's head. Someone always had to hear. Isabel continued. "I mean, not just Pa, but this whole situation with Harry, too."

Sarah nodded as if she understood entirely when she was almost completely in the dark. Isabel would get around to it eventually.

"How did someone find out about Harry? No one walks past our house that early..." Sarah's own thoughts started pounding around in her brain, desperately trying to tell her something. Unfortunately, the telegram wasn't being received. "And why tell Harry's parents, and make it seem like it could have been someone other than Harry? Anyone who knows us knows that..." Isabel continued to prattle on about her misfortune, but Sarah's thoughts had settled on the facts.

Yes, Sarah thought. *It would have to be deliberate.* Again something was niggling at her brain, jumping up and down for attention. Her feet felt like lead as if the polished wooden floor of the kitchen was suddenly swallowing them. The answer hovered at the edge of her comprehension, and it frustrated her to realise she didn't have the brainpower to put it together.

Isabel threw what was left of the eggs onto two plates, liberally buttering some of the bread with butter Marge had brought over from the farm. She'd have to remember to take it out to Connor's if Isabel wasn't going to...

Connor.

Connor had seen Harry at their house. Connor had reason to walk past the house of a morning. Pins and needles stabbed at her body, needling her gut. Surely not? What reason could he have? Harry was his friend, and even if he didn't like Isabel, or disapproved of her, he'd protect her for Sarah.

Right? The wash of words from Isabel had started to slow as her sister reached the end of her diatribe.

"Could you ask Connor if he saw anything unusual of a morning around our place? Or at night when he rode out of town?" Isabel asked anxiously.

"Of course," Sarah replied. "Anything to help you figure this out." And anything to clear this sneaking suspicion from her heart. She didn't want to think Connor capable of betraying her family like that. Of betraying her. But so many things pointed in his direction: his presence at their house, the conversation he'd started and Mrs Ware had overheard... She'd be a fool if she didn't confront him about it.

Blood pounded in her ears. Her vision narrowed to focus solely on the door. Distantly she registered Isabel's quick kiss on her cheek as she left the kitchen.

If he did have a hand in it, she wanted to know the reason why and how deeply he was involved. If he didn't—well, she was sure Connor would forgive her doubt in time. She'd never forgive herself if she dismissed her suspicions and left well enough alone.

There were things to be done today, with the house, the bakery. They'd have to decide what they were going to do in the short term, considering Isabel's wedding was up in the air. But once that was done, once she'd mulled over all the facts and tried to fit the puzzle together, then she'd go see Connor.

Surely he'd understand her need to find out the truth? Her need to see that no stone was left unturned? And Lord, help her be strong, because if he was behind this...violation...of her trust, then there was nothing left for them.

Connor and Sarah would be through.

***

Connor's gut churned as he debated the wisdom of telling Sarah the truth. His conscience was eating him alive. It had been for days, but today was worse than any other by far, considering the scenes from yesterday's funeral. Everything Sarah had experienced was his fault.

Her pa had been dying, alone, and Connor's actions had made the situation much worse for Frank and Sarah than it needed to be. Connor was the one who'd driven Isabel and Harry away, and he was the one who had put his own agenda above the needs of others. Frank dying alone in a pool of his own blood and bile rested on his shoulders alone.

He'd never forget walking into that freezing house with Mr Green at his heels. Thankfully it was cold, because as ignoble as

Frank's death was, they could have walked in to worse. A lot worse, if it were summer. Frank had stared accusingly up at him from that bed full of bloody bile. Shame had coursed through him, stirring Connor to do everything he could to make things easier for Sarah. Right for her.

The worst thing about it was he had still felt a sick sense of excitement and satisfaction when Mrs Ware had publicly snubbed Isabel. When the matron had delivered the ultimatum that should see Harry running for the hills to get away from the girl. Connor had known that Harry loved his farm, and the money it brought with it, above everything else in his life. It was a gamble whether he loved Isabel more than the comfort he enjoyed now. Deep in his heart, he hoped Harry loved his lifestyle more than his girl.

A loveless life was the least Isabel deserved.

His hand curled around the small lump in the pocket of his trousers. He'd found his mother's ring when he was clearing the master bedroom of his parents' things. Mum had stopped wearing it when Connor was still a child, stating she didn't want to get it dirty with all the work she was doing around the property when in reality the proud woman couldn't fit them on her fingers anymore. It had taken some polishing, but the gold gleamed like starlight, the diamond winking within it.

The words he wanted to ask continued to burn a hole in his throat. Connor couldn't do it. Wouldn't do it, when so much remained unsaid. When there were so many secrets he was holding back. He couldn't even be sure he was the man she thought he was anymore. Would a good man have done the things that he'd done?

He clutched at his pocket again, hands shaking as he watched the sun sink beyond the horizon in a fiery streak of red, orange, and pink. It seemed somehow ominous; the mountains being devoured by a blaze of light. And still, Sarah didn't come.

It wasn't until the last of the sun had nearly disappeared behind the clouds that he could make out the hint of dust that meant a rider approached.

She rode slowly, shoulders hunched. Even Daisy seemed to drag her hooves as they rode through the gate.

Connor's heart sank. This was more than the death of her pa. Sarah looked defeated.

And he suspected it had something to do with him.

162

***

"We need to talk," she said without fanfare. Best to rip the dressing from the wound quickly. Sarah looped Daisy's reins over the hitching post, not letting the mare out with Jezebel, who was starting to grow round with her pregnancy. Something in her was convinced she wouldn't be staying the night. She'd learned to trust her instincts over the years. Even if Connor was innocent, he likely wouldn't want to spend the night with a woman who would suspect something that awful of him.

However, her instincts were singing a song she wasn't quite willing to listen to. Yet. Not without the words from his own mouth.

And maybe not even then.

Connor followed silently behind as she made her way into the kitchen, seating herself beside the stove. Her foot continued to tap with an excess of energy but, even though she'd practiced a hundred times today what she wanted to say, the words just wouldn't come. Connor sat down warily opposite her. He was treating her as if she was a snake that'd slithered into his home and had to be treated with the fear and respect it deserved. While she hated to see that look on his face directed at her, it made the suspicions she was nursing flare to life.

"Why do you look at me like I'm about to bite your head off, Connor?" she snapped, then was instantly contrite. She'd condemned him before he'd given testimony.

Connor sighed like the weight of the world was on his shoulders. Then he took a deep breath and looked directly into her eyes. "Maybe because I'm afraid you are."

Her breath caught, foot stopping instantly in its tapping. This was it. Her chance to ask her questions and get answers whether she liked them or not.

And yet the silence stretched further. It was Connor who broke it.

"I have something to tell you, something which, by the way you rode in here and your state now, I'm afraid you've already guessed." A tingle seemed to grow in Sarah's chest, a frisson of awareness.

"Please," she begged. "Please tell me what I'm thinking isn't true. Tell me you didn't play a part in Isabel's situation."

He hung his head in shame, and she knew then and there that everything she'd thought about the situation was true. And that everything they'd shared was a lie.

"I did," he said, voice hoarse. "But nothing I've said to anyone hasn't been true. I've never lied to you, Sarah."

"What do you mean 'nothing you've said'? Please tell me it wasn't you who went telling tales to Mrs Ware. No good could come from something like that, only wickedness."

"I didn't speak to Mrs Ware."

Sarah let out a sigh of relief at his words, her tight chest loosening. Prematurely, it turns out. "But I was the one who arranged for it to be done. I was also the one who spread the rumour in the first place."

Sarah's heart broke into a thousand little pieces. It burned from the inside out, like the tiny shards of her heart were trying to drill their way through her chest. "Why?" she gasped, trying to make sense of it all.

His face twisted into a snarl and Sarah flinched backward. Where was the Connor she loved? This was the dark beast Connor had brought back from the war with him. *This* was what had been riding him, driving him, more than any love he *may* have for her. *May* being the operative word.

"You don't know what poison she has inside her, Sarah."

"Isabel?" she asked, confused by the vehemence in his voice. "How can you speak about her like that? She's my sister, little more than a child."

"A child?" Connor's laugh was wild and bitter, nothing like the full-throated, joyful ones she'd have given anything to coax from him only days ago. "No one is a child when they have blood on their hands, Sarah. All innocence is lost when you take a life."

"What are you talking about?" She was starting to get a little hysterical but couldn't fight her way out of it. Her hands were shaking so badly, she couldn't control them. "For God's sake, Connor, Isabel has only just left school. She didn't even get a chance to volunteer in the war efforts, though I'm sure she would have, if only for Harry."

"Harry? Harry has nothing to do with this conversation, so let's leave my weak-willed friend out of it. Though he's probably better off now if he has given her the shift."

"Harry has everything to do with this conversation," Sarah screeched. "You found a way to ruin both of their lives. How can you say it's nothing about him?"

"Because this is about Caleb and his death being entirely your sister's fault!" Connor spat out.

Her breath left her lungs in one fell swoop. She struggled to pull more in, but it wasn't happening inside this house where she'd made such beautiful memories. All now tarnished by Connor's hate.

How could my sister be responsible for Caleb's death?

She stumbled out of the kitchen and toward the screen door but tripped over her own feet. The ground seemed to loom in slow motion and Sarah had just enough time to raise a hand to protect her head before she crashed into the door.

"Sarah." Connor's voice echoed around her as he gathered her in his arms, frantically pulling her away from the unsuspecting door. Her heart ached for him even as her own continued to splinter away in her chest. Connor's past defined him, and it was full of pain.

"Take me outside." What came out may have been more gurgle than a murmur, like she'd intended, but it had Connor crying out in relief and carrying her to the porch swing. The crisp autumn air cleared her lungs and head, allowed her to breathe where she couldn't in that house full of ghosts. Memories.

She used to like that about it, but today the past hung too heavy in the air.

Ghosts and accusations filled the silence. Not for the first time, she cursed Caleb.

"Why do you think Isabel killed your brother?" she asked when she'd managed to calm down. She shifted out of his arms and onto the swing, as far away from him as she could. She didn't know if she'd be able to think straight if he touched her. And she needed clarity.

Connor's eyes flashed fire again, but his voice remained reasonably calm. His fingers twitched, and he moved to touch her, but Sarah sent him a piercing glare that had him keeping his hands to himself.

"She gave him a white feather, Sarah. In person. He carried it with him right up until the end as a reminder. I assume you know what it means?" His tone was haughty, but she ignored it. Even though his distance made her heart feel like lead in her chest. This wasn't about him anymore.

"Of course I know what it means. Do you think I'm that ignorant? That I don't know what's going on in the world?" She could tell he did think that but forged onward anyway. "How do you know this?"

Connor's face shuttered, a cold mask replacing the fire of a moment ago as if he needed it for control. "I saw him the day before he died. Sixteen years old, on a battlefield he should never have seen. We had time to talk." He looked at her so earnestly she could tell he was hiding nothing. For once Connor was an open book, though that cold hauteur remained. This was the truth he didn't want to tell. Couldn't tell without giving himself away.

Sarah's temper flared again before she tamped it down.

"I just got him back, only the next time I saw him was when I patched almost unrecognisable pieces of him together after Fromelles." His eyes were like ice in his head, leaving her cold when he turned that stare to her. "I say almost because the only thing intact on his entire damn body was that feather, covered in blood, in the inside pocket of his uniform. He'd carried it in with him like a badge of courage."

"I don't know what—"

"To say? Of course you don't," he scoffed. "Your sister and her white feather were what killed my brother."

He was right, and yet this was so wrong. "She was a child, Connor. Not yet fifteen when Caleb left. Surely you don't hold a child responsible for a thoughtless action?" But she could tell that he did and that it had burned a hole in his heart that she wasn't sure she could fill. Or if she even wanted to anymore.

He wasn't the man she thought he was.

"She knew what she was doing. Fourteen or not, she knew what that feather meant, and what most men presented with it would do." Sarah didn't think Isabel did, beyond wild school stories of heroes who defeated armies on the battlefield. But she couldn't tell him that. He wouldn't hear it in any case. Connor was so lost in his anger anything she said in Isabel's defence would make it worse.

Still, she had to try. Maybe he'd reflect on her words later. Sarah could only hope.

She stood, taking care to make sure she hadn't damaged anything in the fall. Her head swam a little when she first moved, but it cleared in seconds. All the pieces were clear now, fitting neatly in her head.

But she couldn't stay here with him. She owed herself more than that.

"I want you to listen to me, Connor," she said, drawing herself up to her full height and hoping her words would hold weight. That he'd think about them later. "You have been judge, jury, and executioner for my sister, who you say was not a child based on her actions. And I agree with you, what she did was despicable, but—" Connor stared so defiantly at her that she almost gave in and left him with his bitterness. But she loved him too much to allow him to live with that much anger.

Even if he'd never get the chance to live with her.

"I want you to consider how much guilt Caleb has in this because I've spent many a night thinking about it." She held up a hand as his mouth opened. "Don't interrupt. You'll get your turn later. How much do you think Caleb's own selfish actions factored into his death? I didn't know about the feather, and knowing Caleb, that would have been the spur he needed to make the decision to leave your mother alone. But it wasn't the only one.

"He continually pursued a girl who had told him quite bluntly she wasn't interested in him. I know, I was there. He left your mother here alone, despite knowing she was not sound of mind. He may have wrestled with his conscience about it, but his desire to prove himself was greater than his concern for Eliza." She emphasized her best friend's faults on her fingers, ticking them off as she went. "He ran away from home and told no one where he was going. The only reason we know he enlisted is because of your letter. And finally," she said, hands on hips as she glared at Connor, "he *allowed* a white feather to drive him to do something he *knew* was wrong, *knew* no one was judging him on, just because he wanted some of the 'glory' he thought you would be having."

"You don't know that," he said, obviously meaning the last point because everything else was glaringly true.

"Oh, I do," Sarah said. "He talked about his jealousy often enough that even I had to tell him to give it a rest, much as I loved hearing anything about you." Her thoughts and words turned bitter toward the end of that statement. "What you've told me about Isabel's actions disgusts me, but she was a child. They both were. And they both made stupid, selfish decisions. You can't blame Isabel without seeing that Caleb was as much at fault in the situation as she was."

She loved Connor, but she had to leave before she did something, said something stupid.

What stupid was right now, she didn't know. It could possibly be forgiving a sad, angry man and letting him heal in her love.

But she had a feeling he needed to heal on his own. And she needed to decide whether his twisted heart would ever put her first, or whether revenge would always trump love.

She strode more confidently than she felt toward Daisy.

"Where are you going?" His voice was breaking, shattered almost as fully as her heart.

Sarah stopped but didn't face him. She didn't want her resolve to waver. "I'm going home. You need time to think. Become a better man. And I need to find a way to start again. Without you."

The squeak of the swing echoed as he surged upward, but Sarah held him in place with a single raised hand. "Give us the space we need, Connor."

No footsteps followed her as she continued toward Daisy and mounted. But his gaze never left her back. She could feel it burning into her as she kicked the horse into a canter and rushed out onto the road. She swore she still felt his stare when she made it into town and slammed the door of her room.

The damn man was with her still, even if he wasn't physically present. She wondered if she'd ever be able to shake him, or if she'd even want to.

As she lay down in bed, her thoughts ran to one thing—how was she going to tell Isabel that she was the reason Harry had broken her heart?

Chapter 18

Villers-Bretonneux. A tiny but strategically important town they'd been sent to ensure remained free of German troops. But the Jerry's were pushing hard. Unfortunately, his commanding officer had passed along the gossip about Connor's dice higher up the chain of command. The general wanted to meet him. Apparently, the man was extremely superstitious.

"What question do you want answered?" Connor didn't mince words.

The general took a moment to consider his words. Smart man. Connor hoped he'd take the answer of the dice with a grain of salt. But with a sick feeling, Connor realised this could influence the entire course of this battle. That was a lot of pressure to put on a young man and his dice.

"Will we be able to push the Germans from their hold on V.B. if we use the Australian infantry? Will we see success?"

Connor took a moment to settle the question in his mind, then shook the cup. The rattle seemed to echo, growing in volume as Connor's focus zeroed in on the dice that rolled in slow motion from the cup. They skipped and jumped across the wooden floor before stopping with a click that rang in his ears.

Five and two.

Connor gathered his thoughts then looked straight into the general's eyes, ignoring protocol and addressing him without permission.

"The answer is yes, but..."

"What's the 'but,' son?"

"The 'but' means it won't be easy, and that you'll have to do it again, and possibly again after that, but you'll be victorious if you use the infantry next battle."

The general exhaled a shaking breath.

"Off with you then, son. Best go wait for your marching orders."

For the first time, Connor was confident about going into battle. At least this was one he knew they would win.

He grinned. They were going to save the day. Over and over again.

They were, finally, going to be heroes.

Connor opened his eyes to the moonlight streaming through the window.

Heroes. Connor's stomach churned. He didn't feel like a hero now, even though he desperately wanted to be—Sarah's hero. Instead, he'd become the monster under her bed and it had him brushing tears from his eyes. He stared at them in fascination. Connor hadn't cried since he'd lost his father, hadn't cried all through the war. Not even when he'd lost Caleb. He hadn't shed a tear when Mr Ware had told him about his mother, even though his heart had slowed to a crawl inside his chest.

But losing Sarah shattered him.

It all seemed so bloody pointless now. Yes, his brother's ghost could rest in peace, knowing that Isabel had got her comeuppance. But Sarah's words had hit home. Did Isabel really deserve everything he'd done to her? Or did more of the blame rest with his impetuous brother?

The questions whirled through his head, keeping him from falling back to sleep. There were no answers there, at least nothing that he wanted to accept right now. But there was one thing he knew, with absolute certainty.

He needed Sarah like his farm needed the rain. And he'd have to find some way to win her back, even if it meant swallowing that he may have been wrong.

He needed to know. Determined, he leapt from bed, shucked off the last of sleep, and strode toward his old room and the dice cup he'd hidden beneath the bed. He'd promised Smith he'd leave Fate to its own devices, but this was important. This was for Sarah

Will I be able to win her back? The sound of the dice rattling echoed in his head, time seeming to crawl in slow motion. When he released them, they bounced once, twice, and landed under the window directly in the moonlight.

Five and two.

Yes, but…

He steeled his spine. This wasn't going to be easy, but he'd never give up. He'd find some way to earn her forgiveness or he'd spend the rest of his life trying.

At least he knew now success was guaranteed.

He only wished he knew when.

***

Sarah woke up in her tiny single bed feeling utterly nauseous. Her belly churned with anxiety. How was she going to tell Isabel about Connor? It made her ill, knowing she'd unwittingly let her sister's ruin into their lives. She didn't know how she'd ever make up for it.

But she also had to consider herself. What was she going to do now her hopes for the future had been dashed? Run the bakery by herself until she died? Would Isabel be keen on that idea? God knows the girl would have plenty of young men sniffing around her if she were to try to find work in another town. A young woman that beautiful always seemed to defy convention.

She sat up and stared out the window at her shed. Its shiny windows seemed to wink mockingly at her in the early morning sunlight. The small building was filled with her dreams, hopes, and aspirations—all ruined now. There was no room for creativity when you were struggling to survive. Her flights of fancy would have to stay in the past now.

An echo of laughter and a man's voice drifted up the corridor. Sarah jumped from bed, throwing on clothes and dashing down the hall despite her protesting belly, hope kindling in her heart. When she burst into the kitchen and saw Harry sitting casually with her sister, her joy came crashing down around her ears.

Shoulders slumped, Sarah joined them at the table. Jealousy ate at her, and then guilt. Surely, she shouldn't feel jealous that Isabel had Harry back??

"Morning, Sarah." Isabel's face was alight with happiness. It didn't take a genius to guess what had her glowing. Harry sat staring at Isabel, looking for all the world like the cat who'd gotten the cream. "It's a beautiful day today, isn't it?"

Sarah looked out the window, where storm clouds were quickly gathering, and quirked an eyebrow at her sister. "I think our definitions of beautiful are very different, chicken. What has you crowing so early in the morning?"

A hot cup of tea was shoved into her hands and Sarah looked gratefully up at her sister. Just what she needed.

"Well, Harry and I have a proposal for you," began Isabel. Interest piqued, Sarah leaned a little closer. She still eyed Harry warily, having not forgotten his behaviour during and after the funeral as Isabel seemed to have. Apparently, all Harry had to do was knock on the door for all to be forgiven by Isabel. Sarah would never be so trusting again.

"Do you just? I'm all ears," she replied to her sister.

Isabel took a deep breath. "Harry's decided that being with me is more important than his inheritance. But, because of his parents' ultimatum, we have no means of income."

Aha. Things were now starting to get interesting.

"Go on," she said, taking another sip of tea to try to get her riotous stomach under control.

Harry took up where Isabel left off. "You know I don't have any trade, Sarah, other than running the farm, but I'm willing to learn. You'll see I can be a hard worker and—"

"What Harry's trying to say is we'd like to run the bakery with you. Harry would become your apprentice." Sarah's jaw dropped. This wasn't what she'd been expecting to hear come out of their mouths. In fact, she didn't know what she'd been expecting, but this certainly was from left field.

She turned to Harry. "You want to be my apprentice?" He nodded. "Do you know what being a baker entails?"

"I have a rough idea, yes. After all, I've seen how hard both you and your father work. Worked," he replied awkwardly.

"I'm up every day before sunup. I don't get home until well after sunset some days. Are you sure you want to do that?"

"Yes," said Harry instantly. "If it's the only way I get to be with Isabel, then I'll be the best damned baker you've ever seen."

"Language," murmured Isabel softly. Sarah shot her an incredulous stare. She'd heard far worse come out of her sister's mouth over the years.

"And where do you think you'll be living when all this suddenly comes to a head?" Sarah asked, already annoyed. Had they even thought this through, or was it some kind of spur-of-the-moment thing that two flighty people came up with in a bubble?

"We have an idea about that too, actually," Isabel said, batting her eyelashes at Harry.

"Yes." Harry smiled fondly down at Isabel. That green-eyed monster still churned in her belly. Or maybe she really was ill. "After breakfast, we're going to head down to the church and see if Father Ben will marry us. Would you like to stand as a witness?"

"Marry? Witness... I'm not sure I understand." Sarah was lost. How was a shotgun wedding going to make things any better?

"It's quite simple really, Sarah," Isabel said. "Marrying me legitimises our love. Harry can live here with us without causing any more scandal, my share in the bakery I'll sign over to him, and you are still a respectable woman, living with her married sister, so you still have a chance to marry your Connor if you wish without the town blowing up in your face."

They had thought of everything. But at the mention of Connor, Sarah's jaw clenched. Should she tell them? Was it really her tale to tell? Whether from cowardice or her own better judgment, Sarah decided to leave the conversation about Connor for another date. One that wasn't making them so happy. She also didn't point out her reputation was already well and truly ruined.

"Shall we go see Father Ben then?" Sarah stood, intending to go collect her coat.

Isabel giggled, turning back to the stove. "If you wait a minute, Sarah, we'll all have some breakfast first. Harry wants to collect his sister from the mayor's office on the way to stand as the other witness. She won't be there 'til eight."

"Ellen would kill me if I got married without her there," he said, smiling fondly over his youngest sister's antics. Ellen was in the same year at school as Isabel, though they hadn't been close friends. That had changed in the last couple of years, however, as Isabel spent more and more time with Harry's family. The vivacious young woman had accepted Isabel without question, regardless of her faults. The same couldn't be said to be true of the rest of Harry's family.

"Will she be able to? What if your dad's there?" Sarah asked, gnawing her lip.

"He won't be. Dad doesn't even get up 'til nine most days. Has too many people doing his work for him, including my sister." Harry's wry grin quieted her concerns, if not her stomach, which was still rebelling.

She must be coming down with something.

"Okay, then," Sarah said and stood. She helped Isabel dish up the breakfast and both Sarah and Harry companionably washed the dishes together. Her heart ached that it wasn't Connor at her side, but she supposed this arrangement was liveable.

Harry was an agreeable sort of person, and if he could follow her directions half as well as he did her sister's, the bakery would soon be running like a well-oiled machine again. Her spirits lifted a little, a weight fallen from the burden she carried. If they could work together, everything would be fine in the end. Even if Sarah operated with a broken heart.

As they finished drying up, Isabel stepped from her room. The pale pink of her knee-length dress highlighted her complexion, making her glow. A tiny scrap of cream lace decorated the neckline and capped her shoulders, making her appear delicate and feminine. It wasn't as fancy a dress as she would have had with Harry's parents organizing the wedding, but it was beautiful and perfect. Harry certainly seemed to think so, if the adoring look plastered over his face was anything to go by.

The three of them collected Ellen from the mayor's office on their walk to the church. Harry's younger sister almost bounced down the road, the optimistic young woman desperately happy for her brother. They must have presented an unusual sight, the four of them all but floating into the rectory, but Father Ben smiled calmly as he motioned them through the door.

"I'm assuming, after that little fiasco at your pa's funeral, Isabel, you and Harry have come to the conclusion if you want to get married, it'll have to be without your parents' consent."

Harry nodded reluctantly, obviously a little disgruntled that the priest had read them so easily.

"So what makes you think I'll do this without your family's approval?" the gangly young man asked.

"You don't really care about what people think, Father Ben," Sarah said quietly. "As long as people are in love. You say your piece to try to stop a scandal then hope the offending couple comes to you instead of living with gossip surrounding them, making them unhappy."

"You're wrong, Sarah. I do care about what people think if only so people can find heaven easily. But you're right about this being about love." The young priest turned to the once again excited couple. "I'm assuming you want to be married now before the mayor gets to work?"

They both nodded eagerly, joined by Ellen, who would prefer to be back at her desk *before* her father arrived and questioned her absence. Sarah quirked an amused eyebrow, happy for her sister now that the ball was rolling.

"Since you've brought your two witnesses with you, we'd better trot over to the church and get started. Give me a minute to put on my robes and I'll meet you over there." As Father Ben left, he rubbed his hands with glee. It might not be a shotgun wedding, but this was probably the most exciting thing the young priest had done in his career. Sarah almost smiled at his retreating back.

Her still-aching heart swelled in her chest as she revelled in the fact that at least someone would be happy. Particularly since those two someones were the couple Connor had tried so badly to destroy. It was a little vindictive, but Sarah hoped he found out about this and realised his efforts had been in vain. That Harry's love for Isabel was truer than Connor's had been for her. Harry's love for Isabel was more important to him than anything else in his life.

She couldn't say the same for the man she was so foolishly in love with. Was it so wrong to wish for someone to put *her* first? To have *her* happiness be the most important thing for someone else?

Because it surely hadn't been for Connor.

A dead man was more important than the living woman who loved him.

Father Ben motioned them to the front of the church where, without fanfare, he began the ceremony. Neither Isabel nor Harry could stop smiling, especially when the priest told Harry to kiss the bride. It seemed the two of them were delighted to finally be called husband and wife. Ellen stood beside Sarah, bawling happy tears, and Sarah handed her a hankie. Her own eyes were dry, heart a shattered mess in her chest.

She shouldn't have thought about *him* while this was going on. That wasn't fair on the two people in front of her, binding themselves to each other despite Connor's interference.

"This was perfect," Ellen said to Sarah as they both signed the official documents. "Even after everything, they still managed to hold on to one another." The younger woman's eyes were shining. "If I ever get married, it'll only be if my love is as great as theirs."

Sarah didn't add that their love was also a selfish love. That, for the most part, they hadn't considered others—but she thought it. Even though she wished them all the best, she couldn't stop thinking about how their decisions had impacted others. Had hers? Had her decision to be with Connor been entirely selfish? With Harry and Isabel, there were consequences of their decisions that could easily be seen. In Sarah's defence, she didn't have all the information to be *able* to see the consequences.

She would never have fallen in with Connor if she'd known what he planned.

Even though the thought of being without him now shredded her soul.

Documents signed, they all, including Father Ben, started to walk out of the church, down to the bakery where Sarah was prepared to give Harry his first lesson in baking—cake.

They were stopped at the gate by Connor.

"Sarah, can I talk to you?" He eyed the others. "Alone?"

She silently handed the key to the bakery to Isabel and the others walked off, though not without confused backward glances. Not two days ago, everyone had known that Connor was her sun and moon. Now here they were, the distance between them greater than the Dividing Range.

When they were alone, she spoke. "If you've come to ruin their lives some more, Connor, you're too late. The two just married."

"I'd already assumed that when Mrs Norton in the hardware store told me that she'd seen you all head up toward the church." He shifted awkwardly.

"What do you want, Connor?" she asked on a sigh. Her soul was breaking in two and the nausea was returning. Half of her wanted to walk forward and be lost in his embrace, the other half wanted to run in the opposite direction.

"You, Sarah," he said quietly. "Just you. Come back home."

She laughed, a little wildly. "Are you serious?"

"Deadly," he replied. "I've never been more serious in my life. I want you, in my life, in my bed, my home. You already have my heart. What more could you ask for?"

She spat out a bitter laugh. "What more could I want, Connor? How about someone who loves me more than anything else in their whole world? How about a man who will tell me the truth and not keep dangerous secrets? Or, how about this one, don't you think I deserve a man who looks after me as I do him, who puts my happiness above his own?"

He ran his hands through his hair in frustration. "But I do love you, more than anything. Can't you see that?"

"No, Connor, I can't. Not when you valued your revenge more than you did our relationship." She started to walk away but stopped short.

Angrily she turned back to him. "Don't come back to me unless you can prove that I'm the most important thing in your life because right now, I feel like an afterthought."

He moved to say something, but she held up her hand in protest, doing the hardest thing she'd ever had to do in her life.

Sarah walked away.

Chapter 19

The road out to the Clearys' place was an easy one, particularly when sufficiently motivated to get there quickly. And Connor had every reason to make the journey as quickly as possible. After weeks of trying to decide how to win Sarah back, and still no ideas how to go about it, he'd decided there was only one person who could help him—Margery Cleary.

He was under no illusion that it was going to be easy. In fact, he'd come out fully prepared to argue his way into Marge's good graces and secure her approval again.

When he pulled a heavy Jezebel up in the house yard, his plans were sent spinning on their head.

Marge stood on the porch, waving a wooden spoon at him like some vengeful housewife. He dismounted, though he wasn't sure it was safe. "Took you long enough to figure out what an idiot you've been, didn't it, Connor Williams?"

And like that, he turned into an errant schoolboy again. He caught himself shuffling his feet and straightened his spine.

"Easy, Marge," he said as he hitched the mare to the post. "I know I've played the fool. I need your help to make it right."

With a self-satisfied smirk, she tipped her head toward the house.

"Come on, you great lump. We don't have all day if we're going to come up with a plan to make you the apple of Sarah's eye again. In fact," she continued, "our battle plan may have to be expanded to outright war. You are definitely not going to win her back with one grand gesture."

"I didn't expect as much, otherwise I wouldn't be here," he muttered.

Marge laughed. "Tried to buy your way back into her good graces, didn't you?" It wasn't really a question, but he nodded anyway. Despite knowing that Sarah wouldn't be swayed by money spent on her, he'd still tried the usual—flowers, chocolates he'd had to go to the next town to buy them. Each had been delivered back to his door by Harry, who'd shaken his head and said when Connor was ready to talk about it, he'd be waiting.

Not bloody likely.

Imagine that conversation: *Hi, Harry, I'm here to talk about how my relationship with your sister-in-law is ruined, all because I tried to destroy your new bride.* Connor was sure that would go down well. It was obvious Sarah hadn't spoken about it with them, if only for the fact that Connor hadn't received a fist in the face from Harry.

He couldn't say he didn't deserve it.

Marge pulled out a seat for him at the enormous kitchen table. "Right, first things first. I'm taking it you haven't owned up to anything yet?" Was the witch reading his mind? She looked amused. "No, Connor, not a mind reader. But I'd guessed you hadn't done it because a juicy tidbit of gossip like that would surely have hit my radar."

He should have guessed as much. "What do you mean, own up?" he asked stiffly.

"You mean to tell me you're still trying to convince yourself that what you did was the right thing?" Marge was incredulous.

He was a little shamefaced. He had been trying to justify his actions to himself over the last few weeks, but always came up short in the face of Sarah's arguments.

She was right.

He was the villain in this piece. Even though Isabel had been in the wrong, his was worse, because he'd made his decisions as an adult, with full knowledge of who he'd hurt in the process.

"Good," she said, nodding at whatever she saw on his face. "I think you're ready, my little apprentice."

"Ready for what?" Connor was uneasy. Marge had an evil little glint in her eye that he didn't like. Not one bit. And what was he supposed to apprentice in? Margery was a notorious gossip. Surely she'd seen how well that turned out for him?

"Ready to apologise to everyone you've hurt. And try to fix the things you've destroyed." Her voice was firm, and Connor knew there was no arguing with her. Not that he wanted to. The guilt had been eating at him for almost as long as he'd been suppressing it. He supposed, now that he came to think about it, that with all her meddling, Marge would probably have a lot of experience apologising.

"Fine," he said to the master of manipulation. "Where do I start?"

***

Five weeks shouldn't seem like such a long time in her life, but when Sarah had agreed to take on Harry as her apprentice, she hadn't realised how totally and utterly inept he was. The man could ruin *anything*. He'd somehow managed to destroy almost every pie he'd set his fingers on, couldn't tell a sieve from a rolling pin, and had managed to drown her pastries in salt.

The only thing he could manage reasonably well was bread. So Harry was taking the morning shifts while Sarah took the evening. It was just as well because lately she'd been waking up terribly ill in the morning and she had a funny feeling she knew what it was about. The thought of it was enough to destroy any peace she may have found, however, so she swept that one under the bed for another day.

She found herself constantly staring out the window, the studio both repelling and attracting her in equal measure. Sarah desperately longed to lose herself in her art, but she didn't have the time or the means to do it properly. On the other hand, the studio was filled with images she'd rather avoid, memories that needed to stay buried, for her own sanity.

She didn't know what she'd do if faced with a room full of *him*.

As today was a Saturday, the only product they'd be selling was bread, and Harry was more than capable of managing that on his own. Sarah had other plans.

Her stomach had only just started to settle when Marge barged through the door without knocking. "Hello, my little muffin. Beautiful morning, isn't it?" Sarah was beginning to hate the fact those around her were unbearably cheery. Did they have to smile so bloody much? Isabel and Harry were positively nauseating. And that had nothing to do with the fact that each morning all she wanted to do was throw up her breakfast.

She ignored Marge's comment in favour of getting on with the day. "I'm ready to go, how about you?"

"Maybe not quite as ready as you, chickadee. After all, I have to live with it. But who am I to refuse the whims of a beautiful damsel?" Marge sighed theatrically, arm across her forehead.

Sarah giggled, and the sound surprised even her.

"Ah," said Marge. "That's more like it. You're starting to sound more like my best friend every day. Give it a bit, and you'll be playing the part in no time."

That last made Sarah a little sad. She had been neglecting Marge, but she hadn't much felt like socialising lately. Which was why today's excursion was so important. Even though she felt terrible, she couldn't miss the chance to see Rachel and little Ewan, Marge's new nephew. To do something 'normal' again.

"If you don't get out front and hop in the buggy, we'll have wasted the day away and my poor nephew will have faded away for want of cuddles."

"Can't have that, can we?" Sarah said with a smile.

"And I have some new dresses for you, so you'll have to try them on so I can do final fitting while we're there." Sarah didn't want to disappoint Marge, but there was no way she was trying on those dresses. Her suspicion would become a reality if she was forced to see physical evidence of it.

To avoid responding, Sarah darted out the front door, ignoring the churning in her belly, and nimbly swung herself up into the seat. Marge wasn't far behind her, taking up the reins and giving them a flick.

"Is that...Bunny...pulling the buggy?" Sarah's tone was incredulous. Was Marge mad? The horse was as likely to kick the buggy to bits as he was to pull it properly. Though she supposed Marge had arrived here safely. She'd have to hope they'd get out to the Clearys' farm in one piece.

"Bunny's been an extra good boy today," Marge spoke in a goo-goo voice as she cheerfully patted him on the rump. Anyone would think the enormous stallion was her baby. "We had a lovely trot into town, though I think we may have broken an axle when Bunny got a bit...boisterous...near the Newmans' place."

Sarah could only imagine what "boisterous" meant to Marge. More like everyone else's "raising hell." She eyed the stallion warily and crossed her fingers for good luck.

Bunny must have worn himself out because he behaved like the perfect gentleman on the way home. When Marge pulled into the yard, the stallion tossed his head as if to say "there, told you I could do it," then as soon as the harness was removed snapped at one of the farm dogs and took off into the paddock left open for him. The horse was spoilt rotten.

At least there hadn't been an international incident on the way there.

The two young women made their way into the farmhouse, a skip in their step. Both adored babies, the tinier the better. Rachel was sitting at the window in the midday sun, thick, dark locks glossy in the sunlight, soaking up the heat with her new bundle of joy. Both looked half asleep when Marge bellowed, "All right, that's enough of that, you two. It's time to give Aunty Marge her cuddle time. Then Aunty Sarah can snatch a quick snuggle before he needs a feed."

Rachel laughed, happily handing over the bundle who, at the sound of Marge's voice, started squirming. "I don't know what it is about you, Marge, but you've had all three of my boys eating out of the palm of your hand from day one."

Marge flipped a hand dismissively. "What can I say? I have a way with the gentlemen." The other two burst out laughing. She may be confident now, but one day all that ego would come crashing to the ground when she found someone she couldn't twist around her little finger.

"How are you feeling, Rachel?" Sarah asked, ignoring Marge's theatrics for the time being. The woman was cooing to the newborn and making duck faces, eyes bulging. It was a struggle not to laugh, but somehow, she managed it.

"Tired," the new mum said candidly. "Thank God we have the family around to help with the other two while I feed this one."

"What are you talking about," Marge teased. "All you do is sit around all day and sleep. I've even had to re-dress you after you've fallen asleep while feeding and left a nipple out for the world to see."

"Marge," Rachel scolded, blushing prettily. Simon's wife really was stunning, even when embarrassed. Lord knows their boys were going to be heartbreakers when they grew up. "You don't need to tell people that."

"It's okay, Rachel, I've heard it all before. Besides, she said the pregnancy was worse for you?" Sarah asked, trying to divert Marge's attention from nipples and nudity. There was no telling what may come out if she was left to wander that path unchecked.

"The pregnancy was awful this time," Rachel said ruefully. "With the first two boys, I could time the morning sickness like clockwork." Sarah's insides started to churn and a chill ran down her spine. "First thing in the morning, right up to around eleven, then I felt amazing for the rest of the day."

That sounded too familiar. Sarah's forehead broke out in a sweat. Her fingers trembled where they rested on her stomach. Rachel's words seemed to echo through a tunnel, all other sounds muffled around her. *First thing in the morning...*

"Dear Lord, you look terrible Sarah. Right, I'm taking you home. No babies for you today, I think you're coming down with something."

Rachel shot her a look of sympathy and Sarah could only smile weakly in response.

Oh God, it can't be, surely?

They'd only been making love for a little over a week when everything came to a head. It wasn't like—

The slap came out of nowhere and set her ears to ringing, cheek stinging.

"Oh good, you're awake now. I thought I was going to have to do something drastic to get you to step up into the buggy." With a start, Sarah realised Marge had already led her outside and harnessed her father's old plough horse to the buggy. Sarah hadn't even noticed.

In her mind she was counting the days since her courses had come last, starting again each time she forgot where she was up to. On the third count, she had to accept it was a number greater than thirty because she couldn't concentrate beyond that number. And that meant...

"I think I'm pregnant, Marge," Sarah whispered in horror.

"Get in the buggy. Now." Her friend pushed her upward, hurrying to get them both off a property full of gossips. Tears filled Sarah's eyes. What the hell was she to do with this new information? How was she going to cope on her own? She was well and truly ruined now.

When they were far enough away from the Clearys' that they could avoid listening ears, Marge drew the buggy to a halt. "Okay, we can talk now."

Sarah couldn't talk. The tears had started and wouldn't stop. Marge gathered her in her arms and made shushing sounds, much as Sarah had seen her do with the babies. Honestly, though, it felt quite nice, so she snuggled into her best friend's shoulders and cried until there were no more tears left to cry.

"I take it this little bunyip is Connor's?" The name had her laughing even as she glared at her friend. As if it was anyone else's. "Okay, no need to shoot those fiery arrows I see being lit in your eyes. Are you going to tell him?" The question was gentle, but Sarah didn't know the answer yet.

"If I tell him, Marge, he's going to want to get married, raise it together, and play happy families," Sarah said, horrified.

"Isn't that what you want, too?" Marge asked, confused.

"It is and it isn't." She sighed, knowing this wasn't coming out well. "There used to be nothing I wanted more than to be married to Connor, raising our children happily on the farm."

"What's changed?" Marge asked.

Sarah hesitated. She didn't know if she was being selfish, but she couldn't go to him, not with everything still between them. "I want to be first, Marge. First for someone. Pa's first was Ma, and then he doted on Isabel, sometimes forgetting his 'good girl' existed when he could see his wife in the other child. Oh, he loved me, don't get me wrong," she hastened to add. "But I was never *first* with him. With anybody."

She took a breath before saying the thing that hurt the most. "And I've never been first for Connor either."

Marge wrapped her in her arms again, not needing the details. She knew already, had been there with her as she tried to sweep up the pieces of her broken heart and put them back together. "If I tell him about this, then I'll always suspect I'm second. Second fiddle to our child. I'll never know whether he truly loves me, or if he's happy to settle. And my heart couldn't take that."

She pulled away from Margery, wiping her eyes on the collar of her dress. Sarah straightened her spine then looked straight ahead. "You can take me home now, chick. Thanks for listening."

Marge clucked at the big Clydesdale, who plodded onward at a leisurely pace. It didn't take long for Marge to start talking. She never could sit in silence when there were words to be said.

"I think you're underestimating Connor," her friend said quietly, all laughter gone from her voice. When Marge was serious, you listened. The woman often had unexpected wisdom to share. "And yourself. But I'll tell you what," she continued, a little more enthusiastically. "You have time. Time for Connor to get his act together and prove to you he's the man you always thought he was, not the lying, no-good devil with the evil plan."

Sarah turned to her best friend, hope in her eyes. "What makes you think he'd even want to?"

Marge hesitated. "Trust me, he does." Sarah stared suspiciously at her best friend. "Hey, don't ask and I won't be forced to tell you about the time when I stole the—"

"Enough." Sarah laughed, wiping off the last of the tears and snot. She'd need to get changed when they finally reached home. "Okay, so I give Connor a chance to prove himself before I make my decision. I think I can do that." She'd have to. It was the only way she'd know if he loved *her* or just the idea of family. And his ghosts.

The draught horse plodded onward, and Sarah steeled her spine. She wouldn't make this easy on him, but maybe she was willing to give him another chance. Their child deserved a chance to grow up with its father and she…well, Sarah deserved love.

And she wouldn't settle for less.

Chapter 20

Connor had rehearsed his speech a thousand times, but like when he'd tried the same with Sarah, in the face of his friend's stony silence, the words wouldn't come. Harry had filled the bread tins and put them in the oven before his patience with Connor's silence broke. It was longer than Connor himself would have lasted.

"Why are you here, Connor? Sarah's not here of a morning, and she's the one you should be talking to. You've broken the poor girl's heart and here you are, waltzing right in as if it was your God-given right." Harry was justifiably angry; he didn't know the whole story.

Unfortunately, Connor was here to make it worse.

Or better, if he was to listen to Marge.

"It was you I came to see, Harry. I've a confession to make." The words seemed to crawl out from the back of his throat, trying desperately to escape when he wasn't sure it was such a good idea.

"A confession? Again, it's Sarah who deserves to hear it. The poor girl's been wandering 'round with a long face since the funeral, and there's nothing Isabel or I can do to cheer her up. She's even gone and made herself sick over it."

Sarah was ill? His heart stuttered into action, pounding erratically in his chest. He needed to go to her, see for himself how she was, but he knew the door would be slammed in his face.

"If she'd let me, I would, Harry. But she's heard all this before. It's you who needs to hear it. You and Isabel. But I'll talk to her at another time."

Harry stared pensively at the oven, no doubt worried about the bread and whether it'd burn before the conversation was done. Connor had timed it deliberately, knowing Sarah's schedule and assuming the woman would hold her new 'apprentice' to the same exacting standards. He wasn't wrong. His chest filled with pride at the thought of his no-nonsense Sarah ordering her brother-in-law around in the kitchen. He'd lay money on Harry never having cooked in his life before.

Sarah wouldn't have been amused.

"Go ahead," Harry said. "I have about a halfer before I have to pull this lot out of the oven. What's so important you need to bother me at work?"

Maybe he shouldn't have approached Harry at the bakery, but it was the only way he could think of to keep both sisters out of the argument that was bound to ensue. Connor took a deep breath, gathered his thoughts, and launched into the explanation that was probably going to earn him a fist in the face at best, a knife in the gut at worst.

"I'd appreciate it if you kept your thoughts to yourself until the very end," said Connor. "I know you're going to be angry, but perhaps you'll understand better if you hear—"

"For God's sake, Connor, get on with it already." Harry's face was a little flushed already, a sure sign the conversation was going to go south quickly, but Connor forged on.

"I think we need to start at the beginning. With Caleb. And his obsession with Isabel."

Harry's mouth turned down at the edges, but he listened through Connor detailing Caleb's efforts to win the girl and the ways he'd been rebuffed. He listened in silence until—

"She gave him a white feather? What a bloody foolish thing to do." Harry's words brought a little warmth to his heart. Someone understood how horrible that act had been. "Hold on a sec while I take these loaves out of the oven."

Moments later that kernel of warmth was squashed when he had to explain the part after Connor had arrived home.

He watched as Harry's ears turned fiery red as he repeated his role in the rumours. The fact that not once, but twice, he'd attempted to ruin Harry's bride and their relationship. Connor saw Harry's knuckles turn white and the veins pop as he admitted to using the knowledge he'd gained from visiting Sarah to help his cause.

So really, he should have seen it coming when Harry's fist flew at his head, landing solidly on his nose with a sickening crunch. Should have ducked, shifted, done anything to avoid what was coming. Instead, he stood there and took it. Let blow after blow rain down on him undefended as he soaked up the pain, knowing he deserved it. He'd ruined Harry's life along with Isabel's, and it was only at this moment, faced with his friend's pain, that he really regretted it.

Blood streamed from Connor's nose, his head felt stuffed with cotton wool, and his vision was blurry when Harry stopped, fist still raised as he looked at the mess he'd made of his friend's face. "Raise your fists and fight back, you piece of shit." Harry's breath heaved as he struggled to contain himself.

"Can't," mumbled Connor through swollen lips. "You don't deserve it. I do." He tilted his head up, offering Harry another free shot with a curl of his hand.

"Christ," Harry hissed through his teeth. "You make it bloody hard to keep hitting you, you bastard."

"Don't mean to," Connor said, swaying a little as the room spun. "Keep at it if it makes you feel better." After all, he'd endured worse.

Sarah had left him. Nothing could hurt more than that.

Harry turned around and disappeared into the office for a moment, grabbing a seat and slamming it down behind Connor. "Sit. Before you fall face-first into the floor." Connor wasn't about to be told twice. Only there seemed to be two chairs where a moment ago there had been one. He stared between the two, buggered if he knew which was real and which a product of his double vision.

Harry grabbed him by the shoulder and shoved him unceremoniously into the one on the left, while the room swayed around Connor. He didn't think he'd be able to ride home like this. Maybe he'd stay the night at the Travellers' Inn? He started to pat himself down, looking for a coin, but nearly slid off the chair instead.

"What on earth are you doing?" Harry asked, horrified.

"Can't ride home." His mouth was stuck together with taffy. Those three words had taken more from him than the whole of his speech to Harry had.

"Just...stay still." Connor obediently sat while Harry raked a shaky hand through his hair. He didn't think the other man would like it if he told him he'd wiped flour through it. Sarah never had, at least. Even though it was when she was most beautiful. When everything else had melted away and she forgot she was supposed to be the sensible sister.

Harry looked at him in horror. With a start, Connor realised tears were trailing down his cheeks.

"Tell me you're not crying," Harry demanded. "You don't get to cry. Not after what you've done."

"I know." He meant that, too. "I've made a right royal mess of things and I don't know how to fix it." Connor drew in a heavy breath. "I need to fix it. Fix us. Sarah. I need her." More than life. Did he even make any sense right now?

"You're not making a whole lot of sense right now, but I'm going to tell you two things, and hope they make it through to the tiny piece of your brain not wrapped in cotton wool right now." Harry paused, choosing his words carefully. "At this moment, I hate you more than I have any man in my entire life, but that doesn't mean I can't see where all this came from. Maybe in the future, I'll be able to forgive you, once life has settled into a routine, but right now... There's too much hurt."

Connor opened his mouth to reply but Harry held up a hand and forged on. "The second is that you need to fix things with Sarah. Much as I can't see how she could have fallen for you now, she, for some inexplicable reason, still loves you. It's making her sick and because I care about her, I'm not going to say you're never to come around home again. But first thing's first." His eyes narrowed and Connor knew he wasn't going to like what came next. "You need to talk to Isabel."

He groaned. Despite everything, Connor didn't know if he could face her yet. And it wasn't about guilt. No. It was because, by the time he did, there'd be no masks between them. She'd know he blamed her for everything, and he wouldn't be able to hide the fact he loathed her.

"You'll do this, Connor, or next time we have words, I won't be stopping when your eyes glaze." Harry glared at Connor, waiting for an answer, so he nodded. It was all part of Marge's big master plan anyway. He didn't think it would have to hurt so much, both figuratively and literally.

"I'll do it," Connor said quietly. "I can't say we'll be friends after this, but I'll tell her the truth and let her explain her actions. That's the best I can promise."

"That'll do for now. We can work on the rest later." Connor didn't want to know what "the rest" was, but he expected there'd be much atoning in his future. That's if he could secure one with the woman he adored who currently wanted nothing to do with him.

Connor stood on trembling legs, wobbling toward the door like a newborn foal. Harry let out a sigh behind Connor's back. "Come on. I'll fetch Daisy and take you home. You think you can get on that leggy mare of yours?"

Already halfway out the door, Connor looked up at the mare, the enormous height of the stirrups, and back to Harry standing protectively near the bread. Harry looked at the loaves too. "They'll keep 'til we get back. I'll boost you up, but you'll have to hang on. When we get home, I'll hitch you to Daisy. You fall off, I ride home without a backward glance. Got it?"

He nodded. Connor got it. Harry may want to appear threatening, but his heart was soft. He wouldn't leave Connor alone on the road, and for that he was grateful. It was far more than what he deserved from his friend after what he put him through.

"Let's go, Frankenstein." Harry's humour left much to be desired, but it warmed his heart that the man was at least trying to be friendly.

They left the bakery together, each lost in their own thoughts.

Connor had a long road ahead of him.

He hoped it wasn't all as rough as this one had been. His face would never survive it.

***

Connor woke the next morning to the sound of a buggy pulling up outside the homestead. His face felt like he'd been hit by a train, while the various cuts stung when he stumbled over to the washstand to clean up. Connor was going to have visitors, whether he liked it or not. He should at least try to be presentable.

Two sets of footsteps surged across the veranda, followed by a knock that echoed through the empty house. Connor let out a groan as he stumbled toward the door, arms lead weights at his sides. His head was throbbing an incessant beat, urging him to go back to bed and nurse his wounds. But it wasn't to be. He opened the door.

Mr and Mrs Ware stared at him, faces pinched in disapproval. Connor swallowed his anxiety. Tried to tell himself it was all part of the plan. But that was rather hard when two pillars of the community he'd manipulated rather effectively were standing on his doorstep. Probably waiting for an explanation.

And according to the plan, he'd have to give it.

He rubbed his nose gently, hoping he wasn't in for another fist to the face. He didn't know whether a broken nose would heal properly if it was broken twice in two days, despite the fact he'd set it himself last night.

"Well, are you going to let us in, young Williams? Or are you going to stand there staring at us all day?" As usual, Mrs Ware's voice cut like a whip.

"Of course," he said reluctantly. "Come in. I'll make tea."

The couple followed him inside, Mr Ware holding the seat out for his wife at the kitchen table before taking his own. Connor went straight to the kitchen, trying to avoid the conversation as long as possible. He felt like an errant schoolboy as he dragged his feet over to where they sat, three steaming mugs of black tea in his grasp.

Setting one in front of each of his tormentors, he took his own seat and waited for what would follow.

He didn't wait long.

"I talked to Harry yesterday, Connor. He had some interesting things to say." Mr Ware was never one for words. While Connor wanted to know exactly what his son had told him, the man wasn't going to give him anything. His wife either, if the daggers she was throwing with her eyes in his direction were any indicator of her goodwill.

"Explain yourself, boy." There was no room for refusal in that statement. Connor wasn't game to try in any case. He needed to do this, to make things right.

He took a breath and began. "I suppose Harry told you—"

"Take it as if Harry told us nothing, and give us your version of events," Mrs Ware said, cutting him off.

So he told them everything he'd told Harry the day before. Everything, from Caleb's love of Isabel through to yesterday when he came clean to Harry. With each word, Mrs Ware's face took on a brighter shade of red. In contrast, Mr Ware's face became paler, perhaps realizing what he'd done to his son.

When he'd finally wound to a close, Mrs Ware stood and, without so much as a by-your-leave, stalked out the door. Her husband hovered a moment longer.

"Those are some terrible things you've done, son." The sadness in the man's voice strummed a chord in Connor's heart. He'd always respected Harrison Ware Senior, and it hurt that he'd lost his regard.

"I know," Connor said quietly, his shame clear in his tone. "But I'm trying to fix it. Trying to right my wrongs."

The other man stared at him a moment, taking his measure, then nodded and followed his wife out to the buggy.

Connor trailed behind them, ingrained good manners having him see his visitors off, despite the circumstances. When the other man had seated himself and taken the reins, Mrs Ware leaned over her husband.

Connor braced himself for a cutting remark.

"You don't deserve that girl, Connor Williams." She didn't disappoint. "You don't deserve her, and I hope to God she realises it before it's too late."

With that, Mr Ware flicked the reins, and the horse walked forward easily, moving into a trot when his master clucked again.

Heartsick, Connor watched as the buggy departed. She was right. He didn't deserve Sarah. Unfortunately for her, he was unable to let her go.

Only when the buggy and the cloud of dust that followed was a speck on the horizon did Connor turn to go inside. There was still one more person left to explain himself to, even if he couldn't honestly apologise. He could concede that maybe he'd judged her unfairly and that he felt remorseful for the mess he'd created, but still. In his heart, he thought Isabel deserved everything that came to her. His only regret was that he'd made himself a villain in his own eyes, and in the eyes of those he cared about, to see that happen.

A kookaburra landed on the porch rail, and he whipped his head around to stare at it, the movement sending his already foggy head into a tailspin where the pain was all he could focus on. He gripped the doorframe hard as he struggled to keep his feet. When he finally returned to normal, it was to find that blasted bird laughing at his misery.

He smiled wryly. At least someone was getting some enjoyment from this. Connor himself had to hope that everything would turn out fine in the end. He had to. Otherwise, anger and pride would have won.

And he couldn't stomach that.

Chapter 21

"Pa, why are you crying?" Five-year-old Sarah had woken in the night, bladder screaming for relief. She'd only just made it to the pot in time. With a great sigh of relief, she'd pulled up her knickers and gone to crawl back into bed. That was when she'd heard the crying.

Her pa wiped his eyes, hiding evidence of his weeping. "No tears here, chook. Not now you're with me. Now come and give yer old man a hug."

Sarah crawled into his arms. There was no better place to be than Pa's lap, wrapped up in his soft, doughy smell. Even if he had lied to her.

The tears were still on his cheeks.

She raised a chubby finger and wiped one away. "You told me no one likes a liar, Pa," Sarah said solemnly, waving her wet finger in his face. Frank sighed and squeezed her tighter.

"I'm missing yer mother a little more today, chook. No need to worry." Instead of snuggling closer, like he no doubt expected, Sarah sat up straight.

"Pa, what makes you happy?" She looked up at him, determined to know how she could make things better.

"You two girls make me happy every day," he replied. "And seeing you do things that make you happy makes me even happier."

Pa watched as Sarah crawled off his lap, stomped determinedly to the coals he'd finished clearing from the stove, and picked up a piece. She started to draw on his nice clean floor.

"What do ya think yer doing, chook? We don't draw on the floorboards in this house." Pa sounded more confused than angry. She didn't know why. Hadn't he just said what makes him happy?

He sucked in a deep breath when she replied, "But I'm happy, Pa. Aren't you too, now?"

Of course her pa was happy. Sarah was drawing, so Sarah was happy. If Sarah was happy then, like her pa said, he must be too.

He gathered her into his arms, charcoal and all, and carried her back to bed. As he tucked Sarah back under the covers, he whispered, "Remind me to buy you some paper, so you don't use my floor as a canvas again."

And she did.

Sarah had never really been overly emotional, but it seemed this pregnancy was bringing out the worst in her. She'd snapped at Harry yesterday when he hadn't made the pastry light enough for her liking. Bawled on Isabel's shoulder as thoughts of Connor and all they could have had overwhelmed her. Panicked then rode to see Marge to find out what she'd need for a baby, even though she'd have at least seven more months to organise herself. She was sure her family thought she was crazy. Hell, even Marge thought she'd lost her mind, and she knew everything.

It didn't help that the mood in the house was annoyingly optimistic. Sarah had walked in yesterday to find Isabel and Harry beside the stove, heads bent toward each other in a conversation that stopped the moment she entered the room. Isabel had tried to cover it up, but her humming and general sunniness was a sure giveaway that something was happening, and Sarah wasn't to be included. Her instincts seemed to pan out when a stiff Mr and Mrs Ware Senior joined them for dinner that night, and though the conversation was awkward, there weren't any harsh words. It made unease stir in her stomach, which had her emotions growing wilder.

But the thing that created the most havoc on her was her damn shed. It sat and stared at her, the epitome of every dream she'd ever had. Dreams of sitting with Connor on the porch, painting while he carved, the two content in each other's company. Of selling her work when the mood struck her. Of being able to create using her God-given skills—in the kitchen and with a paintbrush.

And there it stood. Tormenting her with 'what ifs' every time she looked out her window. Every morning. Every evening. Silently laughing at her pain.

She pulled herself out of bed and got dressed, fully prepared to go and relieve Harry at the bakery when the sight of those windows glinting in the sun was suddenly too much to bear. In a rage, she rushed outside and flung open the shed door. Her anger burnt like a brand within her chest and she grasped hold of it, for without that she'd collapse in a screaming heap and never get up again.

She ripped paintings from easels, tore sketches into tiny pieces that could only be used for kindling. It was as if a tornado had been unleashed within her body, driving her to the destruction of everything that was causing her pain. Paper and paint flew across the room, the perfect visual of her tormented soul.

Ironically, it was his eyes that stopped her. Caleb's eyes and not Connor's.

She stared down at the sketch of her stupid, selfish friend and her legs went boneless beneath her. All of this…this madness. Heartache. Because of the whims of two stupid children trying to be adults before their time.

The tears fell then. An incessant wave that calmed the whirlwind in her heart. Sarah put her hands to her belly, making the life that rested within a promise. No matter what happened, she would do what was best for her child. As her pa had done for her. She'd give Connor the chance to prove himself, but she was not going to bring this child into the world without it knowing that it was loved and wanted. It would be the worst kind of testament to the sacrifices her pa had made for her. She had to put her own heartbreak aside for now and think of what was best for it.

She wiped her dripping nose on her sleeve, looking around at the destruction she'd caused, then calmly walked out, shutting the door firmly behind her. Her baby needed her. Needed its mother to take life by the horns and wrestle it to submission. So she hadn't gotten everything she wanted from life. Who did? Certainly not the men who hadn't made it home to their families after the war. She was being selfish.

The bakery wasn't a bad life. She enjoyed the intricate work and Harry was there to help with the monotonous. She may not have the comfort of her art, but surely she could find some way around that?

With renewed determination she changed, getting herself organised for the new day at work. She would make a go of this. She had to. Her baby needed her to be strong, and she had never run from hard work in her life.

Despite her resolve, a kernel of trepidation wormed its way into her heart. They say heartache came in threes. She'd lost her pa and lost Connor. Sarah wrapped her arms around her belly. She didn't want to think about what more she had left to lose.

The third may just break her.

***

Harry had told Connor when Isabel would be alone at home, trusting him to do the right thing. Knowing the reasons behind Connor's actions, Connor didn't think that if he were in Harry's position, he'd let Connor near his wife. But he wouldn't betray his friend's trust again, even if he had to grit his teeth and fuse his fingers to the table for the entire conversation with Isabel.

He raised his hand to knock at the door, but it opened before he had a chance. His heart decided to beat a staccato rhythm within his chest as Sarah rushed out the door and landed unceremoniously in his arms. It felt so good, so right to have her back where she was supposed to be that he almost missed the dark circles under her eyes and the fragility of her form. His Sarah wasn't taking care of herself. He moved to draw her closer, but Sarah ripped herself from his embrace.

"I have somewhere to be," she said coldly, denying their connection. In fact, he would have believed her totally indifferent to him if he hadn't felt the way her breath caught in her chest when she realised it was him. Or seen the pulse hammering in her neck.

"Sarah," he said, moving to grab her arm, but she moved nimbly away.

"Baking bread burns if left untended, Connor. And I have a job to do." She turned and walked away without a backward glance.

He could no sooner stop himself staring at her departing figure than he could stop the sun from rising. Even after she turned the corner at the end of the street, his gaze lingered on where she had disappeared. Connor had to fix things. He couldn't go on like this any longer.

Steeling himself, he turned around, only to find Isabel in the doorway, a wry smile on her face.

"Harry told me you'd be round, Connor," she said, holding the door open a little wider. "Come in."

Hands suddenly slick with sweat, he brushed past Isabel and into the kitchen. All serious conversations in the Dawson house happened here, and this would be no exception. He settled himself into his seat as she took the one opposite him, eyes hard.

It seemed he wasn't to be offered tea, but that was fine with him.

Connor cleared his throat. "You know why I'm here, Isabel." He didn't bother to mince words. Harry would have filled her in and he'd had enough of playing games.

"I know why you think you're here," Isabel said, her anger leaking through. Good. It would make the conversation easier if both of their tempers were high. "That doesn't necessarily mean that you're right. Or that you have all the facts."

Sarah had implied as much, but so far he'd heard nothing to suggest Isabel was anything but the spoiled, selfish bitch who'd driven a man to his death.

"Then what are the facts?"

"Do you really want to hear it?" Her voice was almost a sneer and somehow made Connor's blood run cold with knowledge. "You aren't going to like it. Your brother doesn't come off the hero at all in my version of events."

"I'll be the judge of that," he said, dropping all pretence at civility.

"Maybe you should have asked before you began your little campaign against me. Didn't your mother teach you there are two sides to every story?"

She had, and it made him a little uncomfortable that his flaws were bring pointed out by someone he detested. He'd let his rage carry him, and that rage had no room for second guesses.

"Well?" They didn't have all day. Though Harry would take his time coming home, there was only so much the man could delay.

Isabel sighed, the anger draining from her as she slumped in her seat. "I don't like talking about this. Have only spoken of it with Harry, and now you." She swallowed, and for the first time since he'd known her, Connor realised that the unvarnished truth was about to come from her mouth.

"Caleb didn't know the meaning of the word 'no,' Connor," Isabel continued. She held up a hand when it looked like he would interrupt, so he swallowed his words and remained silent. "He fancied himself in love and wouldn't hear a word I had to say about the matter."

He could believe it. Caleb had always been stubborn, and the boy had been in love with Isabel as far back as Connor could remember.

"Anyway, after you left, he got so...angry. Persistent. It started to scare me a little, even though I knew he was Sarah's friend. Then one day when I was walking home from school, he followed." Beads of perspiration shone on her pale forehead and he resisted the urge to comfort her. This was Isabel. And she was talking about Caleb. His Caleb. "At first I thought he was going to the bakery, but then he followed me as I turned down the laneway to our house."

The words hung over them like a dark cloud. Connor felt sick. Surely Caleb wouldn't...

Isabel laughed darkly at him. "Not as bad as you're thinking, Connor, but bad enough. Caleb had me backed against the back of the bakery before I could blink and his tongue down my throat." Acidic bile filled his mouth. He couldn't speak, only listen as Isabel's truth rang out. "He wouldn't move when I tried to squirm away, just pushed in closer. His hands were everywhere. I think he thought I was enjoying it like he was." Her haunted eyes remained focussed on a spot on the wall as if she couldn't bear to look at him.

He couldn't blame her.

"When he finally pulled back for air and saw the tears streaming down my face, he panicked. The coward ran away before he could be seen when Sarah came singing out the side door of the bakery." Finally, she turned to look at him. "I know he hadn't always been like that. That determined. He used to be kind. But something after the death of your father and you leaving for the front changed him. He was bitter and lost. So I did the first thing that came to my head to get him to stay away from me. I gave him that feather."

He didn't know what to say. On the one hand, she had still sent his brother to his death. On the other, was it not understandable, what she'd done? Caleb was her sister's friend. Would Sarah have believed Isabel, considering the years Isabel had spent leading other boys on, including his brother? He'd like to think she would, but Isabel had admitted to him she'd told no one but Harry. And that only after Caleb was already beyond revenge.

Connor closed his eyes, praying for the right words. "I understand." His voice was gravel, harsher than he expected. "I understand the why Isabel, but surely you understand my 'why' too? My brother died because of a white feather."

"No, Connor," Isabel said sharply. "Your brother died because he was too proud to admit he'd done wrong. He went to war because he couldn't deal with his own shame." And there was the rub. The truth he had to admit to himself.

While Connor was sure Caleb had loved Isabel, and that the white feather had hurt him deeply, if the young man had been more secure in himself, there would have been no way something like that would have pushed him to enlist.

"I didn't know," he whispered.

"Of course you didn't. But you were so blinded by your own anger you failed to see it from another perspective," Isabel retorted. "Thank God the things you've done are steadily being fixed, though I'm not sure everything will ever truly be the way it was again."

"Harry's parents have been in contact then?" he asked, offering a tentative olive branch.

Isabel looked at him with a raised eyebrow, refusing to answer his question. He knew why. But he didn't have to like it.

He looked Isabel straight in the eye and offered what should have come from both his brother and himself. "I'm sorry, Isabel. For what you've suffered because of Caleb, and for what I've put you through." He didn't add a 'but.' There was no excusing his actions.

Isabel held his stare a moment longer, then nodded. "Next time you go to Sydney you can buy me a new dress to make up for it." And there was the Isabel he knew.

"Done," he said with a wry grin. "Though I think you'd get better quality from Harry."

"That's not the point." She smiled wickedly. "Every time I wear that dress, I'll remember the one and only time I've heard Connor Williams apologise. And you will remember swallowing your pride when you see me in it. It will be glorious." He should have known. "To answer your question, yes, the Wares have been in contact."

"And...?" he prompted.

"We'll see," she said primly. "They have some grovelling of their own to do before Harry and I forgive them."

Unease settled in his gut.

"And what about Sarah?"

"What about her?" Isabel asked, confused. Connor almost growled in frustration. Surely she wasn't this selfish?

"If Harry's parents take him back in, where will that leave Sarah and the bakery? She'll be all on her own again and no one will marry her after...." The words stuck in his throat. After he'd all but ruined her.

"Oh I'm sure she'll manage just fine on her own," Isabel said, tossing her hair flippantly. "And if not, I know someone who'd be willing to take her in."

He did growl then, black dots floating across his vision as he held his breath, trying to control the anger. No man was going to 'take in' his Sarah but him.

"Oh, stop being so dense, Connor. What else is all this apologising for if you aren't trying to win back Sarah?" The anger fled as soon as it had come, leaving a trace of embarrassment. He started to rise.

"Connor?" Isabel's voice halted him as he moved toward the door. "Please don't mention to Sarah what I told you. Not unless she asks. I don't want to tarnish her memories of Caleb any further." They were the first selfless words he'd heard leave Isabel's mouth. The woman was back to looking vulnerable, and he could see why she'd had the boys falling at her feet. His heart went out to her.

He nodded. "Of course. I'll be doing my best to avoid hurting her again. But I won't lie."

She smiled at him, the first genuine one since he'd walked in the door. "And those sentiments will take you a long way with my sister." She hesitated. "Good luck. You're going to need it."

He gave a little salute on the way out, one warrior to another, and went to mount Jezebel and head home. For the first time since Sarah had walked out, he felt real hope.

There was only one task left, and thankfully, he didn't need anyone else to help him with it. Connor had this one covered all on his own. Had already made an excellent start on it.

He clucked his tongue and urged Jezebel into a canter. He had work to do, and the sooner he got it done, the sooner he could bring Sarah home with him, where she belonged.

Chapter 22

"Yer mother liked to bake, chook," Frank said as he watched Sarah kneading her first piece of dough. The motions were soothing, yet she was too nervous to truly relax into it. She really wanted to do this right, to be able to help her pa as much as he always helped her. If he thought she could do it well, then he'd let her work for him in the bakery after school.

"You've told me this already," Sarah said, smiling back at him. "But you can tell me again. I don't mind."

He chuckled. "I won't bore ya with all the details. You need to keep yer mind on what you're doing. But ya definitely have yer mother's deft touch."

Sarah beamed with pride. There was no greater praise from her pa than being compared positively to her mother. "You think so, Pa?" she asked, eager to hear it again.

"Yer more like her every day, chook. Strong like her too. I've no doubt one day ye'll be a woman to be reckoned with."

The loaves she made that day were her first, but her best.

Two weeks had passed since Sarah had last seen Connor on her doorstep, and she ached with everything in her for him to come riding up again. She'd thought about what he'd been doing here, and even though both Isabel and Harry refused to answer her questions, there was a sense of peace about the two of them that she was sure came from the same source. Connor. And possibly Harry's parents, who'd been around three more times in the last few weeks.

Sarah had the morning off as it was Saturday and Harry was doing the bread. She planned to go outside and clean up the mess she'd made of her shed. But first, breakfast was needed. She'd just put the kettle on to boil when there was a knock on the door. Sarah grinned. There was only one person who'd even attempt to disturb her this early on a Saturday.

Marge didn't even wait for Sarah to open the door. She bounced right in, throwing her coat over the rack and sidling up close to the stove. "Good work, pumpkin. I see you've already made me a cup of tea. What're the chances of having some bacon and eggs to go with that?" Marge turned adorable puppy-dog eyes and a wobbly lip on Sarah. She laughed.

"Sit yourself down, woman, before you singe yourself. I'll make your breakfast if you make me a list of what I'll need if I'm to raise this baby by myself." She pulled a piece of charcoal from her pocket, followed quickly by a paper from the other side. Sarah had thought about using the wax board, but she couldn't easily hide it and Isabel and Harry still didn't know about her condition. And she had no intention of telling them any time soon.

"You won't be doing it by yourself," Marge said absently as she started to write. "Give Connor a little longer and I'm sure everything will be fine. After all, the man appears to have made peace with Isabel, of all people. Surely there's nothing the man can't do if he managed that?"

Sarah put one cup in front of her friend then took up the other herself, taking a long, calming slurp. "He still hasn't been to see me though, Marge. I've been working on contingency plans, making sure the bakery is in tiptop shape so I'll be able to earn enough to live from it." She put her hands to her stomach. "Even without Connor, and if Isabel and Harry move back to his parents', Baby and I will still have enough to survive."

"Of course you'd manage by yourself, peahen. You're the smartest person I know. But you won't have to." Marge's usually sunny disposition took on an air of solemnity that didn't surface often. "If it comes down to it, I'll move in here with you and we can be those two crazy spinsters with the kid who knows everyone else's business and make no apologies about it."

Sarah giggled, her heart overflowing. She'd been blessed when Margery Cleary walked into her life. "There wouldn't be a move to Sydney, then, Marge. No fashion design. No string of lovers. Your dreams of a scandalous lifestyle would be ruined."

"Ugh," Marge said with a shrug. "You win some, you lose some. Living with you and a kid seems like a pretty big win to me. Not to mention," she leaned forward conspiratorially, "I can escape the terrible gossip that comes out my mother's mouth. You have no idea what she's been putting me through lately. Why, just last week she came up to see me, so excited that I—"

"Enough, Marge," she said, laughing. Popping her tea on the table, she leaned over, grabbed her friend's face, and gave her a smacking kiss on the forehead. Marge grinned, wiping off the slobber. "You are the best friend a girl could have. How did I get so lucky to have you?"

Marge snorted. "Luck had nothing to do with it, my little dumpling. I chose you specifically, knowing you needed my help, my guidance. After all, your four-year-old self was so adorably clueless in the eyes of my worldly five-year-old-ish-ness. How could I resist taking you under my wing?"

Through tears of laughter, Sarah said, "Is that even a word? And you're only two months older than me."

"Two months more wisdom under my belt, chicken-lickin. And a vastly superior knowledge of the world." Marge wriggled her eyebrows suggestively and Sarah let loose a great belly laugh. "That's better. I'll be needing to hear those much more regularly now, so make sure you keep that frown turned upside down. I demand it."

"Yes, Princess Marge." Sarah saluted, turning back to the stove and the hot breakfast friendship demanded.

They'd just settled down at the table when Marge wrinkled her nose, then sniffed the air. "Did you burn something, chick?"

Sarah frowned, looking over at the stove. The door was closed, the flue open, and nothing remained on the stovetop. "No. Everything I cooked is on our plates."

The wail of the fire siren pierced their conversation, getting steadily louder by the second. Both women looked at each other, fear stark in their eyes, but as one they grabbed their coats and opened the front door. They'd do what they could to help. If it was any of their neighbours, it would be best to contain the fire as quickly as possible before it spread through the rest of the town. Wooden houses in this dry climate and fire did not mix well.

Marge stopped so abruptly when she exited the house that Sarah slammed into her back before turning to see what had her transfixed.

"No," Sarah whispered in horror. Her feet were moving of their own accord, flying up the street toward the one thing she had that would help her support her baby. She knew, even as she charged onward, that it was already too late.

Great, billowing clouds of smoke rose from the bakery while flames ate at the window casings. By the time Sarah and Marge arrived, there wasn't a single entry or exit that didn't have flames wreathing it. The fire truck, donated to the town by the Wares, and the volunteers who ran it were doing their best to battle the flames, but there was little focus on the building itself, just on saving the ones next to it.

Why waste time on the unsalvageable, right?

Frantically, Sarah searched for Harry, terrified he was still inside, but she relaxed when she saw him across the street with Mr and Mrs Ware, looking on with dazed expressions.

She rushed over and patted him down to make sure he was all right, only to realise his clothes were almost pristine, smelling of flour, not smoke. Her heart hammered in her chest while her stomach sank. She backed away from him.

Harry looked everywhere but at her, shifting his feet nervously.

"Why is the bakery burning, Harry?" Sarah asked, the calm before the storm.

"I… Well, I… What I mean to say is—"

"What did you do?" Sarah's voice was ice-cold, all her plans for her child's future vanishing in the flames consuming the bakery behind her. And this man wore guilt like a thick cloak around him.

Harry hung his head, shoulders slumped. His mother moved to interrupt, but Sarah held up a finger, shooting a venomous gaze at the older woman. "Don't think I haven't guessed why Harry wasn't inside, doing his job. You'd be wise to remain silent." She turned to her brother-in-law. Barbara took a step backward, giving them some space. A smart move on her behalf. "Harry?"

Tears were streaming down his cheeks even as the smoke seemed to swirl around their feet. It would probably be prudent to move, but Sarah's feet wouldn't take her anywhere until she knew the truth.

"I'd just put the last batch of bread in the oven when my parents came in." He looked up at her with pitiful eyes, but she needed all of it.

"And?"

"And what?"

"What happened next? How did a brief conversation lead to my bakery burning down, when in the twenty-three years it's been in my family, there hasn't been one single incident? Not one." Her ire was rising with each word.

"I left to have a brief conversation with them, but one thing led to another. They asked me to come home, with Isabel. Told me they were going to give me back my inheritance. My allowance. By that stage, I'd completely forgotten the bread. And the fact I'd left the oven door open and the woodpile too close so I could stoke it quickly."

Sarah could see it in her mind. The loaves catching fire, untended. Flames and coals tumbling out the door as the steadily burning logs shifted and crumpled, rolling out onto the woodpile. There was so much in that store that would burn. That first spark would have had a domino effect. Within minutes the place would not have been salvageable.

Thankfully, it was built of solid brick and that might be enough to save the buildings beside it.

"I'm so sorry, Sarah. I didn't mean—"

"Do you have any idea what you've done to me?" Sarah hissed through gritted teeth. She didn't wait for a response. "You've ruined me, more than Connor ever did you."

Harry swallowed. "What more can I say? I'm sorry, Sarah."

"We can't afford to rebuild, Harry," Sarah said in despair. "Not after Pa. I have nothing now. While you've got your future back, at the expense of mine." She turned from Harry in disgust, silent tears rolled down her cheeks as she watched the last pieces of her dreams vanish with the smoke.

Despite Harry's best efforts to comfort her, Sarah ignored the man in favour of Margery's solid support at her side. Together they stood, silent sentinels as the firefighters tried to contain the blaze and minimise the damage. An hour later, the bakery was a wet, smoking ruin.

As was Sarah's life.

"Let's get you home, chick." Marge took her hand, leading Sarah back toward the house. At least she had one thing left, though how she was supposed to make ends meet now was beyond her. The house was dark when they made their way inside. The stove had long since died. Marge led Sarah to the kitchen table, working to stoke the fire while her friend stared into nothingness.

Hardship always comes in threes, Sarah thought, stroking her belly absentmindedly. Pa. Connor. The bakery. Everything had come home to roost. Her heart was like lead in her chest, crushing her spirit. The *clunk* of a cuppa being sat in front of her startled her from her thoughts, bringing her back to the present.

"Drink up, hun. It'll make you feel better," Marge urged. Sarah reached for it, hands trembling and sooty, despite the fact she'd stayed well away from the action. The heat slid into her bones as she took that first sip, melting her aches.

Sarah looked up at Marge, tears hovering on the edge of her eyelids before spilling down her cheeks in a silent wave. "What am I going to do, Marge? I'm out of options."

"We'll figure it out, chick. Surely there's some way we can rebuild the bakery and Connor is—

"Connor?" Sarah laughed wildly. "I'll have to beg him to take his child and me because within a couple of weeks I'll have no savings to support myself." Sarah's silent tears turned to great gulping sobs as she continued to try to talk through her heaved breaths. "And I'll never know, truly, if he loves me or if he's only being honourable. So not only is the bakery in ashes, my future is as well."

"That's enough," Marge snapped, hands on hips as she glared at Sarah. "No more self-pitying for you, madam. Finish your tea and go to bed." Sarah stared at her friend, incredulous, as she continued to sip her tea, too afraid to disobey orders. Marge had never raised her voice to her before. "Everything will look better in the morning."

Sarah slurped the last gulp of tea. Something didn't feel right. She turned toward Marge with accusing eyes as her brain started to go foggy. Her friend wrapped Sarah's left arm over her shoulder as she manhandled her down the corridor and into her bed. She didn't even feel her toes drag along the floorboards. When Marge took off her shoes and tucked her in, Sarah mumbled, "Whad dish oo doo to be?" Her tongue was like cotton, soft and fuzzy, and wouldn't move the way she wanted even as her eyes started to droop.

Marge pulled the little bottle of laudanum that had belonged to Sarah's pa from her breast pocket, waving it in front of Sarah's nose.

"Knew you'd argue. Thought I'd better be sneaky if I was going to get you to do what you were told."

Sarah tried to berate her friend, but the words died in her throat as her eyelids locked together. Damn Marge. Her scolding would have to wait 'til the morning.

Marge was in for a right royal ear blistering when Sarah got hold of her.

***

Sarah's fingers moved frantically across the page, her eyes darting between the charred ruins of her little business and the paper on the easel. She'd woken that morning to find her best friend gone, butter and bread in the icebox, and the fire in the stove stoked high. Marge had also left a note.

Morning, Pumpkin.

Had to leave early this morning because Rachel's ill and I need to babysit. Mum brought in some butter and fresh bread when she collected me. Please don't tell her the bread is more rock cake than fluffy goodness. It would break her poor, fledgling baker heart.

I'll be in to see you this afternoon. Try to stay out of trouble, and don't make any stupid decisions before you've talked to me. You're too emotional for your own good at the moment, cupcake.

Love you,
Marge.

Stupid decisions. Sarah had snorted out her tea through her nose when she read it. As if Marge could talk. She wasn't exactly the Queen of Sensibility at the best of times.

Sarah continued to draw the devastation of her family business, finding the shadows in the light, the smoke that covered the brick façade. Her memory of the day before kept overlaying the images of the present, so occasionally little flames flickered into existence on her page. Already planning the oil painting, she could see the demons curling through the fire, smiling as they devoured her life. Sarah rubbed absently at her chest to soothe the ache there. The men fighting the fire would have to be haloed in light, giving them angelic power against the demons. It would have to be a large canvas, though where she'd get one and how she'd afford it, Sarah didn't know. She pulled herself up from her dream to the present when a shadow swallowed her drawing.

Looking up, she squinted into the sun as she sized up the stranger hanging over her shoulder.

"Do you mind," she said, voice dead. "You're blocking my light."

The man straightened and it was then she saw he was missing his left arm. Something about that niggled at her memory, but Sarah couldn't place it. It would come to her though. It always did, usually after the person had walked out of her life.

"Sorry, ma'am," he said respectfully. "Just in town to visit a friend and noticed your drawing. A recent loss for the community?" he asked, nodding toward the bakery.

Sarah sighed, resigned to having her solitude interrupted. "Yesterday," she said curtly. Her heart ached, and by sitting here drawing she was trying to keep her mind off her biggest problem—how to approach Connor.

The man's eyes sharpened, seeming to pierce through her. Sarah squirmed under his gaze. "I'm guessing it was a more personal loss, judging from the subject matter of your art." It wasn't a question, so she didn't dignify it with an answer, merely picked up where she'd left off shading the windows.

She knew she was being rude, but really, she was beyond caring at this point in time. She was hollow, as if she'd emptied herself of tears and was waiting for it to fill again before another release. The drawing helped. She didn't want to dwell on the things she couldn't change—she needed to remain focused in the present.

The man sighed. "The name's Smith, by the way, Ben Smith." He held out his hand and she reluctantly shook it. His hand was big and warm in hers, oddly comforting.

"Sarah Dawson." At least she could display some of the manners her pa had instilled in her. It was then it clicked. "Wait. You said your name was Smith? Lieutenant Smith? 53rd Brigade?"

"Correct. And yours is a name I'm familiar with myself." His voice was gravelly but kind. Sarah studied him closely, trying to see the man behind the smiling mask. There was pain there, like with

Connor, and determination too. The man would be a formidable enemy or a wonderful friend. She wondered which side she would be on after the man had talked to Connor.

"You'll be wanting to head out the River Road then, if you're chasing Connor," Sarah told him with a slight smile. It didn't touch her eyes, but at least she'd tried.

"Probably a good idea, if you can give me directions. I didn't exactly tell him I was coming." The man shifted a little on the balls of his feet. Nervous, she guessed.

"No problem," she said. "He's been watching for you since lambing season. I reckon you'll be welcomed with open arms." Far from setting him at ease as she'd intended, her words only seemed to make the man more nervous.

"Open arms, you say? Sure about that?"

"Sure as I could be, given we haven't talked in nearly two months." This seemed to startle the man.

"But I thought…" His voice trailed off when he registered the conversation had taken a turn she didn't like. "Any chance I can get those directions from you now?"

She rattled them off clearly and concisely, eager to be on her own again.

"Thank you," he said, tipping his hat to her as he headed off toward the Travellers.

Sarah sighed in relief as she put charcoal to the page again.

It seemed almost instantaneously that another shadow blocked her view of her page, but the sun high in the sky told her she'd been there for hours. Connor sat on the ground beside her, content to wait in silence for her to speak.

"I can't do this right now, Connor," she said, dropping her gaze to the page. Her fingers were numb. Everything was filtered through a fog now.

"I know," he said, his quiet understanding almost enough to undo her. "But I want you to know I'm here for you when you decide you need me."

"*When* I decide I need you?" Sarah sneered. "As if it's a given that I'll come running to you for help?" The rage was trying to push through the fog, but her efforts were half-hearted at best. Connor looked gobsmacked, at a total loss for words. She packed up her paper and easel as she pocketed her charcoal.

"You'd better head home," she said on a sigh. "Your friend was on his way out to your place. Should probably already be there by now, I'd think." Sarah started walking as quickly as she could back toward the house. She couldn't deal with this right now.

"Which friend?" Connor called from behind her.

"Smith," she yelled, not bothering to turn and face him. If she did, she might have done what he expected and run straight back into his warmth. No. She was better off sorting her feelings out before she gave in to the ones Connor roused in her.

Behind her, she heard the muttered curse and the dull thud of a horse's hooves moving at a quick trot in the opposite direction.

She went slack with relief. Crisis averted for another day, thanks to Smith, who'd helped her avoid telling Connor he was going to be a father.

Sarah wasn't sure how much longer she could do it though. Or if she still wanted to keep it from him.

She was tired, a bone-deep weariness that was a culmination of months of heartache. The only problem she had now was figuring out whether being with Connor would make it better, or infinitely worse.

One thing was certain: she'd better have it figured out soon because Smith was only going to distract Connor briefly before he was back on her tail again. And she'd better have an answer because this baby wasn't going to stay hidden forever.

Chapter 23

Connor cantered his horse up the road toward the homestead, eager to see his friend. The last conversation that they'd had lingered in his mind, causing him to second guess whether this meeting would be friendly, or whether there'd be tension.

He needn't have worried.

"Took you long enough," Smith called, unrolling his lanky frame from the steps. The man was whippet-thin but still as hard as steel. When he met him on the bottom step, their handshake quickly morphed into a hug, Connor relaxing finally when it was returned. Tears welled but Connor quickly blinked them back, coughing a little to clear the lump in his throat.

He was relieved to see Smith's eyes suspiciously wet as well.

"Sorry, had a woman to annoy," Connor said ruefully.

"You always did have a way with the ladies," laughed Smith with an elbow to Connor's ribs.

Jezebel chose that moment to make her break for his veggie patch. "If you give me a minute to see to this little vixen, I'll be right with you."

Of course, Smith ignored him. The man strode lazily after a jogging Connor as he rushed to intercept his mare. "She's a beauty. And already breeding by the looks of her. Is that going to make things difficult?"

"Nah," Connor said, grabbing Jezebel's reins and leading the ornery mare in the opposite direction. "They breed them tough out this way. I'll probably need to borrow one from a neighbour a month before she drops and while the foal is nursing, but she'll be working sooner than you'd think."

He stopped at the entrance to the front paddock, hitched the mare to the post and was about to unsaddle her only to find it done already and Smith with it slung casually over his remaining arm. Connor raised an eyebrow.

"Seems you've managed to compensate well for your loss." He wasn't only talking about the arm. In the months since he'd seen his friend last, the man had lost the haunted look that had stabbed through Connor's heart when last they met.

Smith didn't pretend to misunderstand. "The arm was a matter of training myself to do things differently. You'd be amazed how much more of my body I use without it than I ever did as a soldier." Connor ran a critical eye over his brother-in-arms. He could believe it. The man had muscles where none had existed before. "If you're talking about Susan..." the man hesitated. "I couldn't stay in that town any longer. Watch her with him. I know she's happy with him, but it makes both of us miserable every time she comes across me in town. And Sydney sometimes feels as small as Coona. So I thought I'd come here for a bit, then go home and see if some distance has made things any easier."

"You know, I've heard things are only going to get harder from here," Conner said, concerned for his friend. "Could be you should stay around here for a while. Not enough jobs in the city, not enough food 'coz there weren't enough hands to seed all the fields. This area's better than most. You'd always be welcome here."

Smith hesitated, then forged on. "No, Connor. Not saying I won't come back here eventually, but I need to see what else is on offer first."

He nodded, knowing his friend was right. Smith never had been satisfied until he saw every problem from the inside out. If he didn't go to Sydney, he wouldn't be able to settle anywhere. That didn't mean he didn't want his best friend here though. They made their way together to the barn, Smith still carrying Jezebel's tack.

"Speaking of what's on offer," Smith said, a sly smile on his face. "Met a beautiful little thing in town, flaming red hair and lush curves a man could—"

"You shut your mouth right now, brother, or I won't be responsible for my actions." He knew his words were a snarl, and Smith was only teasing, but hearing another man speak of Sarah like that played with his mind.

Smith shot him a look of understanding. "So you do still care for the woman." Connor nodded, even though it wasn't a question. "Tell me why on earth you're still not married then, and why the woman is walking around with a face as long as that mare you just let loose."

"It's a long story," Connor hedged. He wasn't sure he was prepared to tell his friend about it.

"Got all day, mate." Unfortunately, they had. They were moving into winter, usually a busy time with repairs, but because of the help he'd received when he came home, Connor had very little that needed his attention.

Connor strode toward the house, indicating with a nod for his friend to follow him. When Smith was by his side, he began, as he had done with everyone else he'd explained himself to, at the beginning. Only this time his audience had other insights. Ones that came from close quarters in hell.

"What were you thinking, mate?" Smith asked, horrified. "When you said you were going home to deal with it, I thought you were going to call out the little menace, not become the villain in a bad romance novel."

"I thought I was doing the right thing. For Caleb. Our mother." Connor sighed. "I never really expected any of this to happen the way it has. Thought I could ignore my feelings for Sarah and concentrate on revenge but look at me. I'm apologising to everyone I've hurt, righting my wrongs, for the chance to have her back."

"I can understand why," his friend said. "Even as down as she seemed, the woman was kind and beautiful."

"She's just lost everything, Smith. Her pa and now the business. I'd give everything I have to see her happy, but she won't have a bar of me. But I've one more ace up my sleeve. If that doesn't work, then nothing will."

Smith clapped Connor over the back with his remaining hand. "Whatever it is, I'll help." He grinned. "And when you're happily married with twenty carrot-topped little blighters, I expect the first to be named after me. Deal?"

"I would say yes," said Connor, heart a little lighter, "but I've already requested reinforcement from another source, and she's demanded the same payment."

"She?" Smith's interest sharpened. Connor almost groaned. The last thing he needed was Smith meeting Marge and being smoothly interrogated by the notorious gossip. Even if she only shared some things with Sarah, it could be enough to obliterate his already tarnished image in her mind for good.

"Don't even think about it," Connor warned. "The woman's too smart for you. She'd have you running up and down the road, barking like one of her dogs before you could say 'nice to meet you.' And you'd thank her for the belly rub she'd give you afterward."

"I do love a nice belly rub," Smith mused, pointedly ignoring Connor's warning. "When do I meet this goddess with the formidable intellect?"

Connor sighed, knowing a lost cause when he saw one. Smith was intrigued, and nothing he could say would convince him to back away now. He'd have to wait for Marge to scare him off all on her own.

"She'll probably be round in the next few days, bringing with her the last things I need for my project. Your job is to help me make sure that I have everything else ready in time."

"I'm guessing you need my formidable strength to finish this venture," Smith said, flexing his remaining arm to show off an impressive bicep. Connor laughed.

"Nothing so strenuous," Connor replied. "Though things may get a little…dirty."

Smith shot him a wicked grin. "If you can guarantee the smart goddess is there, I'll happily join your dirty little project."

Connor shook his head. How he was ever going to keep Smith away from Marge was beyond him. Maybe he should introduce the two and let the sparks fly? With any luck, they'd be so preoccupied trying to outsmart one another that they'd forget he even existed.

Connor snorted to himself. *And pigs would fly.*

He hoped he'd managed to tie Sarah down before she found out anything embarrassing about him.

He led Smith to his old room then, as soon as his friend had closed the door, Connor deflated. Shoulders slumped, he heaved in a great lungful of air, trying to clear the weight from his chest. He knew the dice never lied, but he was seriously beginning to question Fate on this one. Sarah hadn't come back to him, even after everything he'd done so far.

He was beginning to think it was too much to hope that his final attempt would see her come back to him. And, if he was honest with himself, it was what he deserved.

***

"That's enough of your lollygagging, Sarah Dawson." Marge's voice seemed to echo through the empty house, but Sarah rolled over instead. What was the point? There was no reason for her to be up, no bakery to rush to at this ungodly hour.

"If you're not out of there by the time I count to ten, Sarah, you're not going to like the consequences." The first stirrings of unease bubbled in Sarah's stomach. Marge could be vindictive when thwarted.

"One…"

Maybe she should get up.

"Two."

Surely if she stayed very quiet under the quilt, her friend would go away?

"Three." The door flew open with a loud bang, startling a squeak out of Sarah as Marge came flying across the room and launched herself onto the bed. "Get up, lazybones."

Then she did the most outrageous thing imaginable.

She put. Her freezing hands. On Sarah's face.

Sarah screeched, struggling to free herself from Marge's grip.

"You'd better get up now, Sarah Dawson," she said, giving Sarah the evil eye. "Or next time it will be my bare feet under the covers. Did I tell you there's a frost an inch thick outside at the moment?" Probably an exaggeration knowing Marge, but Sarah leapt from the bed just the same.

"That's better," Marge said with a nod of satisfaction. "Have a wash, put some clean clothes on. No offence, but you smell like an oven bred with a latrine. Sooty shit."

"Marge," Sarah scolded, though the corner of her lip may have twitched at the observation.

"Don't 'Marge' me, missy, in that scandalised tone." Marge's finger waved in front of her nose. It was all Sarah could do to keep from laughing at her friend. "I'll have you know I've heard worse come out of your mouth when you think no one's watching."

Her statuesque friend waltzed to the door, pausing dramatically when she reached it. "When you smell like a human being again, come to the kitchen. I've got a surprise for you."

Sarah's leapt in fear at Marge's words. Last time Marge had said she had a surprise for Sarah was when she'd decided to give her riding lessons for her fifteenth birthday. Only she'd tried to use an extremely green Bunny as her mount.

Sarah was terrified of any Marge surprise. The last thing she needed now was a broken bone. Marge had disappeared into the kitchen, so Sarah took her time getting dressed, postponing the inevitable.

"I've changed my mind. If you don't hurry up and get out here in the next two minutes, I won't be responsible for my actions."

Sarah haphazardly threw her favourite blue dress on, hoping that wearing it would cheer herself up and make Marge smile too. She wrenched the door open and flew down the corridor, only to come to a grinding halt when she reached the kitchen.

"What's this about, Marge?" Sarah asked warily, eyeing Connor as he sat, large as life, in her kitchen. She didn't remember giving him permission to enter her home. In fact, she distinctly remembered telling him to leave her alone.

Unfortunately, her heart took that moment to leap in her chest and start racing in excitement. And baby decided it needed her stomach empty. Even though there was nothing in it.

Sarah rushed to the sink, dry-retching for all she was worth. Both Marge and Connor made a move to go to her, but she waved them away. It would pass soon. It always did.

"Can one of you get me a glass of water and some bread?"

"Are you sick?" Connor demanded, panic lacing his voice, while Marge did as she was asked. Bless her. "Do you need me to get the doctor? We have the Clearys' buggy out front, I'll be back before you know it. How long has this—"

"Sit down before you hurt yourself," Sarah said, wiping her mouth with the back of her hankie before accepting a cup of water from Marge. "And if you want to hear what's going on, I suggest, as your mother would say, you 'haud yer wheesht.'"

Connor fell silent, his eyes fixed on her with the intensity of a hawk. She'd already resolved to tell him about the baby, but now she was faced with it, and she hadn't had a chance to plan what to say, she was totally tongue-tied.

"Let it out, peanut. It'll make you feel better." As always, Marge was right.

She sucked in a breath, praying that the baby didn't force another incident, and blurted it out.

"I'm not sick, Connor. I'm pregnant."

If he wasn't sitting already, Sarah was sure in that moment Connor would have hit the floor. His knuckles were white on the table and his eyes were darting around the room, having trouble focussing on anything. It would have been laughable if it weren't for the honest confusion in his eyes.

"What….? How…?"

"Oh, I've got this one, Sarah," Marge said with enthusiasm. "Now it's like this, Connor. When a man and woman really love each other, sometimes they—"

"Enough, Marge. He knows how babies are made."

Connor cleared his throat and immediately became the focus of both women. "I'm hoping it's mine?" he asked hesitantly, heart in his eyes. "I mean, not that I think…but I don't mean to imply…I just can't—"

"Of course it's yours, you fool." Marge was righteously indignant on Sarah's behalf but the woman herself was trying to contain a crazed laugh. The situation was so ridiculous. "When did she have time for a roll in the hay with some other bloke, between her looking after her father and the bakery?"

"I think it may be time for you to take a little walk outside, my friend," Sarah said firmly. Her heart was drumming in her chest and, even though she loved her best friend dearly, she didn't need any witnesses to this conversation.

Mouth opening and closing like a laugh-less kookaburra, Marge stared wide-eyed at her, then promptly stomped out of the house.

"I'll pay for that tomorrow," Sarah muttered under her breath, then turned back to Connor. "Yes, it's yours. And I know you wouldn't think that of me." She eased herself into a seat. Her hands surrounded the cup of water with an iron grip, hoping it would disguise their trembling.

"Does this mean you'll marry me then? Come back to the farm? We can get Father Ben to marry us today…" His voice trailed off as he looked closer at her. Sarah wasn't smiling. In fact, his words had only seemed to confirm her earlier fears. Connor would marry her because she was pregnant. Not because he loved her.

"I don't understand. I can provide for our child, you'll live in comfort. You have nothing here, Sarah," he said passionately, moving to take her in his arms.

"Exactly," Sarah cried, launching herself from her seat and whirling away from him. "I have nothing. You don't love me and the only reason you're so happy is because you have a ready-made family on the way to replace the one you've lost." She was so lost in her own tirade she didn't notice the hurt that lanced across his features. "I don't even have a choice about it anymore. I can't provide for our child by myself, so now I'll have to go out there and spend my life wondering 'what if?' 'What if' you really loved me, put my needs before anything else? As I have you.

"I've bent over backward to try to make you happy, Connor, to try to coax the heart into the shell that came back from the war, but I feel like a miserable failure. You put revenge before love. Before me. Do you know how that makes me feel?"

Sarah's chest shook with great heaving sobs. She was battling both anger and heartache, and it was undecided yet which would be the winner. Yet the tears still fell, and it made her furious that she couldn't stop them. "Yes, you've apologised, maybe even fixed things between the parties you injured, but you still chose revenge over me. And now I'll never know if you were apologising because you loved me, wanted me, or because you realised what you did was wrong. I was hoping it was both." Her voice shook and she tried valiantly to steady it. "But I guess I'll never know now."

She turned her back to him, unable to face him in her moment of misery. Connor was having none of it. Gently, with his hands on her shoulders, he turned her to face him.

"I think you need to come with us after all." His smile was weak, but it was there. "I still have a surprise for you."

She sniffed. "I thought that was just Marge trying to get me out of bed."

"No, there really is a surprise. Are you coming?"

She hesitated, but reality intruded. Did she have much choice?

As if reading her thoughts, Connor said, "There's always a choice, Sarah. I'll support you, whatever you decide. But I choose you. Please, choose me too." And he held out a hand. "Let me show you I love you."

His words were her undoing. Tears continued to flow down her face, but she placed her hand in his and followed him outside to the waiting buggy.

"Good Lord, what did you do to the girl, Connor?" Ben Smith, the man she'd met the other day outside the bakery, said from the driver's bench. "There's an overflowing waterworks there and I'm pretty sure it has nothing to do with indoor plumbing."

Connor helped Sarah up into the buggy, sitting her beside a testy Marge. "Just shut up and drive," Marge snapped, glaring at Smith, then muttered an aside to Sarah, "You owe me a *huge* favour for leaving me with that one."

Sarah smiled through a haze of tears. It would all be over soon. Hopefully, things would work out for the best. If not, there was always Plan Spinster.

Chapter 24

The buggy drew to a halt outside of Connor's place, beside a haltered Jezebel, but Smith didn't get down when the others did.

"I'll wait out here for you, Marge." For once the man seemed to be serious, as was Marge, who rushed to do his bidding. Sarah didn't think she'd ever seen her friend move so fast. The young woman swept a bag from the porch, tied the reluctant mare to the back of the buggy, then leapt back on, all in the time it took Sarah to make it to the veranda.

"Don't wait up for me," Smith said to Connor. "I plan on spending some quality alone time in the hayloft in your barn when I get back." He turned to the woman in the buggy with him. "Could always do with some company." He wriggled his eyebrows suggestively at Marge.

"I don't think so," Marge said disdainfully but with a dangerous gleam in her eye. "Even Bunny has smoother lines than you, and he hooked Jezebel because he was the only stud on offer. I, meanwhile, have far too many men lined up to consider you."

Sarah smothered a cough at the outright lie, but Smith roared with laughter. "Let's get you home, you sharp-tongued she-devil." With a flick of the reins, they were off, leaving Sarah alone with a nervous Connor.

Instead of heading in through the front door, Connor led Sarah around the back of the house. Her steps slowed when they rounded the corner, trying to sort out what she was seeing. The wide back veranda had been partially enclosed, only the left side with the swing remaining open to the air. However, that wasn't all. The enclosed area wasn't totally closed either. Instead of windows, there were large shutters, almost the size of doors, with Connor's signature scrollwork chasing itself across the panels.

It was stunning. And it hadn't been here last time she visited.

Sarah swallowed, throat dry and hand suddenly clammy in Connor's. "What's that?" she asked, voice tight.

"It's your surprise," he countered. "Are you ready?"

She nodded limply, following him onto the veranda and through the door.

What she saw brought her to her knees.

The room was filled with canvases, boxes of paper, half-drawn sketches and paintings. Some of the materials were new, some of her old ones, waiting for her in a new home. Marge's work, she guessed. The shutters were closed, but she could imagine what it would be like when they were open to the world. The view would be amazing, air and light for her to paint her dreams and reality, yet those same shutters would protect her work from the elements as Connor would protect her and their child. Eager to test her theory, she threw open the shutters and melted. The view about stopped her heart.

The farmland faded into the distance where it met the silhouette of a mountain range, blue in the morning haze. Sharp stone spires pierced the sky, but it was the light that held promise. A world of promise for a brighter future.

Her vision became suddenly blurry and she swiped at her eyes and she reached forward to touch the wonder of his work, running her fingers over knots and vines so similar to the bedroom. Only someone who saw into her soul could have done this. Someone who would hang the sun and the moon for their one and only.

Connor *did* love her.

She turned to him, hands still on the carvings, only to see a suspicious gleam in his hand. Her mother's opal ring. Her legs ate the distance between them before she threw herself into his arms, fusing her mouth to his and plundering it for all she was worth. A great weight lifted from her shoulders as her body melted to his, strong arms pressing her as close as she could get into that broad chest.

Breathless, she leaned her head on his shoulder and sank into his embrace, sliding the ring onto her left hand and admiring the colours that flared within. It was only when she felt his shoulders shaking that she looked up, about to give him a piece of her mind for laughing at her, only to realise that tears were running unchecked down his cheeks. She reached up in wonder, tracing one's path to his lips, where she brought her own in a tender brush across his.

"Why are you crying?" Sarah asked, confused. Her own tears she understood, but not his.

It took him three tries before he found his voice. "I thought I'd lost you. That I'd never be able to prove to you how much you mean to me." He laughed self-deprecatingly. "I even rolled the dice, to see if I still stood a chance."

"They obviously said yes," Sarah said softly. "Did they give you any other advice?"

"No," Connor said. "But I did get some advice on how to fix things with your sister. This," he indicated the room around them, "was my idea. I couldn't think of anything you'd love more than time and space to paint."

"I can," she murmured against his lips. Connor groaned.

"What?" he asked, a little desperately. "Anything, Sarah. I'll do anything if you just give me another chance."

She nipped his lip. "Take me to bed."

And he did.

Epilogue

The church was almost empty when Sarah and Connor made their vows, but Marge wasn't surprised. Neither her best friend nor Sarah's soon-to-be-husband was a showy person. Everyone who mattered was here with them. Harrison and Isabel sat front and centre, looking the picture of marital bliss. If they weren't in a church, Marge would quite cheerfully wring both of their scrawny necks for everything they'd done to Sarah. And yet still, the woman wanted her sister at her wedding.

It was too bad her best friend was the forgiving type. Marge had some creative ideas for how she could make them both realise the error of their ways.

Or maybe not so bad. It was probably a good thing she didn't meddle with them further.

Her gaze was drawn back to the happy couple as Father Ben started to wind up to the conclusion of the ceremony. If Sarah wasn't the forgiving type, this whole saga would have had a very different outcome, and Marge's intuition said none of them would have been happy. She'd learned to trust her gut over the last few years. Especially when it came to Sarah.

Sometimes, she felt her practical best friend would have died a nun if it weren't for Marge's interference.

"I now pronounce you husband and wife. You may kiss the bride." Finally. Marge was a sucker for a love story. Connor pulled Sarah close, tenderly cupping the back of her head as his lips sampled hers in a kiss a little too hot for the church.

Marge discreetly fanned herself until she noticed Smith watching. She quickly snatched her hand away from her breast, clasping them demurely in front of her, but the man only arched an eyebrow. Unfortunately, Marge couldn't help but notice how well he filled out his uniform, both men having stood up in their military apparel. The man had broad shoulders and, even with one sleeve pinned neatly up around his stump, a look up and down his taut body had her panties damper than they'd been in her life.

Even when she took matters into her own hands.

Shooting him a glare, she raised her hands and clapped, cheering as the happy couple walked back down the aisle as husband and wife. A tear or two may have trailed down her cheek, not that she'd admit it to anyone.

He noticed, however. He seemed to always catch her at the most awkward moments.

Thank God he'd be leaving for Sydney in a couple of weeks. Marge ignored the pang in her heart, charting it up to a little indigestion from breakfast.

So what if he was the most fun she'd had in her life?

Marge had a plan, and no man was going to take it from her, with his smiles and his broad shoulders.

No way. Not now, not ever.

Now could someone tell that to the damn organ currently trying to beat its way out of her chest?

ABOUT THE AUTHOR

S.E. Welsh is a self-confessed bibliophile who moonlights as a writer when her day jobs of secondary school teacher and mother allow. She is happiest with a book in one hand, and a diet coke in the other. A two time winner of the Northern Territory Literary Awards and finalist in the IEUA Queensland and Northern Territory Literary Competition, her short and flash fiction have been highly acclaimed. Shona has a book of poetry published, and her short fiction features in a variety of anthologies. Shona has been weaving her passion for history with her weakness for love. Exploring the past and giving troubled souls happily-ever-afters is proving exciting and challenging for the fun-loving wordsmith.

Connect with S.E.:
website: sewelsh.com
instagram: @sewelshauthor
facebook: facebook.com/SEWelshAuthor
twitter: @sewelshauthor

www.BOROUGHSPUBLISHINGGROUP.com

If you enjoyed this book, please write a review. Our authors appreciate the feedback, and it helps future readers find books they love. We welcome your comments and invite you to send them to info@boroughspublishinggroup.com. Follow us on Facebook, Twitter and Instagram, and be sure to sign up for our newsletter for surprises and new releases from your favorite authors.

Are you an aspiring writer? Check out www.boroughspublishinggroup.com/submit and see if we can help you make your dreams come true.

www.ingramcontent.com/pod-product-compliance
Lightning Source LLC
Chambersburg PA
CBHW031327170626
46807CB00002B/603